A.E. Snelling-Munro

First published in paperback by
Michael Terence Publishing in 2018

www.mtp.agency

Copyright © 2018 A.E. Snelling-Munro

A.E. Snelling-Munro has asserted his right to be identified as the author of this work in accordance with the Copyright, Designs and Patents Act 1988

ISBN 9781912639205

All rights reserved. No part of this publication may be reproduced, stored in a retrieval system, or transmitted, in any form or by any means, electronic, mechanical, photocopying, recording or otherwise, without the prior permission of the publishers

Cover images
Copyright © Balázs András Bokor, Smikeymikey1

I dedicate the following to Paul, Trudy, David, Sophina, Ellis, Bailey & William being the new and next generations that follow in the family's ancestry. Wishing all good fortune in their futures.

BOBBYJAC
THE FINAL CHAPTER

A.E. Snelling-Munro

CHAPTER ONE
Return to Duty

The recipient of a long drawn out marital separation whose wife had lost interest in their fifteen-year marriage, Bob Benyon, Police Constable had returned to local duty from his recent absence on a one month's residential course off division.

During which he had many quiet moments to reflect on his marriage, and the strain he was under, as to how they first met, her background, her love and aspirations for him and what their futures held for both.

He remembered their first date together, her lithe figure, her flaxen unbleached hair that gathered many complements from others, her pink toned freshness of her face and eyes that radiated a bright sparkling blue, and now today a complete opposite as to her change of personality in all her thirty-six years as she languished in her own toil and torment, as gone was the sparkle from her eyes, now dull and lifeless.

It seemed that their own credentials that brought them together was not sufficient to sustain a loving relationship that would last their lifetime, Bob was confused from her being so vibrant both mentally and physically in every way he could describe in the beginning and now heading for the most likely outcome to their marriage a savage and distressing divorce.

It was as he remembered their fourth year of marriage had been a very stressful period for both back and forth to the family planning clinic, and sadly the most damning news for his wife was to be told that she was barren and not able to have children. The outcome from numerous tests and visits was a final statement on her femininity that the news was irreversible, her heartache, and her desperation of wanting to be a mother began to fester in her an ill-judged wind in the years that followed to the present day of their separation.

Bob never lost sight of his responsibilities, although his wife found it difficult in the long term of him doing shift work, sometimes the hours and days were long when his duties were for the good of the community and not for her that festered a deep anger and frustration that made her realise that as a Police Officer she would always have to share him for as long as he remained in the Police service and this was now her growing enemy of resentment, and wanting out of their marriage.

His wife remained in the marital home during his absence away, he thought perhaps she would take the opportunity of staying with her parents. As she also remained undecided at the time on whether to be the Constable's wife at home or seek her own career, she also knew that whatever her choice Bob would support her wholeheartedly, but that was not the gnawing issue that burned deep inside her feelings, it was motherhood and Bob wanting a family, but she was not prepared to adopt it was her own flesh and blood she longed for.

Arriving home was more of a cordial and sedate welcome than to the rapturous screams and kisses he hoped for *(dreaming with perplexed thoughts of what it could have been)*. Within the half hour of him arriving home, his wife left the house to shop for groceries alone in the house, he aimlessly wandered between the ground floor rooms, lounge, dining room and kitchen, nothing had changed in his absence as once again all his old emotions came flooding back and the solace of his acknowledgement was not enough to encounter as he too wanted to be held and cuddled on his return.

His thoughts became sexual in wanting to feel his wife and touch her in the most intimate of places, unbuckling and pulling down her jeans, pulling her knickers to one side and fuck her in the hallway, the lounge or over the kitchen sink it did not really matter to him so long as he could enter her with flowing passion and she would reciprocate and respond and not push him away and kick him in the crutch as that was going to be the most likely outcome to his thoughts if he approached her, and now left the house to go shopping, what a home coming she clearly did not want to be around him, it was obvious to Bob's thoughts.

Unpacking Bob was well capable in looking after himself as he loaded up the washing machine and programmed for a one-hour wash. His uniform was returned to the wardrobe, other clothing returned to the appropriate draws for storage, and he changed into a casual style of dress. Once downstairs he was soon handling a mug of coffee and ferreting for biscuits as there were none to found, he left the kitchen by the backdoor and walked down the garden path to the wooden bench positioned on the edge of his garden and beyond was thick undergrowth and woodland belonging to private landowners.

Bob took many an opportunity to sit under the canopy of trees that over hung his garden, the position of the bench was just so and never in full sunlight, the cover and shade was tranquil and perfect for him to sit and contemplate many issues and thoughts that came into his head. This was one moment as he sat with hands clasped round the coffee mug, as he watched the breeze open and close the branches that swayed and bowed with bursts of sunlight breaking through the canopy in long streaks of light. But for Bob the best was yet to come, nature never loses its sounds and none more so than the melodious harmony of the many songbirds that flew in and out of the trees around him, often heard but rarely seen hidden by the leaves. It became a guessing game as to which song was from which bird and who was the best whistler or songstress it was a whole new world. A plateau that few people would perhaps appreciate or recognise as in hindsight so many lived and worked such busy lives and one Bob found nauseating in having a regimental life, he preferred policing and the openness it provided in experiencing so many different factions of society and the unexpected that made the adrenalin flow and to make one's hair stand up on the back of the neck. Variety was indeed the spice of life and that came with sincere thoughts and responsibilities to the public he served and why would he want to run for the early train on a full English breakfast he thought, as he witnessed many who did at the local railway station when he worked an early turn shift, panic stricken souls not wanting to miss the train or hoping to grab the next available seat, the rat race of life was not for him, he shuddered at the thought preferring the career he had.

It was a good hour when Bob was disturbed by the soft strokes and touches he felt on his face, stirring he realised that he had fallen asleep on the bench and it was the figure of his wife who leaned towards him. Bob closed his eyes and remained still believing that he was in some dream, he felt a hand rubbing gently his face, eyes opened, and he just stared and stared until he came to his senses and realised that it was not a dream but his wife touching him. He pushed himself back into the bench and stretched both arms out before giving one almighty sigh with a parched throat, as his wife leaned in and kissed him, then another kiss that became longer than the first and it continued like this until her hands clasped his head as she was pulling him towards her locked in a very long passionate kiss that left Bob gasping for air. He was shocked at her sudden outpouring of passion for him as with both hands he held her shoulders as he steadied her as she leant right over him and pressed his head into her breasts, she held his head vice like against her body as he let both arms fall to his side, then she let go and stood upright in between his legs and he just stared at her waistline realising something was different, but for the moment he did not know what as he was somewhat confused by her sudden actions and attention. When the penny dropped Bob realised that she had changed into a dress and held the material with her hand as she swished the hem back and forth, just like the 'Can, Can girls' then without any words being uttered between them, she stopped and lifted up the front of her dress exposing her nakedness underneath, with just a thin pubic line showing which was the way to her silky lining, Bob could not believe what he was witnessing, does this mean he can reach out and touch or must he sit as a voyeur being teased to the sexual limits of his endurance, she hadn't made him wear a blindfold (muttering and giggling under his breath) 'God! Forbid,' he thought.

His wife pulled down the shoulder straps of her dress to expose her naked breasts that were full and rounded with nipples that had struck accord with his moistened lips as her nipples were bewitching to his eye, then realised it had been many months since he last saw them both exposed on one sitting (mentally giggling to himself)

"What the fucking hell is she up to," he was thinking,

Then looking past, her towards the house, nothing looked out of place, so what has brought this sudden sexual urge, could it really be that she has missed him or was it simply to meet her sexual needs and desires to get fucked at the end of the garden, he thought,

"Nothing makes sense, but I am not going to complain," said Bob again thinking to himself.

His wife grabbed with both hands the waistband of his joggings and pulled then down as Bob quickly reached out to steady himself from the force of her tugging, at the same time he used his feet to free the garment as he opened wide his legs exposing his gormless looking, half hearted, couldn't make its mind up time penis that bounced from limp to a half limp and then when she touched the foreskin pushing gently back the flesh he felt the flow of blood rushing in defence of his manhood, as she bent down and kissed the tip and rolled back his foreskin even further as she took more of the fleshy member into her mouth, the warmth was exhilarating as she sucked gently as he continued to grow and harden, by which time she had lifted up her dress and was astride him in quick time as she reached between her legs and found him rock hard she took hold and gently eased into her as she raised her buttocks off her haunches letting out a loud whimper as she felt him travel deep into her as Bob joined the sexual ritual by thrusting his haunches towards her, she by this time had pushed her breasts into his face with one nipple squeezed at an angle against lips as she again with both hands held the back of his head, she was now in full flight she was fucking him. Bob had no control other than to let her ride him and in such a furious manner, she was really going for glory without by your leave it was all wife and wife it was she who was fucking him hard and the nipple he managed to entice into his mouth as the more he squeezed her nipple the more outrageous she became with her movements. Her orgasm was one of those savouring moments that men folk love to watch and few experience in a lifetime of relationships, she was oblivious to his presence and then suddenly he felt hot and very wet as she let out a scream and shouted,

"I am a squitter, am I not," said his wife, as a long stream of liquid appeared from her lower region that soaked them both.

Covered in dripping perspiration and a nipple tingling from Bob's sucking she pulled on her shoulder straps, leant forward and gave him a long passionate kiss, got off his lap, turned and walked back up the path to the house and disappeared. Bob remained seated and realised that his body was covered in gaps and ridges outlining the shape of the bench slats from the movement and pressure of his wife upon his torso.

Bob was still not sure as to what had taken place, as all this happened without either of them saying a word and why did she change into a dress, why did she rave such sexual prowess after such a prolonged period of abstention. Now realising how wet he was and clearly needing a shower and a clean change of clothes he too returned to the house and went for a shower. His wife was already in the shower, when Bob entered the bedroom undressing he was a stiff as a board, his foreskin had crept back over the pink and purple flesh that it protected and now he was ready to try fucking his wife on his terms as he entered the shower and stood behind her as he ran his hands down over her breasts, tummy and then between her legs as she bent forward slightly, but then he thrust his hands in between her thighs and pulled her buttocks into his groin area, one foot tapped her ankle as she widened her stance, to where she placed both hands on the wall of the shower, while Bob had knelt down behind her and was holding her buttocks apart whilst his tongue went in search of the good life to be had from her, he used his tongue to open and tease her lips, having placed a thumb inside her pudenda and pressed on her pubic bone, as both their bodies were bathed in the warm shower droplets that bounced from their naked flesh. Having tasted her juices Bob stood and kept his wife in the same position as he parted her buttocks and pushed his penis right into her and pushed and he pushed and held her round the waist as he lifted her feet momentarily off the floor as she was perched only on his penis that kept them together and now Bob was determined to ride her well, to fuck the life out of her and to show her what she had been missing as it was fortunate for them that the wet room was of sufficient size as Bob lowered his wife to the floor, she remained on her knees whilst he thrust hard and deep, her hair wet and dishevelled as Bob placed a finger into her mouth as he moved back and forth as his wife sucked his finger, then Bob pushed her down onto her tummy as her whimpers became louder and clearly she was having an orgasm, then he withdrew and turned her onto her back with arms outstretched and face covered in wet hair as he parted her legs and went down and found her protruding clitoris which he took between his lips and continued to gently pull and suckle until that moment of truth when she thrashed around the floor of the shower as she screamed out that she was coming again, Bob moved back and saw the squirting fountain that came from his wife as she continued to buck and thrust and then silent as she turned onto her side and placed herself in a foetus like position as the water continued to splash over their bodies, Bob stood and reached for his bathrobe as he sat for ages with his head resting on the back of the armchair in the bedroom. His wife remained curled up in a ball on the shower floor and then finally standing and laughing she turned off the shower and appeared in the bedroom wrapped in a large bath towel, as she sat on the corner of the bed, now topless, Bob watched from afar as her breasts moved in different directions as she rubbed and dried her hair.

Bob's physical strength had now evaporated and left him tired and weak all over as his muscles came to be so relaxed and the stickiness left from his ejaculation could be felt on the tops of his thighs, finding a tissue he took hold of his penis and slid back the foreskin and wiped gently round the rim at the same time he squeezed the tip of his penis to expel any further remnants of sperm before finally wrapping tissue around it to avoid any further seepage later.

Bob remained with eyes closed and simply confused as to what had actually taken place in the last couple of hours, it just didn't seem real no matter how or which way he looked or turned the situation was bizarre beyond words and his comprehension having been so sexual together, having been fucked by his own wife and vice versa no words had been spoken between them, her only sounds were sexual whimpers with every twist and turn she made, but no words uttered between them, how can this be, she never objected to his touch, she never stopped him entering her, she never objected to the various positions she found herself in and why was she such a willing partner, why after all these months with arguments and long spells of silence between them and then today after a month away they both fuck like heaven has no fury and my goodness it was needed to brush the cobwebs away and to stabilise some order into their lives and perhaps bringing them closer together in the times of so much pain having been shared between them, Bob was never one to give up on their marriage, although, physically it clearly was a fucking that they both needed, the intimacy may well be the answer without worrying her and wanting her to explain or make a statement, Bob decided to except what had taken place and hope that perhaps a corner had been turned as he had loved this woman for all their years together, even without a child, he knew nothing could replace her whatever her judgement of him.

CHAPTER TWO

Strengths and Weaknesses

At quarter to nine o'clock on the Monday morning, Bob arrived for duty after a month's absence in the small village police station. A radiance of sunbursts glowed on the stone work of the 1930's building. The day began with bright sunshine and a warm breeze, as he left the police car on the forecourt of the station and entered the building. Hanging baskets were an abundance of colour, adding some real country charm to the local surroundings.

A colleague greeted him with the first comment of the day,

"Morning Bob, first day back mate."

"No mate, early turn yesterday," said Bob.

"Kettle's on, skipper will be here soon," said his colleague.

"Okay Andy, I am popping up to the office first," said Bob.

His colleague Andy, on Bob's return, was rambling on about the good old days at the station and how nice it was to see him. Bob's mind was elsewhere as he gazed around the office. His thoughts were on the fire at 'Marshalls Green'. He had vaguely remembered the fine old rambling house set in beautiful surrounding woodland with a valley to the rear and below, the house with a river running through the property that made it so picturesque.

Andy's voice broke his train of thought,

"What beat you working today?"

"Two," came Bob's reply.

"Yeah, that is a lovely beat. It's nice this time of year, not much excitement though," said Andy.

"I see there was a nasty fire at 'Marshall's Green'. Bloody shame that," said Bob on a fishing expedition with Andy's knowledge.

"Yeah, that's right. That was a bastard; they reckon there were two people in that place when it went up. I only work days, but I got called back to open the station that night. I heard a couple of firemen talking and apparently, when they were digging out all the rubbish and damping down the ashes, they thought they had seen a fucking ghost. Something loomed out of the ashes. Seems as though it was a dog and the back half had been burnt away. Can you imagine, it was still alive? It shook them up quite a lot, poor bloody dog, it must have died in terrible agony. It slipped back into the burning ash and wasn't seen again," said Andy, in a rather sad tone of voice.

"What's the story behind the fire, do we know?" asked Bob.

"You gotta be kidding mate, it's a secret squirrel job. Typical CID, nothing on the grapevine. Can't help you mate," said Andy.

"But surely there is an incident room on division?" said Bob.

"No, not really, they were working down there for three or four days and Scenes of Crime were sodding about up there picking this and that up. To be honest, I don't think anyone has a fucking clue as to what really happened and what really went on during the early hours of that morning. Much of the debris was sent to the science lab. The fire service is putting it down to an electrical fault. That is a load of bollocks, all political. How come a tanker lorry is embedded into the side of the fucking house with a dead body in the cab? The skipper was a bit uptight. He did try to find out as to what was going on. It's his patch, and even he is none the wiser. None of us have been up there; we've not had any cause. All that's up there is the bloody gypsy camp and they are a couple of miles beyond the property. I know the skipper was told to stay out of it, typical CID job again. Three more years mate and I will be gone. I just don't want to know about this fucking job anymore, too many self-appointed agendas and all the political bullshit that comes with it," said Andy now speaking on his soap box.

"Yeah, I know what you mean, but don't start me off as I am as pissed off as you and many more with long service who feel the same way. I've had a lot of hassle lately and I must get back in the swing of things," said Bob.

"Yes. I've heard you are separated mate," said Andy.

"Well mate, it's just one of those things. I mean, it just went from bad to worse and this bloody job doesn't help with all the cut backs. Government have got their heads up their own arses, poor vision, the bloody lot have stuffed this fucking country. I am like you Andy, really treading water as the years tick away and retirement looms," said Bob, looking at the time and wondering about Sergeant Anderson.

"What is the skipper working today?" said Bob.

"He is on a split today, twelve to four and eight till midnight," said Andy.

"Well, I better show the flag and have a run-around with the Panda," said Bob.

"Are you on cover then?" asked Andy.

"Well yes, there are no driver's apparently, only probationers," said Bob.

"That is a load of bollocks. They're always swinging that one on us. The trouble is, they're letting too many take time off for this and that. Management wants to put its foot down and shut some of them up. They are real piss-takers at sub-division," said Andy now with a livid voice.

"I had better check the Panda, make sure there is no damage or surprises that I might get caught for," said Bob, laughing.

"Well that doesn't surprise me. I'll dig out some old telex files on the fire. It's just an incident log that went up to HQ for the old man's consumption. Everything else was removed and taken into town," said Andy.

"Did you say constipation or consumption Andy?" said Bob jokingly.

"Well, who knows these days, we are none the wiser," said Andy.

"Do you know who the officer in charge would be, D/I or D/C/I? Can't help you their mate," said Andy.

Bob decided, on leaving the station, that he would make a visit to 'Marshalls Green' and in his absence. Andy left the telex messages in Bob's docket for later.

Near to midday, Bob returned to the station,

"I went up to 'Marshalls Green' earlier and had a poke around. It's a right bloody mess. It's been turned over well. I can't imagine the gypsies leaving it alone. How bad is the problem round here with them Andy?" asked Bob.

"Nuisance value really at times, real aggro, but not much

happens on our patch, thank Christ. We just get a call as to who has recently been checked, otherwise, others arrive and do early morning turnovers, that is it mate," said Andy.

"Fuck me, what's the matter with this bloody place," said Bob.

"Don't worry about it mate, I'm bloody sure that I am not too bothered at my time of life. The bloody Governors don't seem that bothered either. Anyway, all I can say is the skipper was told to stay out of it. Have a word with him when he comes in," said Andy.

"Yeah, I bloody shall mate, no mistake there Andy, I am going upstairs for my breakfast," said Bob, as he closed the office door behind him as Andy answered the telephone.

Nothing changes round here as Bob laughed to himself. The same old creaking staircase, stopping on the first floor and from the window that overlooks the courtyard, saw the same old white painted fire buckets casting neat shadows on the brickwork. As usual, everything in its rightful place. Climbing the next floor level, Bob entered the kitchen. The earlier fragrance of bacon still lingered in the air. It was obvious that a traffic crew had stopped over from their motorway patrol and had a fry up. Whilst taking his meal break, his attention was drawn to the kitchen window as he heard a vehicle draw up on the forecourt. The slam of a car door and footsteps across the yard indicated perhaps that Sergeant Anderson had arrived for duty. At the sink, Bob threw the coffee dregs away as he washed and rinsed his mug, by which time a voice echoed out behind him. He turned and saw Sergeant Anderson standing in the kitchen doorway,

"Hello Bob. Nice to see you old mate, I heard you were joining us," said the Sergeant.

As he went to turn away, Bob said, "Sarge, before you go, what's the story on 'Marshalls Green'? Is it a murder? Only earlier, I had a run up there and saw the shocking mess that's been left," said Bob.

"That's been a bastard affair from the start," said the Sergeant.

"What's behind all this hush, hush then Sarge? The fire must have been massive," said Bob.

"There is no answer at the moment. Forensics results are not known yet, although the intimations are that it was a tragic accident," said Sergeant Anderson.

"And," said Bob eager to know more.

"Well, there is more, but I'm afraid we're going to have to sit on it. I've been told to stay out of it by CID. The fire service found some odd things among the debris. I informed CID, but no-one's taken any notice," said Sergeant Anderson, as he was slipping off his jacket.

"This bloody amazes me, I thought we were all in this together, all doing the same job. I would have thought the station would have been the first to know what's going on. The job is well and truly fucked, all secret squirrel stuff these days," said Bob in a somewhat frustrated voice.

"You know what it's like Bob, in a few weeks CID will get fed up and it will be filed away, with one CID to keep the file up to date should there be info arriving on someone's desk or someone important like the County's High Sheriff, then arseholes will start to tweet and headless chicken's will be running all over the place, just like the good old days," said Sergeant Anderson, laughing out loud to his final words, "The good old days, did they ever exist, I wonder?"

"Well, I've finished my meal break, so I am going to have a wander," said Bob.

"Hold on Bob, I'll just check my tray and dispatch and I'll have a run out with you. Do us a cuppa, while I sort myself out mate," said the Sergeant.

Heading away from the Police Station, Bob and Sergeant Anderson were very much in the small talk of what served best the community and the village in general terms of crimes.

"Out here you will find this to be the focal point for many ramblers to meet up on most weekends. They travel in by train and are well organised, I must say. Well prepared for changing weather, they are no trouble," said the Sergeant.

Many years had passed since the early days of Bob's service and the brief tours of duty he performed in the village, speaking out loud,

"It's funny, you know Sarge, years ago we patrolled this village from sub-division. It's bloody strange how things have changed. No wonder people get fed up with us. We really don't offer them a good service. We ice over the cake and yet, over the years, we have always said the fucking wheels will come off one day and yet we go on struggling and no one gives a fuck," said Bob, as he changes gear of the Panda and accelerates out of the village.

"Well Bob, that's the powers that be. It's called man-management. You know as well as I, they think with their balls in their mouths," said the Sergeant.

Bob laughed out loud at his last remark,

"That's funny Sarge, balls in their mouths," Bob continued to laugh at the remark and said, "I'm glad I've come back. I need the peace and quiet and it's always been a beautiful place, so green. I only wish I had the money to buy my own place round here, that would do me away from life's aggravations," said Bob as he also remarked on his separation being somewhat confusing in the way his wife behaves.

"I'm sorry to hear that mate. This job doesn't help, it takes a special kind of woman to put up with the shift hours and the disruption to family life, but they are out there. I found one, touch wood," said the Sergeant as he also tapped his head. "We are known as 'Wooden tops' by the city boys. They think we are country yokels, bumpkins, working out in the countryside," said the Sergeant.

The Panda car drew up to the front gate of 'Marshalls green'; Bob rested his arm on the driver's door at the open window of the vehicle, his flat cap rested on his forehead with the peak pulled down to shade his eyes from the sunshine. Both officers sat in silence, each with their own thoughts as the scene of devastation could still be clearly seen at the loss of such a large building collapsing and disintegrating to nothing, other than burnt ash that gets caught in the wind from time to time and swirls up into the sky like a swarm of bees and then disperses just as quickly to nothing as it rises.

"Christ, I wish I had the answer to this," said Sergeant Anderson in a rather frustrated tone.

Bob listened with a blank expression,

"I had a brief wander round here this morning. I get this old stomach-churning feeling that there is more to this fire than we have been given credit for. I just can't explain it. Bloody suspicious, yes, but too easy to say an electrical fault on such a large building, I don't buy it. Why the petrol tanker and the body found in the cab? Has the body been identified yet? This place grips me as if I have had some connections to it in the past, but my mind is blank, but whatever I still believe that the answer to this mess is still here," said Bob in a contrite conspicuous manner.

Then rubbed his arms as he felt the gooseflesh creep over his skin as he shuddered. Sgt Anderson was scanning the ground from the passenger seat as he listened to Bob. Clearly, the undergrowth was thick in places and able to see the new growth emerging along the edge of the copse and woodland. Nature is always evolving and overwhelming at times, it never stops moving, like marching soldiers.

Bob left the police car to stretch his legs and walked down the gravelled driveway to the edge of the blackened surface that circled the house. Then he turned and looked back towards the front gate. In doing so, he realised that they were being watched from the woodland on the opposite side of the lane. He ignored the figure and continued to wander round, eventually moving close to the front passenger door. Sgt Anderson had wound down the window as Bob whispered and informed him of the watchful eyes that were upon them from the opposite side of the lane. Sgt Anderson then sat back and looked into the vehicles internal mirror hoping to capture some movement behind them.

Moving away from the vehicle, Bob moved closer to the copse, keeping the ashen remains to his right as he followed the burnt line that outlined a circle effect, but how was this formed? Bob was mesmerised at what he thought he had discovered. He had to blink a number of times as his thoughts were fixed, as a stare on the burnt ring that formed the circle round the house, even the stench of burnt timber remained in the air as he followed the burnt perimeter of the ground, thrusting both hands in his pockets as he rocked back and forth on his heels, thinking, just thinking at the pattern of events he feels he has discovered. Then, turning to face the copse and woodland, what searches have been made in there, Bob thought. Does that place hold a secret clearly untouched by the fire, although much of the tree line was showing signs of singeing among the leaf canopy, crisp and curled over and yet remained on the tree? None appeared to have fallen as one would have expected with such an intense fire close adjacent.

Bob widened his search and beckoned Sgt Anderson to join him on the ground. Bob ran through his thoughts and explained in some detail about the shape of the perimeter, the circle that went around the building,

"How did this burn and remain in the shape it has on the ground? Let your eyes follow from the front of house to the rear, that is a definite pattern emerging here and that was caused by liquid, petrol in fact from the tanker, it must be the answer. Slope from the front gate, vehicle is against the building on the other side, so how did the ground end up in this shape? The only way it could, was if petrol was flooding the ground, the liquid was a flowing stream that crept over the ground and formed this shape with the contours of the ground," said Bob gesturing to the Sergeant.

And with a wary eye on the woodland opposite and the prying eyes that were somewhere in the undergrowth, who may be watching their every move.

"Just think about the shape. How was this formed? It had to be by liquid flooding the ground and, of course, when on fire, it simply engulfed all in its path, hence the shape of what we are looking at. So how can this be an electrical fucking fire, I ask you?" asked Bob, whispering in frustration to the Sergeant.

"You are right. How was the shape formed at the time of the fire? It had to be liquid. It had to be petrol and that can only have come from the tanker and they are designed for heavy impact, which only leaves the valves and they have to be physically turned by hand to let the fuel flow," said the Sergeant, "which means only one thing, there had to be others here on the night and the valves were deliberately opened for this one purpose to set ablaze the house. Vengeance, could it be vengeance?" asked Sergeant Anderson.

"Why are you laughing Bob?" asked the Sergeant.

"Skipper, you have come to the same conclusion as I and I have not influenced you with my opinion. You have taken the signs that I have shown you and the answer is clear as to what we believe. This is a deliberate act of some kind and one of murder, murder most foul, but were there others in the house at the time or was the property empty at the time? I read a report that mentioned, at the time, the building was in total darkness, even with the raging fire and the noise that was clearly generated from outside. No lights came on, no windows opened, no screams, no shouts. I believe the house to be empty for some reason but as to how many people does this involve I have not got a fucking clue," said Bob in a rather jovial mood of what had been discovered by them both.

Streams of sunlight emblazoned his position as he left

the side of the Sergeant and walked on flat ground away from the building and looking up towards the leaf covered branches which gave the effect of an umbrella, protecting the ground below, when his foot caught on something hard which stopped him in his tracks, having almost tripped over. Bending, he rubbed his ankle and then searched for whatever caused his near fall. He found something hidden in the grass and it felt like metal of some description that jutted out from the ground. Clearing away some of the long grass, he could see the rail that descended into the hollow ridge. Wooden steps appeared overgrown and trailed down into the hollow. Counting the steps down, Bob estimated that it was a depth of around fifteen feet.

"Christ," he thought for a moment.

Coming to the bottom of the steps, his hand lent on what could only be described as the remnants of a tree stump. his train of thought was quickly interrupted by the crackle of his radio,

"Bloody hell," cursing the damned interruption.

He realised that he would have to climb back to the ridge due to poor radio reception. On his way up, he could hear the intermittent voice of Sergeant Anderson calling him,

"Okay Sarge I am coming." He shouted out as he took one last look below him, vowing to return under his breath.

"A burglary has been reported. It sounds as if it happened overnight," said Sgt Anderson.

"I suppose there's no CID on again," said Bob.

"You guessed right, no CID," said Sgt Anderson.

Bob finished duty at five o'clock that day and already he

was troubled by his visit to 'Marshalls Green' and also the way his wife behaved towards him two days earlier,

"Squirting, where did that come from, that has never happened in all the years of their marriage, so how did she know it was going to happen? When did this all start and why pick on me the way she did, and we fucked without any words spoken between us. We were all animal, all grunts and groans. I could have been drowned if she hadn't warned me," said Bob laughing his head off.

And still none the wiser as to how all this comes together and yet officially we are still separated; confused to say the least,

"And the fire gives me the gip. Something is very wrong here. Why are the signs not being read or ignored? Could this be a political matter? Who lived in the Mansion house? I need to be careful and not tread on toes," said Bob muttering to himself on his way home.

Next day, Bob was down at the local authority planning office.

"Bill Sheffield please," said Bob to the receptionist. Leaving the central office, she returned with Bill.

"Goodness me, what a surprise, I heard you had moved on Bob," said Bill as they both greeted each other with a handshake.

"No, I have moved to Chessbury Town," said Bob.

"Bill, I have a slight problem that I would like solved unofficially," said Bob quietly.

"Come through to my office and let's have a chat," said Bill.

Bob explained further his reasons for being there and

the nature of the enquiry he was hoping to solve.

Bill Sheffield returned from the archives with a series of ground maps and survey reports concerning 'Marshalls Green'.

"You know it's burnt down to the ground Bob," said Bill.

"Yes, that is why I am here on the 'QT'. It's on my patch, but nothing is coming from CID and I am left wondering as to what is going on," said Bob.

"Yes, I know your CID has been up to the office and had a look at the house plans," said Bill.

"Only the house plans. Did they say what they were looking for?" said Bob.

"No, they didn't sorry; apparently they just wanted to look at the buildings outline, nothing else, that was it. I spoke with them when they came to the office. Why? Is there something else?" asked Bill.

"Well yes there is, but I don't know if your department can help me," said Bob.

"Well, just try me," said Bill, spreading out a survey map.

Bob pointed to a space around the house,

"Here to one side of the house is a hollow, shaped in a circle with a ridge all round and flat ground on top. In places, the sides are sloped with shrubs and bushes growing and woodland on top. It's hard to explain, but something keeps niggling me and I feel the answer is in the landscape around the house. Been up there yesterday and I feel that I am missing a piece of the jigsaw, but I have no idea what it is. So, checking your records and comparing details with the survey maps might provide me the clue I am looking for" said Bob, more in an appealing voice of hope and prayer language.

Whilst Bob waited for Bill to return, he became rather inquisitive of some rather old framed photographs on the wall of Bill's office,

"You found it then?" said Bill.

"Sorry, found what?" said Bob.

"Well, the house, you are looking at the Mansion house," said Bill.

"You are joking Bill, that is the house?" asked Bob pointing to the photograph.

Bob stood staring at the photo and realised that looking down at the building from the lane, the land on the left-hand side of the house was flat, and there was no copse or woodland shown in the photo.

"About hundred years ago, that is where the huntsman congregated for the local hunt; they used that open paddock before jumping the lower fence that leads off into the valley and river below," said Bill.

"Do I kiss you now or later Bill?" said Bob with a big grin from ear to ear. "I am very excited about this. That is what I am looking for. That copse and woodland is modern day. Who put it there? Who built it? Why is it there?" asked Bob.

The survey maps confirmed that the copse and woodland are not shown on the national survey maps. Bill checked further for planning permission and it was clear that whatever the reason, there was no involvement from local authority.

"I reckon it is about fifteen plus in height and runs from the front of the property downhill towards the rear boundary fence. There is a dried river bed that circles round the base like a private road, it has those plastic grass sections stamped into the ground so that it acts like a road. It would take the weight of a vehicle, Christ, a vehicle, a vehicle, this is ringing bells with me now," said Bob, now becoming very excited at his discovery.

"Can you bury this for me Bill, until I have had a word with my skipper? He might want to come and check for himself, that copse hides a secret, but what is the secret? I need to find out and get back down there and have a good scout around," said Bob.

By nine o'clock the same evening, Bob tucked away his papers and draft of papers that he had been drawing on. In doing so, he cleared the table for the morning as he intended to be up early for duty the next day.

Entering the kitchen next morning, just after five o'clock, Bob unlocked the rear door and stood in the warmth of the rising sun, uttering swear words under his breath from a sleepless troubled night. He needed to be gone for duty at six o'clock am.

Bob was kept busy over the next few days and failed to inform Sergeant Anderson of his find. It was apparent that his actions were deliberate. He had decided to play his cards close to his chest and not involve others for the moment. He needed to be sure of the information he had put together and that the facts would stand up for themselves once he revealed his evidence.

The next day was Bob's rest day and he decided to go rambling up near 'Marshalls Green' and spend much of the day up and around the area with a mapped-out route leading over the copse down on to the footpath beyond. Should anyone take an interest in him, he had an alibi ready.

By ten-thirty o'clock the next morning, Bob had reached his destination and had descended the steps down into the hollow, leaving his nap sack hidden in the bushes. Bob wandered over the flat ground of the copse, prodding and kicking as he moved around but the ground failed to reveal any secrets.

Finally, he conceded and sat down on the wooden steps to eat his sandwiches. It was during this time, his eyes caught sight of a change of grass colour on the opposite bank to where he was sitting. Puzzled by the change, he went to investigate. Moving on to the bank, he pulled on the tufts of grass and immediately saw the colour change.

"It's different alright, I wonder what this will tell me?" said Bob,

He placed the tufts of grass into his nap sack and found his way back to the lane. Walking back down the hill to the village, an old flat back lorry passed with several young gypsies on board. He watched as the vehicle continued heading towards the village, but not before he had noted the vehicle's registration number.

Later, arriving in the village, whilst shopping on his way home, he stopped to assist a young woman who had been struggling through the swing doors of the local supermarket, after one of her four bags had collapsed spilling her shopping onto the floor. Bob offered to help her to her car. Did she have transport, he thought. She indicated as to where she had parked.

"I am trying to do too much as usual. I think I'm jinxed," said the young woman.

Bob just grinned and beckoned to follow her as she stood, having gathered some of her shopping. Bob was already holding an arm full shopping.

"Where's your husband?" asked Bob.

"He hates shopping, I have to do it all on my own," said the woman.

She sighed. By this time, she was on her feet.

"Oh! God there go my tights." She realised, that by kneeling to gather her shopping, she had torn her tights on the rough surface.

Unlocking her vehicle, she moved into the driver's seat, her legs swung round revealing her damaged tights. Bob couldn't help but notice her shapely legs. When she turned in her seat with both feet on the ground she said,

"Excuse me; I must just get rid of these."

Her hands wrenched at her torn tights and then stood up as the remainder of the material was pulled from her body. As Bob stood close by just watching her actions of intent, he grinned at her frustrated face as if looks could kill. She could feel Bob's eyes on her bare legs.

"Looks great to me, nice legs," said Bob with a big belly laugh.

She beamed a return smile as she returned to the driver's seat.

"So, you are a leg man," she grinned as she was ready for the off,

"I appreciate beauty when beauty needs a compliment," said Bob.

The woman raised her eyebrows at his comment and nodded as she thanked him again before driving off. Bob stood and watched her move off, it was clear that she was watching him from her interior mirror. Once on the main road, she cast a wave in his direction.

It wasn't until the following week that Bob caught sight of a little green car parked near the local school. Not wanting to draw attention to himself whilst in full uniform, he walked past the school gates and saw nothing. Then passing the recreation ground adjacent to the school, he saw the young woman with the torn tights throwing a stick for a brown spaniel to chase and retrieve. He watched her chase after the dog. She certainly appeared fit with a hugging blue sweater and tight jeans and a well-shaped arse, as he noticed that as a prominent feature of her when she bent down, petite and neatly trimmed, he thought.

The woman finally retrieved the dog and stick and was approaching Bob, who remained standing on the footpath. As she came closer, he grinned in her direction.

"Hello again, I didn't expect to see you again so quick," said Bob.

The woman looked puzzled until Bob mentioned torn tights.

"Oh! My god that was you I am so sorry, I never recognised you in uniform," said the woman.

They faced each other. Bob seemed to dwarf the petite figure who looked up into his face smiling, and certainly out of breath. Her dog pushed up against his trousers. She apologised as to the hairs her dog left on his uniform.

"I don't suppose your wife will be too pleased with dog's hairs," she said, concerned.

"Separated," replied Bob as he continued to look into her smiling face.

"Sorry, I wasn't being nosey," said the woman.

"That's alright. Do you live local?" asked Bob.

"I live on the new estate. I do schoolwork for those with special needs," said the woman.

"Do you have children of your own?" asked Bob.

"No, no children yet," said the woman.

"Did your husband treat you to a new pair of tights?" asked Bob.

"You must be kidding," said the woman, as she continued to laugh and shake her head, "My husband forgets that we are married," said the woman. "No, he wouldn't have noticed. Anyway, I buy my own things. We are not what you would call on the same wavelength. My friends think he is strange. He won't change. My brother often tells me I should leave him. I don't think he cares anymore. He makes out he does," said the woman humping her shoulders.

"It's that bad is it?" said Bob.

With the sounds of noisy children, she turned and quickly walked away.

"What is your name?" asked Bob, calling out as she quickened her pace.

"Sandy," came back a loud shout and a wave from her.

It wasn't until the following Monday night that he returned to duty. His first patrol was on the high street, going from shop to shop, shaking door handles, with an occasional 'goodnight' from passing members of the public. Glancing down the street once more before he moved off, returning to his parked police car, Bob exchanged his helmet for his flat cap. Driving away from the village out into the countryside, he travelled a few miles where he stopped at the Forestry Plantation, parking up the vehicle in a secluded spot. With torch in hand, he left the vehicle to examine discarded rubbish that had been dumped in an adjacent lay-by, looking for evidence as to the culprits who were litter dumping. Whilst rummaging, he heard the roar of vehicle engine racing, the revs echoed through the trees of the plantation.

"Christ, what the hell is that?" said Bob muttering to himself.

In the distance, he could make the outline of a vehicle, with the slamming of doors echoing and unknown numbers of moving figures and voices could be heard. Using the trees for cover, Bob moved slowly, his eyes peeled for signs of movement. Mot sure as to what might be happening, he continued slowly forward. It was clear that the vehicle had been racing across the golf fairway. Adjacent, laughter was loud with blaring music blasting out. Remaining under cover, the vehicle travelled at speed in his direction and Bob knew he needed to take immediate action to hide from the blazing headlights and the spotlights on the roof. Bob realised that they (whoever they were) were night lamping, shooting rabbits in the glare of a spotlight, the creatures freeze and easy prey to be shot, and the word 'Shot' came into his thoughts. It meant shotguns or small-bore rifles, which, again, brought the question of gypsy to the surface of his thinking, but how many remained back in the trees?

Now hidden from view, Bob watched as the vehicle passed, banging, rattling and thumping hard on the springs as it hit rough ground before grinding to a halt some distance from where he remained. It was only minutes when he heard a whoosh sound and then out of the darkness sprang an orange ball of flame and a glow that lit up the night sky. Then there was a loud explosion as the vehicle had been set alight. Bob moved further away into the darkness, as it was clear that should the flames reach the woodland, then considerable damage would be caused by the oils in the conifer trees. With weeks of sunshine and dry and parched ground, a major fire could easily become a greater nightmare.

He saw the silhouettes of at least six figures, but now his priority was to get back to his police car and call for the assistance of the fire service. During the early hours, Bob was able to resume patrol and headed back into the village, eventually finishing his shift at six o'clock that morning and for once, in need of a shower as he felt scruffy and dirty from his nightly experience in the woods and undergrowth.

Within the week, Bob had managed to verify from the voters' register that no persons had been registered for many years, although, a company from overseas paid the local authority a rent of some kind, making the arrangement all legal-like and nosey parkers would be kept at bay, but why pay monies if the place was empty? It was, after all, a residential property and not a trading business address. Bob was very much on a learning curve as to how all this comes together, meaning someone is very business-like in their preparation that made the mystery even more intriguing and he needed to find the reason as to why one or more persons should go to great lengths as to disguise their existence. Bob hoped that his tenacity would bear fruit and reason in solving the why 'Marshalls Green' was raised to the ground by fire.

CHAPTER THREE
Chance Meetings Keep Happening

Bob stirred from his final night's duty on the Monday, and now making ready before he left home for his quick change-over duty, starting at two o'clock with a ten o'clock late finish. This always seemed the graveyard shift with little rest in between, and in quick succession, the two tours of duty he always found to be a drag on his mental and physical abilities. It made him more lethargic than any other working day, with two rest days that followed on the Tuesday and Wednesday that meant more freedom to search for clues of the Manor House and use the knowledge he had obtained from his contact at the local authority office.

Whether by design or another coincidence, he realised that the word 'Design' was more in keeping with his thoughts as to her deliberate actions on 'Sandy's' part, as she was always popping up at the most opportune [should this be inopportune?) moments for contact with him when he was on patrol.

He began to suspect that there was a game to be played; she was disappointed with her marriage and a husband who showed little interest in her, but also a man who spent prolonged periods working away from home.

Bob was also aware of the private comments he had made about his own marriage during the first contact with 'Sandy' which, perhaps, was more of a trigger in her mind and the loneliness she felt within her own relationship, that she had found Bob's friendly help and earlier attention a lifeline. She felt, perhaps, that she could nurture in the absence of the male company she longed and hankered for.

Bob was always polite to everyone he met and 'Sandy' was no exception, but it was the time factor that crossed his mind more than anything. Working time was a premium to him and he needed to exercise caution on his part before others began to notice a pattern and one of life's big evils, 'Local Gossip', that would cause him concern with his colleagues and, again, station gossip that weaves its way back upstairs to management, although, many of them needn't talk out of turn for the shenanigans and tales he often hears about the ivory towers (muttering and giggling to himself).

Bob stood with a more Policeman-like stance as if duty called, when he addressed 'Sandy' as she approached from kerb edge, having just parked her little green car, having given a wave in his direction. He waited on her presence as her open coat exposed an open necked blouse and a blue-buttoned fronted short denim skirt that hugged her hips, that exposed her naked legs with striking muscle tone that he could not ignore. She gave the appearance of a well-kept and fit individual, her hair tied into a pony tail. He, in his mind's eye, began to see her in a sexual light and true femininity that was going to waste, (to waste what the hell was he thinking – he was whispering to himself), when he caught 'Sandy's' voice as she greeted him with a smile that told him more about her facial expressions in the way she looked at him. But then the deliberate trip and a shoe that came adrift from her foot that slid across the pavement, her hand reached out, as she used Bob's arm to steady herself and then the shoe was kicked back to her by a passing stranger. Bob was all smiles as he knew that he had been caught in a deliberate trap by 'Sandy', as he saw right down the front of her blouse. She wore no bra exposing a slight tan to her naked flesh. Then, on standing, she again gave him a 'come on smile', if that is how he would have described it. Tempting well his mind, was that of a man, whether embarrassing again, the jury was out in his mind, but behind his façade, Bob never dropped his guard, other than being professional as he remained on the public thoroughfare at the time.

"Are you teasing me?" asked Bob with a smile.

"Am I?" replied Sandy, responding as she looked into his face.

"Well I caught sight of your belly button, just then my girl," said Bob with his banter.

"Only my belly button, now that does surprise me," said Sandy as she gave a more intriguing look.

Bob grinned and nodded and said to 'Sandy',

"You should do your coat up as you might catch cold."

"Well if that's the case, I would need my chest rubbed and someone to put me to bed, don't you think?" said 'Sandy', enquiring about his thoughts to her words.

Bob soon realised that his banter was as good as hers in replies and clear that a corner had been turned, as their comments were now becoming flirtiest to say the least.

"I ought to buy you a coffee or a drink for helping me," said 'Sandy'.

"That can't happen, I am on duty," said Bob, rather bewildered at her openness.

She was becoming persuasive in her manner. She obviously had made a beeline for him and the way things were going, she wasn't about to stop her flirting which she had taken to another level.

"I know that, I don't mean now. Do you want to meet up sometime?" asked 'Sandy', as it was clear that she was anxious for a 'YES' answer from him.

"Why not? I finish at ten tonight. Pubs stay open late and I know just the place to go," said Bob,

Realising that he needed to visit the 'Bull and Butcher' pub and see Judy in the next village, as he had promised on his return to duty.

"How are we going to work this? if I pick you up somewhere away from your place, would that be okay with you?" asked Bob. "Better still, if you give me your number, then I'll give you a call to make sure that I am free and not caught up in work."

He gave her pen and paper from his tunic pocket and remained in a professional stance. As 'Sandy' returned paper and pen, as Bob left her side and continued his patrol, 'Sandy' went in the opposite direction to a line of shops.

Bob never looked back in her direction, so nothing looked out of place to any spying eyes and no tales to be told by the wicked. His working day was quiet and remained at a slow pace. No panics and emergencies to contend with and the kind of day he needed having done a quick change over in duty terms. His brain always seemed scrambled on this back to back duty roster.

Bob kept his meeting with 'Sandy' later and drove to the next village as arranged. Judy's greeting was a good indicator to 'Sandy' as to how popular Bob was in the lives of the locals when his presence was mentioned by Judy. Bob introduced 'Sandy' and ordered drinks. Judy fetched Dan, her husband, to bring down the box that had been left for Bob weeks before. Judy explained about the other man in the bar that night and you mentioned gypsies to him and obviously your conversation struck a chord with him, because the next day, he appeared and asked us to look after the box until you returned from your course.

"I have got no idea who he was. He never said, and I never bothered to ask at the time," said Judy, in a friendly gesturing manner. "So, I took the box from him and Dan stored it for you."

Bob frowned with a look of curiosity, as Dan produced the large cardboard box and placed it on the bar. Bob just simply turned it around and looked for outer signs on the box.

"No labels or note attached," said Bob with a very inquisitive look and tempted to open it then and there and decided not to.

"I need to be careful with this. I'll take it back to the station with me, just in case things are not right with whatever is inside," said Bob.

As he removed the box from the bar and left it on a table nearby, while he continued to sit and socialise with 'Sandy' and the other patrons of the pub who came and went in their conversations as they both sat at the bar.

Bob had noticed that 'Sandy' had not changed her earlier clothing, except for a different outer coat and, from his position on the bar stool, he, from time to time, tapped 'Sandy' on the knee when he spoke to her. It was a long-term habit of his but realised what he had been doing and apologised. 'Sandy' rubbed her hand over her naked leg.

"I don't mind, feel you can't ladder my bare flesh," said 'Sandy', with whispers and a smile.

Then her hand laid over his, as he went to touch her leg. She stroked the back of his hand as he laid his palm on her knee. She gently pulled her hand with his underneath back along the top of her thigh.

“My skin is so smooth, I loathe pimples and gooseflesh,” as she laughed out.

As her short skirt was revealing more of her naked thigh as she turned towards him on the stool with his hand now between her legs as she continued to rub his bare arm as his rolled shirt sleeve gave her the opportunity she was perhaps looking for, tempting him more, encouraging him to touch her more intimately between the legs as she felt the warmth of his hand on her skin.

Bob drew back from her touching and sat up and turned as he ordered further drinks. In fact, he decided on a coffee as he was driving, but that didn’t deter ‘Sandy’ from further glasses of wine, as she whispered to Bob, a big thank you for his company, as it was clear that she had not socialised for some time in another man’s company and her flirting was clear in the way she had held Bob’s hand.

Finally, both said their farewells to Judy as Bob carried the box and ‘Sandy’ held back the door as they headed outside to Bob’s parked car. Once both were seated in the vehicle, it was ‘Sandy’ who leant over and placed a kiss to the side of his neck and thanked him for their time together. As her mental thoughts were rather mixed here, she was enjoying the company with this gorgeous man beside her, then also quietly thinking of her husband who never displayed his feelings to her. It was simple to analyse, as Bob had returned the kiss more on her lips than cheek as his hand on her chin turned her in the right direction towards him, as half of her wanted to stop and the other half wanted more than just a good night kiss. Slowly, her inhibitions began to subside as she was the one leading the flirting earlier and now she has reservations and had become more hesitant in her manner towards Bob.

'Sandy' had a change of mind as she reached out and touched his face with soft strokes and gentle touches, with her fingers running over his lips as she stared into his face, her eyes were in a fixed stare, as if she was wanting to climb into his mind and feel what he was thinking at that moment.

"Well me girl, we better make a move," said Bob with a smile and glance in 'Sandy's' direction.

"Can we go somewhere; do you have to get home?" asked 'Sandy' as Bob went to change gear. She took hold of his hand and placed it between her legs then held his arm.

"Please, please can we go somewhere quiet," said 'Sandy'

Bob realised how inviting this was all becoming, but clearly not a situation he was looking for as he had genuine issues of his own and had no intention of adding to his demise. He was in two minds as to whether to return home, rather than listen to 'Sandy's' pleading words. But then she let go of his hand and rubbed between his legs as he accelerated away from the pub. He was so bewitched by her touching and feeling like any red hot-blooded man ought to be at this moment and amorous to say the least. His mind worked overtime as to the situation he was walking into. He needed to be sensible about her behaviour and to level with her, even though sexually he fancied the pants off her, but still taboo with a big sign which read 'Untouchable'.

Bob drove to a quiet place off his patch and parked up. 'Sandy' had moved back her seat and placed her feet on the dashboard as she poured her heart out to Bob in the way she felt she had to, and so neglected by her husband

and her need for male company and it was she who suggested that she wanted a friend with benefits. She wanted a sexual partner to determine her own needs as a woman and to explore more of her femininity and in return, to compliment a new male friend in her life who would be compatible with her and not demanding and criticising her every five minutes they are together. She looked for the peace and tranquillity that quality in the sexual and physical sense could give her and not go looking for one-night stands. Quantity was not on her menu, but a solid friendship from a trusted source she could rely on without leaving her husband, without divorcing and giving up her lifestyle and hoped that Bob might want to fill that gap in her life and what she may be able to attribute to his life without becoming bogged down in all the emotional factors that come with eventual new relationships, not being in each other's faces and boring, but alive and sharing each other's sexual favours and needs and to experiment in the real art of deep love making in pleasing each other physically, with a solid bond of togetherness.

Bob was frank and honest about his sexual feelings to her and remarked upon his own needs of being close to femininity in ways that he took for granted in his younger years and in marriage, lying together skin to skin and to feel the warmth between bodies and the strokes and touching that he so longed for. He explained further that he had no desire to divorce as he had settled into a routine where his work was now the most important thing as his years became less as he was heading for retirement and had no wish to rock the boat on either work or his domestic life.

"Give me your hand Bob," said 'Sandy' as she thrust his

hand up and between her legs. "This has a need, I have a need, I feel neglected and I want to be fucked by one who enjoys fucking. Is that you Bob? Am I wrong to act like this? Why should I live a life of a virgin with a husband whose absent? I want a fuck buddy, a partner who also feels neglected without any commitments other than the trust of a solid friendship," said 'Sandy'. "God, I have said it," as she blurted and gasped the last few words.

Bob remained silent, as with one hand up her skirt and the other gripping the steering wheel of the vehicle, he closed his eyes many times and shook his head in disbelief of 'Sandy's' request. She is wanting him as her lover and yet he fancied her rotten from the moment he saw her bare legs and torn tights in the car park.

Bob had secreted his vehicle well off the road and hidden behind thick undergrowth, when he heard the door open and the interior light come on as 'Sandy' left the car. He simultaneously turned to his door and alighted and in doing so he never noticed that 'Sandy' had unbuttoned her skirt and deliberately left it on the car seat when she got out, but of course, wearing only blouse and briefs, her lower torso was hidden by the coat she wore that reached to her knees and closed at the front, so Bob was completely unaware that 'Sandy' was out to seduce him this very night by any method she could.

Together, they both walked a short distance away from the vehicle and it was more of a rise in the ground they had both trod, when, in one direction, they were able to see lights in the distance and in the other, it was pitch black and led into an open field with long grass, both eventually coming to rest in the long grass, although, 'Sandy' had kept the front of her coat closed so that Bob remained unaware of what she had done. Their conversation was in whispers, as 'Sandy' confided more in Bob than he had with her, but laying full length on her back, she pointed skywards to Bob as he was prone and, on his side, propped up on one elbow as he looked over her into face. She then knew they were going to kiss as she placed her hand on his neck and drew him down towards her lips as they finally met with such a long lingering kiss, as if it could be described as though she was about to eat him alive with such passion, and whimpers were plentiful as he felt her whimpers vibrating his lips as they continued to kiss as he leant more across her body. 'Sandy' had already opened her legs wide, although the coat still covered her modesty and that was soon to change when Bob began to use his hands as he explored her body. 'Sandy' felt the gentleness of his hand glide over her blouse as Bob pulled on the material to reach her bare flesh underneath, exposing her waistline as he continued to stroke in slow gentle movements and yet 'Sandy' was more in a rush to get him to touch her more intimately. She felt a deep sense of urgency striking out and wanting him to stop and fuck her hard, but Bob was Bob and he was not going to spoil this night of nights. Why spend a penny when he can get more for the pound?

Bob recognised her beauty, her touches and her candid manner she had enticed him into her sexual web of intrigue. As some women were not very responsive with their partners, even those of long standing, it was time to rid herself of any inhibitions she may have had and really get down to the nitty-gritty with Bob, as she was so determined that he would fuck her that very night, but hadn't considered the long grass and stars overhead in what was now becoming a more romantic setting than she had planned by being fucked in his car. Whether in the front seat or back, it would not have made any difference to her, it was the result she sought.

Bob began to be more productive as his hand went down on to the lower buttons of her coat. Finally opening the garment, he saw only bare legs and thighs, mentally thinking, "The skirt, where is it?" Without further ado, Bob began to be more relaxed as he knew he had gone past his limits of no return, he just could not resist the temptation that she had laid bare in words and now, in deeds of her nakedness, that he was about to encourage as he knelt by her side as he pulled on the sleeves of her coat and removed her arms, one by one, and then pulled the blouse over her head, leaving her wearing only her briefs. Using her coat as a ground sheet, 'Sandy' laid back with her arms down by her side as Bob stood and undressed himself, even taking off his 'Bloody Socks' she thought. Her copper, now bollock naked, standing at her feet with a limp truncheon that looked rather small for such a tall man as he in the darkness looked down at her almost naked frame, as the night sky glistened upon her toned body, making shapes and shadows on her flesh and the cherry nipples with a larger than life brown patch that circled both, even able to see, and what could only be described as, little goose bumps dotted inside the brown patches, uncanny and so bloody stupid, but then he was noticing more of the femininity as being the woman, than he had noticed on other occasions with other women, more as an episode of taking things for granted and that really was the issue of most relationships. Being eager to engage that much is left behind in understanding the woman and the emotions that are so often ignored by men.

'Sandy' was more mindful of seeing such a small

truncheon come to her rescue in her time of need, but as Bob remained standing at her feet, 'Sandy' sat up and slid her legs underneath him, as she came face to face with a large hanging scrotum and a wee fellow that needed some nurturing as she moved her lips on to his foreskin and kissed gently, and then two fingers held him at the hilt of the pubic line as she placed her lips over his member and gently cradled, sucked and used her tongue to raise some interest in her. It was as she had hoped, a penis that raised its game like self-raising 'Yeast' waiting for the baker to see the readiness that awaited him.

As she slowly withdrew on the member, as it continued to grow in her mouth, and by which time Bob had realised the intensity of his sexual feelings as gently with both hands, he held 'Sandy's head as he moved his member back and forth in her mouth. Her hands held the back of his thighs as she moved with him, then, letting go as she came up for air, gasping and panting from the sudden surge of Bob's energy towards her.

Neither had uttered any words. It was a solid physical interaction between them. Words were meaningless. As for her, it was that moment of the unknown as to how he would perceive her. How would he fuck her? Would he be gentle? Would he be rough? Would he last, and fuck her as any woman would want to be fucked by a deep sense of love making that provides the art of enjoyment for them both? And now, 'Sandy' was about to find out about Bob's prowess and whether he would satisfy her as she would with him. Who was going to be the teacher or the pupil? What would they learn together? Or, would he be the greedy one and leave her unfulfilled in a sexual famine that was of long suffering on her part, or to masturbate herself silly, but only ever in the shower or in bed alone surrounded by her toys, like most modern women of her age.

Bob made the first move. He turned 'Sandy' on to her tummy, and on his knees, he pulled her back with legs wide open. She resembled more of the wheelbarrow laying across his lap. 'Sandy' was beginning to wonder where this was taking her. She had never been manhandled into this position before. Even so, she wanted to experiment and now was the opportunity to note his behaviour. Both of Bob's hands came into play as he stroked, caressed and gently touched her back shoulders, arms and every part that was exposed to him. By this time, 'Sandy' had folded her arms underneath her head and just lay in the warmth of his touches and gentle massage that tingled throughout her body. Then, pulling down her knickers and peeling them from her legs as he bent, he began to kiss her slowly with deliberate butterfly pecks and kisses that made her even more sexually moved by the way he was conducting himself. Finally, he encouraged her on to her back and moved her legs back and wide to expose more of her hidden vagina that he was now taking a greater interest in, as he moved with protruding tongue as he really went to town on her clitoris. She wriggled her arse but kept pushing her body towards him as she felt the intense pressure on her public line. She neared orgasm, but managed to hold back and, in fact, Bob had been doing that from the beginning. He was very much in control of his shooting sperm, he was not ready to be the expendable one, when he knew that a good forty-five minutes were needed to get any female in the mood. Without screwing up, he kept a focused mind.

Eventually, he took hold of his penis and tickled and teased 'Sandy's' front door and clearly well moistened by her own female magical ways of control, no dryness, no burning or irritation and Bob was feeling good as he slowly pushed back his foreskin as he slowly and gently eased back and forth, and she felt it where she could not control herself anymore, as she grabbed him with both legs round the waist, her ankles locked as she physically pulled him on to her and then, together, they found each other's rhythm, and my goodness me, Bob realised the tight fit of her vagina as he felt her grip on him. As she laced and bathed him in her inner juices, it was as good as she hoped. It was that long-awaited fuck that blew away her cobwebs and made her feel a wanted woman again. She also felt how good they performed with each other. He showed a caring side that was unexpected. His kissing, cuddling and the way he fucked her with real consideration for her and not just for his own needs, and that little truncheon she saw earlier had come good when it was needed to expand and bring forth the truth, the whole truth and nothing but the truth in one hell of a good fuck. Bob rode her well and tried a couple of other positions, until they both fell into each other's arms, knackered, and well and truly pleased with each other's performance. What more does a wanting woman want from her man (muttering giggles and whispers), as she finally reached out and cuddled him for all his worth.

It was gone two o'clock the next morning (Tuesday), when Bob dropped 'Sandy' off at her home address and he returned to his home. Leaving the cardboard box in the car overnight, he needed a clear head before he made any attempt to open and find out what was inside.

CHAPTER FOUR

Change of Direction

Five o'clock on the Thursday afternoon, Sergeant Anderson and PC Bob Benyon were three hours into their late turn duty, having parked up among the shrubs and bushes of the forestry woodland on the north side of the village. Both sat listening to the cat and mouse game being played out elsewhere on their radio, hearing the operator describe the offending vehicle involved in the ongoing Police chase some eight miles away from their location.

"All mobiles wait out, message to follow. 'A' division mobiles, two white males described as of scruffy appearance were seen to drive away from a dwelling subject of a burglary at Wilton Drive, zero eight minutes ago. Vehicle described as (pause) small orange Datsun saloon, index number not known at this time. Vehicle last seen heading towards Chilton town. If seen, stop and detain and inform control, message ends," said the Police radio operator.

"I wonder if they will come our way," said Bob. "Sounds like gypsies of scruffy appearance - could be from our patch".

"Sounds interesting, two scruffy males," said Sgt Anderson, pondering on his words.

"What you thinking Sarge? Travellers the same as me" said Bob.

"Mmmmmm, I am. Would they come this way or go around and over the top?" said Sgt Anderson, turning towards Bob who was sat in the driver's seat.

"Control didn't say a bloody word as usual as to what's

been stolen. This is a tosspot bloody job we are in. We only ever get half the fucking story, it really pisses me off as to why we ever bother chasing villains," said Sgt Anderson in a real frustrated voice.

"Listen to all those silly arses giving their locations, all eager to join the chase. What the fuck is wrong with them? Gypsies are just as capable as listening in as any other bugger. The press will soon be on this, you wait and see," said Bob, shrugging his shoulders in annoyance as to the last radio broadcast.

"Christ, did you hear that, even CID have joined the chase. Must be something big that Burglary. I wonder whose house?" said Sgt Anderson.

In silence, the hunt continued as the two officers listened as their radio crackled with pip tone sounds.

"What the fuck are they doing? We can't hear with this bloody thing sounding," said Sgt Anderson,

As he referred to the radio pip tones, Bob pushed himself down in the driver's seat, his flat cap pulled down over his eyes. He was in deep thought to his last contact with 'Sandy', as she had not surfaced since he dropped her off last Monday night. It wasn't until Sgt Anderson made him jump with the words,

"Come on England, wake up, let's go," said the excited voice of the Sergeant. "It sounds like they are coming our way Bob".

Without a moment to lose, Bob, with engine roaring, broke cover from their hidden location.

"Right, go left and straight on," was the Sergeant's instructions.

Bob roared through the country lane, twisting and turning with every bend, driving within his safety limits, dreading to meet a farm tractor coming from the other direction, driving with headlights on, no blue light or twin horns sounding, just speed to get them where the Sergeant wanted to be. Two miles out, they came to a 'T' junction with flat grass verges on both sides of the lane.

"Right, pull over and let's see what the position is," said Sgt Anderson.

Other police mobiles were feeding the radio controller with updates on their negative searches of the local areas.

"I am sure two-one has a sighting, fuck what is wrong with them all jabbering on at once, too much excitement here Bob," said Sgt Anderson. "Bloody poor reception again. Listen, it's all intermittent. They're breaking up on their broadcast. I reckon they are coming our way Bob," said the Sergeant.

"Two-one is behind it, it's coming up through Hotley Bottom," said Bob, ready to join the chase with engine revving.

Sgt Anderson sat holding the radio handset, waiting anxiously, wanting to get in on the broadcast. "Fuck it", as he broke into the previous radio transmission, trying to relay their position.

"Go ahead Delta Three, pass your message," came the operator's call.

"Wait one Delta Two, (pause) what is your position Delta Three?" came the controller's request.

"We are parked up at Herbert's Hole," said Sgt Anderson as Delta-Three. "We are double crew," he further replied.

"Delta One, say again," said the controller's voice. "Say again. Mobiles wait one, say again Delta One".

Then that moment all Police officers dread to hear with any ongoing vehicle chase.

"Polacc, (Police Accident), we have been rammed. Decamp two on foot making off across the fields," came a sudden burst of voices over the radio. "No injuries. I say again, no injuries. Vehicle damage only," came the radio call by Delta Two. "Road is blocked."

"Come on Bob, let's make a move, I have an idea," said Sgt Anderson.

"You thinking what I am thinking? The bins are in the boot, you are going to need them," said Bob, turning and grinning, two minds alike.

A quick stop to retrieve the binoculars from the boot of the police vehicle and then driving off towards the known gypsy camp on their patch. It was on route that a uniformed officer flagged them down. He stood waving in the road and pointing. Both officers realised that a foot chase was in progress. Sgt Anderson was first out of the vehicle; Bob stood half in and half out of his vehicle whilst the skipper was scanning the chase with the binoculars from a higher vantage point. Sgt Anderson came back to the vehicle and conversed with Bob about the direction of travel the two burglars had taken.

"Right, we need to take our friend with us, the chase has moved on towards the direction of the gypsy camp. If we can get down there 'ASAP' we might be able to head them off before they reach their camp," said Sgt Anderson, his thoughts working two to the dozen.

Driving back over the route they had taken earlier, then finding a place to hide the police vehicle, all three officers now out of the vehicle and on foot, now camouflaged by the trees and undergrowth. Sgt Anderson saw only one running figure ahead of the chasing officer. He hesitated for a moment.

“One missing. I can only see one of them ahead of the copper,” said Sgt Anderson.

“I’ll go back up the lane skipper if you keep track of the other one,” said Bob.

As he left, both officers watching the chase, he headed back up the lane, with slow deliberate strides. Bob was sure that the other figure had doubled back and was probably hiding somewhere in the hedgerow alongside the lane. Then, having walked about two hundred yards up the lane, when he saw the crouching figure of a person moving backwards, feet first towards the hedgerow. The figure faced in the direction of the chase as Bob settled into his task of observation hidden from view on the opposite side of the lane. It was obvious the figure was covering themselves with leaves and grass, intending to remain secreted for some period. Bob realised the typical strengths and characters of these young gypsies in being fast learners in decamps and the lengths they go too to avoid detection, always amazed at the risks they took. By this time, more Police officers arrived on the scene and voices heard from the field where the hidden figure remained. Dog handlers had arrived and had begun to search the open ground and woodland away in the direction of the running figure. Bob remained watching his potential customer. Not a twitch or sound could be heard from him. Other officers came up the lane to join him. Bob whispered that the other one was nearby and well camouflaged from view. He suggested that they (two of the three) go up the lane and find a way into the field and walk back to our positions in the hope of flushing out the hidden figure. Quietly, Bob and the other officer remained seated on the bank of the hedgerow and waited and waited for the other two colleagues to walk down the hedgerow. It was then that a pair of feet, then legs appeared, sticking out of the hedge. The figure was slowly propelling backwards in a crawling motion out from the hedge and intending to escape the approaching officers searching the field. It was to the shock of the figure that Bob, and his colleague grabbed his legs and torso as they pulled him free of the hedge. He twisted, he turned, he kicked, trying to break free from their grasp and lastly, the filthy habit of spitting into their faces, which was now becoming all too familiar in recent months. The figure was indeed a gypsy youth now in custody. Handcuffed, he was marched back down the lane to the main body and collective congregation of other officers who had arrived on the scene to assist. Later, the other youth had been captured by the assistance of a dog handler. It appeared that he too went to ground just like his mate, so both captured and in custody was the result and now to unblock the road of the two crashed vehicles left abandoned, including the damaged Police car. Sgt Anderson gave Bob a great hug for a job well done.

"We got the action then mate and the result," said the Sergeant.

With a beaming smile, as he and Bob returned to their vehicle, he was still rubbing his hands in excitement.

"Fucking marvellous Bob, great job," said the Sergeant. "That was a good crafty nick that will hurt CID. They can stuff that up their arses, uniforms can deliver".

By seven o'clock that evening, both had returned to the station for their meal breaks and a freshen up. Left in Bob's docket was an envelope addressed to him which he took into the kitchen to read. It was from 'Sandy' – she had written a brief note offering him friendship and benefits along with a new mobile number with an explanation that it was just for the two of them, meaning private and confidential, if he agreed to her desires.

After their meal breaks, Sgt Anderson asked Bob to drive him up to the gypsy site as he wanted to look for himself.

Arriving twenty minutes later, the Sergeant was astonished at the number of caravans that had parked on either side of the lane. It seemed endless as the officers approached.

“Good grief, I didn’t realise there was so many,” said the Sergeant.

“There was quite a number here the other night when I came through and clear that more have arrived from somewhere,” said Bob, “It means more local aggravation,” he muttered.

Bob pulled the police vehicle off the road in between two caravans, more near the tepee tent positioned alongside the hedgerow. It was then, Old Ben Witney appeared and sat down with his back pressed against a wooden stave fixed in the ground, as he puffed away on his pipe with rising clouds of smoke swirling above his head and as he watched both officers approach. Greeting Ben, as he spat spittle from his mouth and then reinserted his pipe back into his mouth,

“Hello governor. What do you want for your car?” said Ben, with a wry smile on his face.

“You’ll be lucky my old china, you wouldn’t want that after we have finished with it,” said Bob, answering with a joking voice at Ben’s question.

Old Ben raised himself off the ground and ambled

awkwardly over to the Police car. Old Ben was a wily old fox, he was not interested in the car, he was anxious for a chat with Bob whom he had met on other occasions and he knew that Bob could be relied on. Peering from under his thick eyebrows, he made out he was looking into the vehicle.

"They are a bad lot, the new ones," said Ben whispering as he continued to puff on his pipe. "The big house was bad business, our young ones are cider crazy, choring every night," said Old Ben,

Still, following a rouse with Bob making out they were talking about the Police vehicle, Ben bent down and banged the wheel hub.

"Hiding bling in the grease cap," said Old Ben.

Other travellers began to appear. Women with folded arms stood silent as their men folk ambled around with their hands in their pockets, some jibbed Old Ben.

"They come for you then Ben," said one voice from the group.

"He been a choring governor 'as Old Ben," said a traveller woman.

That brought a raucous laugh from the group. Bob was all ears to their spoken slang as he laughed along with them. The outsider, Sgt Anderson, stood and watched fascinated by the way Bob interacted with some of the old gypsies who now joined the growing throng.

"Have the council been up here yet?" asked Sgt Anderson.

"They came up on Monday morning sir," said the voice of a woman.

As Bob turned and looked in her direction,

"I thought that voice was familiar," said Bob.

A lean slip of a young woman, now heavily pregnant, stepped forward.

"Christ, Annie when is the baby due? I didn't think you were old enough to get married," said Bob, with concern in his voice.

The group of travellers laughed and jeered loudly.

"What's going on here then?" asked Bob, "Who's your man then?"

"Leafy," came the gruff reply from somewhere in the group.

"What old Teddy's boy? Bloody hell, I haven't seen them since I left the old place," said Bob.

"He's sick, is Old Teddy, governor," said another gypsy, "Ain't he," Ben, "Sick is teddy".

Old Ben waved his pedlars certificate around.

"Am I alright with this governor?" asked Old Ben, as he beckoned Bob over to his grotty looking truck parked away from the group.

Bob leaned through the open window as he waited for Old Ben to speak.

"Shhhh, you want to watch them, governor, they're nasty bastards they are sir, you watch them," said Old Ben, whispering to Bob.

"Who are you talking about Ben?" asked Bob, also replying in a faint voice of a whisper.

"At the top of the lane, then new ones," said Old Ben.

"Are they choring (stealing)?" asked Bob.

"At it every night, governor, they are sir," said Old Ben. "Done some foreigner folk, supposed they say, got some big stones, but they're gone, been nicked from them," said Old Ben still whispering.

"What is the family name, do you know Ben?" asked Bob.

Quietly whispering and eyes everywhere scanning and being sure no one was approaching them.

"How many are we talking about Ben?" asked Bob.

"Seven caravans at top of lane," said Old Ben.

"Where's the stuff going Ben? Do you know?" asked Bob,

Sounding more inquisitive than ever, as he wanted to find answers now and not tomorrow or another day after that. It was imperative for him to come up trumps.

"They've got a farm at Ampthill. Generators, chainsaws. They have been doing the allotments and farms for miles, some doing burglaries. They got chased by the dweller they did, sir, chased them for miles. They abandoned the car and ran off. Three big fellows came looking for them. They speak funny, not like a traveller speaking," said Old Ben.

Bob decided that he had had enough. He was taking too long with Old Ben, gesturing to his certificate that he handed back to him.

"Do you want some earners (Money) Ben?" asked Bob.

"Yes governor, I would," said Old Ben,

Smiling and clutching and fingering his pipe as he spoke to Bob,

"I'll get something organised," said Bob. "Can we meet tomorrow morning? Give me a place and time," said Bob.

"By the burnt-out house, I'll be there early. I spend time down there watching who comes and goes," said Old Ben.

"Okay, I'll catch you tomorrow Ben, I'll find you mate," said Bob.

Sgt Anderson had already returned to the vehicle when Bob appeared with Old Ben.

"Pedlars Certificate, Sarge," said Bob. "Old Ben does it proper Sarge."

They both laughed together and loud enough for the other travellers to hear, as it was obvious many a beady eye was watching them go.

"Who else wants Pedlars Certificates?" said Bob to the waiting group.

Driving back to the station, Bob remembered that in the boot of his car was a cardboard box that he had forgotten all about.

"Bloody hell, I have a box left me. I left the bloody thing in the boot of my car, I have clean forgotten about, Jesus Christ," said Bob, rather shocked at his forgetfulness.

"He won't help you mate," said Sgt Anderson.

Bob laughed at the comment as he continued to drive.

"Near knock-off time skipper," said Bob. "They're a crafty lot of sods. You see how their eyes followed us, they watched our every move. Old Ben has given me some ideas. We have some nasty ones further up the lane, out every night apparently. They're supposedly being chased off from a burglary by foreigners. They decamped and left their vehicle. I bet that's knocked off. They really are some bastards when they get going," said Bob.

"Yeah, I did notice how their eyes followed us around, the smell of body sweat is awful though," said Sgt Anderson.

"They really do fuck us about though. You never get a straight answer, always in riddles," said Bob. "Well, it's like back there, Old Ben talks in riddles and expects us to work out the rest of it. That's the way they are. That to them is not snitching, but can earn them a few bob from us, so it is very important to listen to them. I speak their language, I don't let on, I am always picking up a few extra words when around them. The word 'GAVVER' is for us 'POLICE'," said Bob.

"It might be an idea for you to spend a bit more time up here and keep an eye on them. We need to keep this to ourselves until we have something to really work with. Let's play it by ear Bob," said Sgt Anderson.

"Well, there is no harm in trying. Something has got to give, and I hope we are the ones to pick it up," said Bob.

Back at the Police station, they each removed their things and Bob completed the mileage book before locking and leaving the vehicle parked up for the night. He realised that he was clutching 'Sandy's note as he entered the back door of the station, just after ten o'clock. Bob left the station and sat momentarily undecided as to whether he calls 'Sandy' or goes to the pub for a drink, or just simply goes home and forgets about his desiring thoughts. Instead, he calls 'Sandy' and tells her he is coming past her junction and to be there should she want picking up, and as expected, 'Sandy' was waiting in the shadows for him to arrive. Once in the vehicle, he drove slowly away as he gave 'Sandy' a gentle pat on the knee and she greeted him with a smile and said,

"I've come prepared tonight Bob, just in case. I am naked under my coat, so you obviously got my note," said 'Sandy'.

As she leant forward and looked him in the face for his reaction, Bob was just grinning to himself as he continued to drive out towards the countryside. It was a good five miles before Bob found what he was looking for, an open driveway that was secreted by undergrowth at the lane edge. This has been an isolated place for years, used by the military and now abandoned, only used by the local farmer to store animal feeds and hay bales. Parking up alongside one of the old buildings stuffed with hay bales, the couple left the vehicle and stood out in the open as they greeted each other with a long lingering kiss. Then, as 'Sandy' turned away, she laid across the bonnet of his car with her arms outspread and said,

"Take me now Bob, fuck me here," she laughed in whispers as she said it. "What here, out in the open?" said Bob, laughing.

"Well you do have a hot bonnet Bob?" asked 'Sandy'.

Gesturing, as she stood up and walked with her arm entwined with his, as Bob led the way to the front opening of the old building, the heavy smell of fresh hay was hanging in the air as they found themselves newly placed bales to sit on. As 'Sandy' cuddled up to Bob, as they spent some time while discussing their personal arrangements between them and what friends and benefits meant to both. 'Sandy' made it plain about her sexual needs and regarded Bob as a desirable choice as a lover and what she experienced with him on their first night together had left her with fantastic vibes as to how he had fucked her and why she sent the note. She wanted more of what he had to offer, and why, tonight, she came naked, hoping that he wanted to fuck her as she was ready for him. Eventually, Bob led 'Sandy' further back into the darkness and away from the front of the old building as he looked for perfection and means of comfort. Finding soft loose hay to spread them down on, using the blanket she had dragged from Bob's back seat of his car. Bob, giggling at what he had realised, she was well and truly ahead of him in her preparation for them being together this night. In the beginning, it was nothing more than silence and one long big cuddle and lots of gentle pecks and kisses on lips, face and neck. No groping from either, no intimate touching, just gliding lips over their facial features. Neither wanted to rush and spoil the moment. 'Sandy' was happy with herself in her choice of lover, and the respect he had shown her throughout since their first meeting. Bob was very much alive to the emotional stimulus that women need and not just simply hard and gripping penetration. It was the cuddling itself that made them so relaxed with each other and, of course, both were not tied to time, as time together was theirs for as long as they wanted on this very night.

'Sandy' removed her coat and in doing so, revealed her nakedness. She folded and used the coat as a pillow for two. Bob, at the same time, peeled off his clothes and folded each garment neatly, then returned under the blanket with 'Sandy'. As she lay on her side, he cuddled up against her back, at the same time pulling the blanket over them both. Bob had cupped one of 'Sandy's' breasts, as he pulled himself tight into her. Neither had spoken but laid her hand over his that cupped her breast. Skin to skin, their warmth's engaged their silent togetherness and outside, darkness became more overshadowed by the moving night sky. It was perhaps a more romantic setting than she had expected, being naked and locked together and being cuddled was unexpected, and it was a nice feeling to relax with somebody of her choice and drawing on the smells of the countryside added to her moment of bliss, as they lay upon the bed of sweet smelling hay.

It was the early hours of the morning when Bob had woken, having both fallen asleep much earlier when cuddling her. He gently parted from her as he coaxed her on to her back, whilst she remained asleep, he then began to stroke her breasts and stomach area. A finger followed the contours of her belly button as he continued to move his hand over her naked flesh in slow deliberate strokes. At the same time, he had placed his lips against the lobe of her ear, kissing and sucking gently with occasional blowing air from his pouted lips. It was then 'Sandy' turned on to her side facing him, with her hand and arm touching the small of his back. He had done the same where, from the small of her back, his hand reached down and fondled her buttocks in smooth strokes and touches. 'Sandy' began to stir as he continued to arouse her. She placed a leg over his, bringing her buttocks closer to him as he continued to reach and touch parts of her inner thighs, As the side of his hand brushed against her vagina, as he continued to manipulate his hand deep between her thighs. Then, 'Sandy' rolled on to her back as she pulled Bob with her. She was encouraging him. She was wanting him as he rolled between her open legs, now spread wide, to receive him and at the same time, remained with her eyes closed and gentle whimpering sounds purring from her lips. Bob was ready for her, as he gently moved himself above and on to her as, on his first try, slipped into her moist opening, as he really was giving his all in not being a 'Bull in a China shop'. His movements back and forth were so, so, gentle, that it was her who lifted and pushed her buttocks to greet him. 'Sandy' was blissful at being taken to another level of the quality she sought, reaching a plateau of her design. She found this to be a captivating moment, as she awakened like 'Sleeping Beauty'. As she became more active with Bob, who was teasing her with very slow and deliberate motions, making it last, not being expendable, but then he hadn't reckoned on 'Sandy' reaching orgasm so quick, but more of wrapping her legs around his waist and pulling him tight to her as their pubic areas rubbed and vibrated, as her whole body shook and trembled, as she let out gasping whispers as she continued to murmur, "Yes" "Yes" "Yes", and then became calm as she relaxed her grip on him. He withdrew still with a hard on, chuffed to say the least. He had produced as to his teachings of his younger years by mentors older than him.

He was very much a toy boy in his late teens and early twenties with women much older than him, who taught him plenty about the emotional values of women and to understand the signs and mood swings that often raged in pleasing and pleasuring femininity, as all had different thoughts, expectations and desires to be met by their husbands and lovers they challenged, and sadly, so many women are left unfulfilled by their sexual experiences, with partners lasting only minutes, some can be only seconds. Understandably, such incidents leave women confused, as if it is their fault that their sexual partners can't cope with the physical pressures. Love making is very much an art form, but so often men cannot be bothered, as their excitement and adrenalin is ahead of them, more of mind over matter and sadly, masculinity and the macho man is not always the deliverable type, as a greater care needs to be considered for women and not themselves. Practice makes perfect, so don't end up like the sleeping Lion, be the Rabbit with energy to match.

'Sandy' turned again on to her side as Bob tucked himself in behind her, as she clasped his hand to her tummy, as they cuddled up with a glowing warmth and affection, as their surroundings was so peaceful, with a heart that skips a beat of her contentment, as time was never an issue, so it was hours later at the break of dawn, when Bob stirred and realised they had been wrapped naked and cuddled together with only a blanket for company the whole night, as they had slept and after their love making, had brought them to a place of calm.

It was near six o'clock the same morning when Bob finally dropped off 'Sandy' on the corner of her street. He sat and watched her walk the short distance to her house before he drove home himself. So, when is an affair not an affair, he thought, with intimate conversations and she is being so outgoing and flirtatious with him from the beginning, as mentally, she was a strong and determined woman who knew what she wanted in an open relationship without making demands on him.

Whilst showering, he could not believe that they had both slept, not only together for the first time, but in a hay barn of all places and nothing seemed to detract from such a fitting and pleasurable experience, that neither had disturbed sleep but woke feeling electrified and so relaxed with waking smiles for each other and sharing a lingering caress between them before they finally left for home. Certainly, a fit lady with such a trim body and beautiful skin and so soft and smooth to touch. He smiled as he finished showering.

CHAPTER FIVE

Travellers on the Move

Bob remembered his promise to meet Old Ben up at 'Marshalls Green'. It was extraordinary as to the fascination this place held for so many people locally. Perhaps the mystery is real in all its times as to who the occupants were.

Friday morning, coming on seven o'clock, Bob decided to forgo a quick coffee and get himself up to where he hoped to meet Old Ben, and fortunately Bob had the time as he was on late duty at two o'clock that same afternoon.

No sooner had he arrived at the Manor House then he saw Old Ben appear from the copse standing on the embankment. Then he slipped back out of view into the bushes. Bob parked his own vehicle just inside the gate of the property and locked it, when again, he felt a shudder down his spine. The boot, the boot came to mind and the cardboard box he had completely forgotten.

Climbing the embankment, Bob stood surveying the landscape, before he too stepped backwards into the bushes where Old Ben was waiting for him. He slipped Ben a few quid out of his own pocket in the hope that he could obtain more direct information and not riddles needing answers, he thought.

"Bad lot we have on us governor. We got stoned and shot up last night, shotgun pellets all down some of the caravan's mister. I saw two big black cars come up from the bottom and boom, boom. Then the stones broke windows, very bad, it was very bad last night," said Old Ben, as always, fiddling with his pipe in his hands.

"Did the Police come", said Bob, frowning at the story.

"No one called them governor. You know traveller's sir, we ain't going to the gavvers, traveller's deals with it themselves," said Old Ben.

"Was anybody hurt?" asked Bob, with concerned voice.

"No sir, some of the pellets missed the babies," said Old Ben.

"The black vehicles, whose are they? Do you know? Has any traveller seen them before up here or locally?" asked Bob, rather inquisitively as he listened on every word that Old Ben uttered.

"I heard a whisper that they are the dwellers that got chored, but not from around here. They were the foreign-speaking dwellers who had the bling stones," said Old Ben, as cool as a cucumber; nothing seemed to disturb him whatsoever.

Old Ben fascinated Bob in the way he moved and drifted around the area, always turning up at the right time. He was very much the eyes and ears of the fraternities and was well trusted and left alone to his wandering.

"What about the fire here Ben? Anything you can tell me old mate?" said Bob, hoping Ben had some answer to what he was seeking.

"Two geezers from the big city lives here. One has dogs and the other has a big black Range Rover, he drives it at night time. He just drives through the night. They alright governor. They had two women here a couple of weeks ago. (Ben with a big smile on his face), I saw one couple fucking down by the water trough. The other one was down in those trees (he pointed). He was fucking the other woman standing up. I ain't seen the women since," said Old Ben.

"What about the fire Ben, what was that about?" asked

Bob yearning for the truth to be told?

"It was a traveller who done it. Took revenge of the geezer in the house," said Old Ben, as he began to puff on his pipe, as you could hear his lips smacking on him, drawing breath.

"What was the revenge for?" asked Bob.

Now eager to get to the nitty-gritty of the story, as the story was slowly unfolding.

"The bling they chored from the dwellers, they hid in the grounds of the house and it's gone. Someone has taken it," said Old Ben.

"How do they know it was the people in the house?" asked Bob trying to piece together the events.

"The young'uns came back one night and got caught by the geezer and they kicked and fight him. He fights back and hurt one of them. He crushed young'uns balls in his hands, so they lashed him and then run off," said Old Ben. "I heard them talking about taking revenge in Old Teddy's caravan. It was 'Leafy' who flooded the petrol. He was burning up as he got covered in the stuff and his clothes were wet with petrol and they took another traveller who was run over and hurt to hospital a long way from here. His leg is in plaster. Some of the others did a runner and left the area very quickly. 'Leafy' and the other one in plaster are back up the top," said Old Ben, as he continued to reveal incredible details of what had happened on that fateful night of the fire.

"They found a body in the cab of the vehicle. Do you know who he is Ben? Was he a traveller from here?" asked Bob.

"No sir, he be a stranger who came down with the others. They from another camp near the foreigner's dwelling.

He be more Black Country. I don't know him sir, we don't know his name, we don't," said Old Ben. "Big trouble coming soon governor. We don't want them new ones to stay with us, they are bad people and the women too, very bad people," said Old Ben as he looked woeful at Bob.

"Christ, why aren't the Police doing more? What about the people in the house? Did they die in the fire? Who knows," said Bob.

Trying desperately to gauge the depth and the crisis that has befallen the local community and clearly, violence was the mainstream that appears unstoppable without Police knowledge and intervention, it was not for him, but a more collective operation is going to be needed to bring this to a conclusion.

"They didn't die sir. They were not here when the house burnt. The other man and woman came next day. I saw the man in the field (he pointed towards the fields beyond the boundary fence). He was hiding at the back of here (pointing behind the copse). He found his dog and down there (pointing) by the river, he found the other two and he left. He went back across the fields in the direction of the village. They ain't been here since governor, none of them have," said Old Ben.

"Bloody hell Ben, you have seen it all. Look, we must forget about us talking today, alright. I must think this through with my people. I need to know more of those in the black vehicles that came last night, as someone is likely to get killed with shotguns blasting," said Bob, in a rather serious tone to Old Ben. "I am working this afternoon, so I will be up and around here to see what I can find old mate. Leave it with me and I'll catch you later,"

Old Ben stood up and walked off through the thicket unseen. He disappeared from Bob's view. The only trace of Ben was the smell of his tobacco drifting in the morning's breeze.

Bob remained in situ, thinking through Old Ben's words and knowledge on the night of the fire; it had to be him that was watching him and Sgt Anderson, the other day, when they first visited the scene together. Bob was back and forth over the ground scouting the ground for the slightest disturbance of a sign that might indicate an interest for him to investigate. Remembering also, what he had discovered in the office of the Local planning authority that the copse is not shown on the survey maps. So, what is the reason for this large mound of earth covered in shrubs and bushes? When, eventually, Bob came across the manhole cover at the opposite end of the bank and more towards the lane, he knelt and saw the edging of the cover was clean and appeared to be maintained, as the grass edge had been cut back and, in fact, looking back over the ground, Bob realised that someone had flattened the ground away from this cover. He dug his fingers into the indented grip in the lid and pulled. It lifted rather easily and then realised that the water trap surround was packed with grease to seal the lid from the weather elements outside. Clearly, this confirmed his suspicions that this was well maintained but by whom he wondered. Finally, removing the lid, he looked down into a blackness where a ladder was attached to the inner side of what appeared to be a chamber, but then his mind turned to sewers and water flows. Was this for that purpose, as he strained his eyes by not seeing further into the darkness, but how far did it go down? Was it dangerous? Could there be methane gas? Much went through his mind, but Bob wanted instant answers to his mindful questions.

Returning to his vehicle to fetch a torch, he again, whilst opening the boot of his vehicle, was confronted by the cardboard box he left in there a couple of days ago and still it remained unopened. Bob realised, now was the opportunity to quickly look inside the box and see what it contained. Minutes later, he stood aghast at what he had seen. Various bits of electronic equipment from surveillance to hi-tech photography gear and recording devices and much more besides.

"Fucking hell, where the hell has this come from?" thought Bob, in deep thought.

Taking the torch from the boot, he closed the box and shut the boot of the car. He now was in earnest to know what he had stumbled on as he returned to the copse. The torch provided the answer he was looking for. Just below the rim, he saw a light switch as he reached in and turned it on exposing a well-lit region at the bottom of the ladder, as he lay on his stomach with his head below looking down. He noticed an echo as he muttered. Then, banging the steel ladder, further echo's. This must be a vast area underground, he thought. He then decided to enter and climb down the ladder as he listened for any signs of life, finally reaching the floor of this construction, but what construction, he thought. He then realised that he was standing in a corridor of sorts, as the light went in one direction away from him. He used his torch to flash in all directions as to the height, and what were the black shapes on his left that was clear to see with the torch? Slowly, he moved down this narrow corridor and realised that the black shapes were rooms containing a variety of equipment and tools and much more that needed to be listed on a proper property inventory, as this was clearly part of the property belonging to the Manor house. Finally, the biggest shock of all was being confronted by a large covered sheeted object. As he pulled back the cover, he saw the black Range Rover Old Ben had earlier mentioned. Bob realised that he had hit the jackpot. This was a big job, much bigger than he could ever have imagined. Leaving it as he found it, he went back to the way he had come in and climbed back out of the underground tunnel. Securing the manhole cover, Bob remained hidden, having moved back into the woodland and climbed down on to the flat ground below and over the fence to the lane. Very conscious that he may have been seen by prying eyes and spending a little more time than he had intended to be sure that the manhole cover had not been discovered by others before deciding to drive off.

Returning to the village, Bob stopped off at a local restaurant for breakfast and reached home by nine-thirty the same morning. First, he removed the cardboard box from the car and placed it in the garage for safe keeping. On the kitchen table, he was left a note by his wife. She had decided to take off for a few days. Bob regarded his life was becoming more bizarre by the day. Not since the extraordinary sexual events that took place some weeks prior with his wife in the garden and later in the shower, no further contact had been occasioned between them. Since then, he had worked nights and now late turns and their paths in the house had not crossed due to the unsociable hours he worked.

Bob took this opportunity to ring Sergeant Anderson at home and bring him up to speed with his information and findings from his contact with Old Ben. Bob realised that prior contact was better than leaving until duty time and the privacy needed to explain in some detail. Sgt Anderson had agreed that at the earliest opportunity, he and Bob would get themselves up to 'Marshalls Green' and have a proper run through before bringing in CID.

By mid-afternoon, Bob had returned to the station and collected Sgt Anderson, now armed with some sensible torches they returned to 'Marshalls Green' and parked the police car just inside the gate. Both officers walked down towards the boundary fence and disappeared behind the copse into the woodland. Both found convenient places to hide themselves for a good fifteen minutes before climbing the bank through the undergrowth on to the top of the copse, having made sure that no prying eyes or wandering persons were looking or seeing them. Bob was soon lifting the manhole cover as he entered and climbed down into the darkness of this tunnel construction, then switching on the light as he continued down to the floor with the Sergeant following behind.

"Fucking hell, what the hell is going on, what is it?" asked Sgt Anderson.

Astonished at what he was seeing for the first time, slowly both officers walked from one open bay area to another. Each had been connected to mains electric and clearly had its own power source integrated into the construction, then, realising that each of the rooms was constructed from steel containers.

"I'm staggered, some engineering feat is this. Would have cost a few bob I bet, but what's it for? Why go to all this bloody trouble? Where did you say the vehicle was, Bob?" asked Sgt Anderson.

"Right at the bottom, the last room, it's covered by a sheet," said Bob.

Finally, the vehicle was the last to be examined. Removing the sheet, the officers saw the immaculate body finish of this Black Range Rover, it was an awesome sight.

"What a beauty. Fucking hell, just look at it, this is some money Bob," said Sgt Anderson.

"Well old mate, you really have fucked up CID with this lot. I'm going to contact the Chief Super first and get our oar in place before we get written out of this story. What you are thinking Bob?" asked the Sergeant.

"Crime, this is crime, I reckon big time. Those four workshops are for a particular purpose. If you noticed the type of equipment in there and the vehicle, well, I just don't know what to make of this. There must be a way out. It's more like sitting in a garage, its facing this wall like a garage door. Look at the height and the width," said Bob.

As both officers looked for answers, was there some device, a switch that would make them believe that this was some kind of garage for the vehicle, designed purposely for this vehicle? Checking underneath and around the vehicle, it was Bob who touched and twisted the light switch. As the lights went out, as what they suspected was a garage door which began to jerk open, then stopped, held back by an internal chain. Turning back the switch, the door reversed its self-slacking off the chain. Bob unhitched it and turned back the switch. Once again, the door opened up and over and from their position, both officers were looking directly across to the Manor House as to where it once stood. The Range Rover was now facing in the same direction, leaving the confines of the construction. Both officers scoured the ground looking for vehicle tracks. It was only when Sgt Anderson lent on the wooden post that the garage door began to close.

"Fucking hell, skipper, look at this. The fucking door's closing. It must be on a timer or something that brings it to operate like this," said Bob.

He remained mesmerised as he watched the door close, also realising that the exterior had been designed and constructed to camouflage into the surroundings and no one would be any the wiser. When Sgt Anderson removed his hand from the post, the garage door began to jerk open again. Both officers stood gawping and laughing at their discovery.

"Christ, a lot of trouble has gone into this Sarge," said Bob, astonished at the efforts made. "This is very deliberate in its construction. It's just not normal to go to these lengths, unless it's for the dark side of life. It's just unbelievable and the vehicle has got no plates on it, have you noticed?"

"No, I didn't notice that. I just don't know where my head is at the moment. This has cost a pretty penny, but as you say, what for?" said Sgt Anderson.

Both officers again stood looking into the opening at this immaculate painted vehicle. The paintwork just shimmered in the light of the storage unit.

"This has got to be for crime purposes. I can't think of any other reason, can you Sarge?" asked Bob, still very mystified at their find.

"Well mate, I have got to agree with you there. It just does not make any fucking sense," said Sgt Anderson. "I'll put a call into the governor and get him down here and go with his guidance on this, Bob. Cover our arses, as I can see the wheels coming off this mate."

Sgt Anderson put a call into the station with a request that their Chief Super gives him a call. Twenty minutes later, the Sergeant was speaking with his most senior superior and so outlined what they had found and a request that he attend and bring himself up to speed on their find. Bob, meanwhile, had gone back into the bowls of the construction and began to pay more attention to the array of items and objects that were stored in cupboards and boxes, and it was boxes that he noticed first. It looked identical to the one in the boot of his car, frowning, as he continued to examine more carefully and had come to realise that the various photographic and listening equipment had the same maker's labels, and, in fact, some products were again identical to what had been placed in the cardboard box. He just stood and fingered some of these items, becoming more confused by each touch as he moved to the other containers, in trying to paint a bigger picture of what he was confronting.

"The governor's coming up for a visit, he will be about half an hour, so let's see what we are looking at. What you found, Bob, anything of real interest?" asked Sgt Anderson, inquisitive to know more of their surroundings.

"Well, yes, but I need to get my head round something first. I wonder if this a security operation, spooks. What about spooks? Could this be one of their locations?" asked Bob, looking at the skipper and gesturing with arms outstretched. "Think about it. Either for crime or security, that's all I can think of," said Bob, trying to sound more convincing.

"That's an idea, I never thought about security," said Sgt

Anderson.

"Look, for now, I don't want to say anything to you, but I was left a cardboard box by somebody I had contact with in the local pub. This was over a month ago. In fact, it was the evening before I went on my course. Whoever it was, left this box with the licensee's wife to look after until I returned from the course, and we were talking about gypsies beyond that. I am at a loss, but first I need to look more carefully at what I have in the box. What it does give us is a starter, because there will be fingerprints on those items and I could get them seen by 'Scenes of Crime' and that might give us a lead to this place. It might be the piece of the jigsaw we are missing as to the identity of whoever was living here," said Bob.

His enthusiasm at this point was now sky high, realising that maybe the missing link to the puzzle has now been found.

"I'll cover you on getting that stuff in for fingerprinting. If it is the same, then book it into Miscellaneous Property with a mark-up query of tracing owner via 'Scenes of Crime' and put me down as first reference of contact," said Sgt Anderson.

"I can understand why there is no energy in this by CID. Well, what we have, as I see it, is a house burnt to the ground. Suspicious - yes, but is it an accident or arson? – Who knows? Then we have the body in the vehicle. That, again, is suspicious, but died because of the fire. No other trauma was found, and smoke was found in the lungs, but nobody has reported anybody missing from around here. We've got the hill, a tanker vehicle which could have been a run-away, but nothing that directly ties this all together as a major incident and, of course, the occupants of the property are missing. Their bodies, if they were caught in the fire, have not been found. It's all fucking conjecture and now we have this, and our problem is, now we have found it, are we going to record every bloody item in here or just lock it up and leave it as we found it? This will be a big job to record it all, otherwise 'Scenes of 'Crime' could video for future evidence and we, I suppose, could get one of our alarms in here to protect it, otherwise it means us wasting a lot of Police time for what, speculation on a crime, supposedly, that may not exist. We ought to find the owner's details from the Land Registry. There must be some lead to go on. What do you think Sarge?" asked Bob, looking for an agreeable viewpoint on his thoughts to the present situation and whether senior officers would agree, otherwise they are going to be lumbered until someone responsible for the property comes forward.

Both officers walked back to their Police car and waited for their Chief Superintendent to finally arrive. It was whilst standing near the main gate of the property, that Sgt Anderson was in conference with the Chief Super. When a large black foreign vehicle approached from the village direction and slowed nearing the brow of the hill, it was then Bob's attention was drawn to the vehicle and questioned – "Why slow down?" Strange. Then it dawned on Bob.

"Fucking hell, Russians," said Bob.

Muttering and chewing over mentally as to what Old Ben had told him earlier and the burglary and jewellery theft from these people, clearly, was a big issue for them and was not going away. If they are visiting our patch, that means trouble and that means a very big score in value had been stolen. He was slow to admit that he missed sighting the vehicle's index plate as it passed, by which time, Sgt Anderson and the Chief Super had walked down to the copse and the hidden Range Rover.

Finally, the Chief Super left, and Sgt Anderson said,

"That's it mate. 'Scenes of Crime' to video and install a couple of our alarms and that is it. No crime, but at least we have covered our arses as the governor has suggested and stick your stuff in the Miscellaneous Book and let's see what comes out of the woodwork."

"We need to get 'SOCO' out now and get this sorted 'ASAP', Sarge, otherwise it will end up being another late nothing day for us," said Bob, anxious to get moving.

By seven o'clock that evening, Bob dropped off Sgt Anderson at the Police Station and headed off for his meal break – 'Fish and Chips' local takeaway. Bob was more relaxed, as he felt that they had done the right thing and now with 'SOCO' (Scenes of Crime Officer) involved and the place now alarmed, he could concentrate on more mundane matters that concerned his local beat area.

Off duty by ten o'clock that evening, Bob decided to visit Judy at his local pub in the next village, as he was feeling good with himself, having achieved more than he thought he would when he came on duty at two o 'clock this afternoon. Bob remained there until kicking out time, when he made his way home to an empty house, although his mind did turn to 'Sandy', but discouraged himself from calling her that late at night.

CHAPTER SIX

Lenny and Karen

Miles from 'Marshalls Green', Lenny and Karen had rented a bolt hole well off the beaten track and clearly remained in seclusion since their last visit to retrieve the dogs. During which time, Lenny had bought a new 'Pay as you go' mobile and, again, travelled many miles with Karen to use and contact Frank and others. Frank was a godsend. In the heat of the moment, he took the pressure off Lenny, contacting Tim's Barrister firm to alert him and for immediate enquiries to be sent from abroad in establishing a go-between with some Estate Agents to take control of the situation and act for the overseas company as their UK representative, leaving no UK trace back to London and others involved. Although the mystery remained as to Tommy and Toni's whereabouts, not one whisper on the grapevine had been heard since that weekend of the operation and fire. It wasn't right that no bodies were found in the fire debris, but as Lenny realised he couldn't come forward and break his cover, without Tommy's crime operation being publicly known and the media would have a field day, with every journalist this side of the Atlantic on Tommy's trail and that he couldn't allow it to happen, only to rely on his own confidential sources he can trust and even those were not informed as to where he was held up with Karen. He always wrapped the mobile phone in aluminium foil after each use to conceal the signal; it was more a one-way contact to keep up to date and ahead of the game. It was through Frank that Lenny became aware as to how successful the crime operation had been, and all the operatives were sent home soon after each job was completed. So, it all ended very well on the night and the firework display was plastered all over the International news. It was those astronauts who raised the alarm from Space. They saw all the colours exploding and radioed their base and one thing after another, it all kicks off and 'Bob's your Uncle', the whole bloody world gets to know about it in minutes.

The Police soon became aware of the Estate Agent's interest in 'Marshalls Green', having provided a solicitor's letter and contact details of those representing the owners of the Manor House, which happens to be an overseas company, whose details remained confidential and all enquiries were directed through Solicitors. No individuals are mentioned in any of the documentation concerning ownership and those who were thought to be resident up and until the fire. The mystery continues throughout and made the police more suspicious. But the point in reckoning is a simple one. They have no evidence that any crimes have been committed. Without evidence, without witnesses there, is nothing that can be attributed to Police work other than an unidentified body lying in the mortuary and that will be a Coroner's job to decide on the outcome of the evidence to hand.

Back in Lenny's bolthole, he and Karen had become more of an affectionate couple than on the night at the village pub when he became aware of her being a Customs Officer and, of course, since she has resigned, and what both have since learned of each other, the relationship has gone from strength to strength, as today, they do everything together as a couple. Running the dogs and taking their long walks in the countryside was idyllic and more inviting than being in the glare and spotlight of the media, and that could easily happen by making just one small mistake in the process. So, Lenny kept everybody in the dark as to where they were living, but then who was hunting them? Who knows that they were residents of the Manor House? Who really is interested in either of them questions, questions and no answers to explain his thoughts on the whereabouts of Tommy and Toni, whether dead or alive.

Mid-afternoon on the Saturday, Bob was patrolling the back lanes off the motorway, when he passed a grey-haired man, with sleeves rolled up, leaning on a five-bar gate as he smoked a cigarette. Reversing back the police car, Bob pulled up alongside him. The man turned to acknowledge him. At first, Bob spoke to the man from the police car. The man then approached the police car with window down and gripped with both hands the driver's door of the Panda as he said,

"That was quick of you," as he looked into Bob's face.

"Quick? Sorry I don't follow you," said Bob, rather bewildered at the man's remark.

"Well, I have just rung your station. I asked for CID as I have a theft to report," said the man.

"I see, and who are you?" enquired Bob.

"Derek Adkins. I farm this area".

Derek gestured with a hand pointing across the surrounding fields.

"What have you had stolen?" asked Bob.

"Well, my small fuel tank, it's on wheels," said Derek the farmer.

"When did you last see it?" asked Bob.

"I don't really know. It was some weeks ago when I last

saw it," said the farmer.

Bob left the police car and walked to the field gate and stood with the farmer as he surveyed the field area, pondering on the fact of another fuel tank stolen, but this was not a tanker. The farmer continued his story as Bob listened as to the tank's description of being capable of holding one hundred and fifty gallons of petrol for two stroke appliances, chain saws and Strimmer's. His workers are clearing woodland on the hill over yonder as he again pointed across the field.

"I've got twenty sheep missing and all. I can't find them anywhere, so I reckon they have been nicked as well," said the farmer.

"Sheep, that means transport, so we have to be looking for some kind of truck and not a van of sorts," said Bob.

"Yeah, that would be right. They would be frisky, so they would need a few hands to keep control of them," said the farmer.

"Have you had any problems with gypsies?" asked Bob.

"No, not really. They use my farm to collect water. They have been coming to me for years. I treat them fairly," said the farmer, "I've used some for labouring in the past, potato picking."

"What direction is your farm?" asked Bob.

"I'm over that ridge about three miles, 'Mantles Green Farm'. The names on the gate" said the farmer, as he pointed in that direction.

"Did you hear about the Manor House?" asked Bob.

"Yeah, we all did. That is a bad do, mark my words," said the farmer.

"You didn't know who lived there by any chance?" asked

Bob.

"I once saw two fellows, one of them had an Arab horse which was kept in the paddock next door to the house. The stable girl whose friends with my granddaughter looked after it, but that was a couple of years back now and she has moved on. Oh! Yes, and a vehicle which had immaculate body work, black it was. I think it was a Range Rover, lovely job though," said the farmer. I never paid any real attention to them, but I would have thought they were in their forties. Never saw any women about," said the farmer.

Keep chipping away, was the only answer Bob had, as bit by bit, he was beginning to see a picture being painted. "Two men in their forties," he muttered. "It's all coming together slowly. Now sheep stolen and Russian villains, talk about variety being the spice of life," he laughed. Who would believe it? A right old copper's tale, he thought. He felt more impatient, sometimes anxious, in not knowing sufficient details at what had taken place. Had CID discovered the identities of the occupants in the fire? Then, a flash of inspiration came to him,

"Fuck me. Two men and the telex message made mention of one man and one woman, so if that is right on what he had been told by the farmer and what Old Ben had mentioned, there is another fellow, so why hasn't he come forward? No one's said anything about a second man, other than what he has been told from his own enquiries, which means no one else is poking around other than him," said Bob, really speaking out loud his thoughts.

Bob was beginning to feel that progress had been made and more than he was realising, when his sits down and thinks through all the pointers and information he had collected, and in the order, he was now following, it was beginning to make sense.

Having passed over to the 'SOCO' Department, the cardboard box and contents for fingerprinting and requiring the return of the contents to enter the items into the Miscellaneous Property register, Bob now knew that he was in a 'wait and see' situation and hoped that science would come to his rescue.

Recording the two crimes from the farmer with a circulation notice regarding both, the stolen sheep was a growing problem for farmers, as it did appear that many foreigners from the former Eastern Bloc Countries were very much involved in the numerous crime gangs springing up across the counties and night time raids were not uncommon.

At the Police station, Bob read the note left in his docket from Sgt Anderson giving him a change of duty the next day to a ten o'clock (am) start to cover the Sunday Church parade and fete with a six o'clock (pm) finish, this suited Bob enormously giving him some free evening time off.

Before going off duty at Ten o'clock, Bob texted 'Sandy' with his Sunday change of duty, in case she was free and interested in meeting up. By the time he had arrived home, 'Sandy' had replied – 'House sitting for friend. Come and spend the night with me?', the message read. Bob smiled and muttered,

"This is a turn up for the books. Dear me, I can't decline this invitation can I now?" Bob replied with a 'YES' acceptance to her invitation.

It was whilst leaving the Police Station just after ten o'clock that two Black painted foreign vehicles passed by, driving away from the village and heading in the direction of the motorway. It was one of intrigue on Bob's part, that once again, these foreign vehicles kept appearing in the area and obviously looking for something or someone. Again, it didn't make sense, but he knew that he needed to be doing more to identify the occupants of these two vehicles as clearly, they were driving mob-handed and once again, he didn't catch the index numbers of either vehicle.

CHAPTER SEVEN

Overnight with 'Sandy'

Constable Bob Benyon's Sunday morning ten o'clock start saw him meeting local church leaders who were organising the parade and fete. Six Special Constables had been booked for duty to assist in the day's events. The day continued in the way Bob hoped, with many families out enjoying the parade with the many attractions arranged in the local Recreation Ground, from food stalls to children's entertainment. By mid-afternoon, Bob took time out for a coffee round the back of one of the refreshment tents, when he caught sight of 'Sandy' walking among the crowd. Bob stayed in the background unannounced as he watched her every move, as he decided to avoid any compromise for the moment, as he was more comfortable with his coffee and a sandwich sent out to him by the staff.

Sometime in the early afternoon, 'Sandy' caught up with Bob as he stood watching some of the social events taking place. The Special Constables were also patrolling in three pairs among the spectators and organisers. Bob managed to listen among the noise to what 'Sandy' was trying to relay to him about later when he finished duty. It was obvious from what 'Sandy' had managed to briefly explain that the house sitting concerned a rather palatial place that she had been asked to look after for a couple of days, as her business friend had workmen on site, and she needed someone to keep an eye on them and manage a couple of small dogs in the making of the arrangements. This, 'Sandy' had agreed to do and now extended her invitation to Bob to stay over the Sunday night, which he agreed to, and it was her turn to pick him up and act as chauffeur for the journey.

By eight o'clock on the Sunday night, Bob now passenger in 'Sandy's' car, was relaxing for the first time in a long time, not to be driving. The journey was more of idle chat and now and again, Bob teased her with touches and his style of gentle groping techniques was becoming a distraction, as 'Sandy' was beginning to warm up to the attention with her giggles and laughter.

"Policemen should not make this so tempting," said 'Sandy.' "You are a right teaser Bob," as her hand reached down to grope him between the legs. "Touché. We can both play that game," as her laughing was becoming infectious.

Finally reaching their destination, a house situated on a private gated road with a manned security post was extraordinary, to say the least, and the first Bob had experienced. "One of 'Sandy's' friends, bloody hell," he muttered to himself. "This is big time," he thought.

'Sandy' organised the entry into the property, having parked her vehicle on to a hardstanding opposite the front porch. Once inside the house, she was the first to turn and place a long lingering kiss on Bob's lips, and with both arms around his neck, she was not in any hurry to move her position. Bob had responded, by holding her round the waist and knew this also could be the night of all nights in the bed of strangers.

Eventually, they both toured the house together, finding also the two small Terrier-type dogs left in the utility room, both excited and friendly. When let out, obviously, that was their place of residence, as both dog baskets were deliberately placed with water and feeding bowls to match on the floor.

By ten o'clock that evening, Bob and 'Sandy' had taken

an uneventful shower together. Wrapped in large bath towels, they were both curled up on a large settee together watching television. 'Sandy' had been doing her toenails as the couple relaxed in their new surroundings. Hardly any conversation had taken place between them and what was exchanged was more of idle chat. It was the sharing time for both, for once again, time was never to be a rush between them in parting this night. Bob was surprised at the enormous size of bed. Even a greater surprise, when 'Sandy' was riding the crest of the waves, she was bouncing up and down every time she moved. She was giggling loud to Bob for him to join her which he did and then realised it was a water bed with mirror tiles on the ceiling. He couldn't stop laughing. This is more like a bordello, but nice, nice, nice, as he too was in hysterics at how they both bounced up and down together with little movement.

"Do we get a life raft or a sailor's hat to wear in bed 'Sandy'?" said Bob.

He was in awe of the raptures of his own laughter. A new experience, one most men would try, and he hoped that it didn't make him run for the loo every five minutes with the sounds of splashing water in his ears.

Climbing naked into bed, Bob remarked that perhaps they ought to leave a map on the bed to pinpoint where they would be due to its size and where they could be found should anyone come looking for them. Bob's mind went haywire, thinking that perhaps six people could sleep abreast as normal in the bed and still have a comfortable sleep. 'Sandy' was laid on her tummy just giggling at Bob's funny comments as her body was bobbing up and down, as he continued to move and explore the size of the bed.

Eventually, with a couple of stiff drinks between them, they both settled for the middle of this enormous bed, as they sipped their drinks surrounded by extra-large pillows that determined their positions. Within the hour, 'Sandy' had managed three glasses of wine and Bob had two whiskies, when finally, they slipped under the duvet together for a little tender groping between them. More than ever, 'Sandy' enjoyed their kissing, so soft and warm the feelings, that she just let Bob butterfly his pecking kisses over her face and neck. It was the tenderness he was showing her as she laid so relaxed against his neck. As he stroked her back, nothing more was needed, as she felt the growing hardness that she held in her hand having attempted to masturbate Bob for the first time. He was controlling his events of mind over matter and, of course, her hand movement was tiring to her, as she turned and laid her arm across his chest, as she rubbed his shoulder and arm and then down to his pubic area. As with her fingers she twiddled his hair and then smoothed her hand around his open area with his legs spread wide as she cradled and cupped his balls in the palm of her hand, time after time, gentle and caring, as not to hurt him, as at times withdrawing her hand to rub over his stomach.

'Sandy' left the bed to use the loo and to turn the main light switch off, leaving on the side lights, as she did the same with the television, changing channels to a music radio station before returning to bed, but she also carried what appeared to be a larger-than-most makeup bag. Bob paid little attention at first. Then 'Sandy' produced some body gel samples in different flavours, realising that the gel was designed for sexual purposes and arousal more of the female than the male. Reading the label, he saw one had a sting in its tail when used on the clitoris of the vagina. Also, internal lubricating gel for fingers, sex toys and rubber gloves for ringing the anus and instil a greater sensation with an inserted penis and a hand on the arse to encourage movement of the female. Bob was perplexed as 'Sandy' reminded him that she liked to experiment and that perhaps, on this night, he might like to join her as she produced three sex toys from her bag, clearly dildo vibrators of some description. Each, 'Sandy' switched on as he listened to the buzzing noise. All three were battery powered and ready to go, if that was the right expression and, in the manor, served. Life is too short to be embarrassed and inhibited.

"Nature really is designed for reproduction, not for us to have a fantastic sexual social life. If that were the case, then men would manage more than their five minutes fucking us women and not rolling off and going to sleep in minutes. They would stay awake and play with us girls. We need foreplay, lots of hugs and kisses, then you can mount us and fuck us with a stimulus that rocks our emotions," said 'Sandy', as she waved one of the vibrators in his face as she giggled.

"These save a man's energy and so they can play longer with our vaginas and give us the orgasms we richly deserve from you men," said 'Sandy', as she continued to giggle.

Bob took one of the gel's and squeezed a small amount on his fingertip and he tried to prise open her legs. 'Sandy' was awkward in her present position, so she slipped down on to her back as Bob's hand came between her legs and placed the gel on her vagina. She felt the tingle and made her twitch and wriggle as Bob again placed more of the gel on her clitoris. At the same time, he inserted a finger and gently soothed the roof of her lining that was becoming rampart from his gentle strokes. She was working herself off on his finger, when he withdrew and inserted the dildo vibrator that she had handed him earlier into her vagina. She remained with her eyes closed and sucking her lips, as Bob gently manipulated the sex toy as he continued for some time to move it back and forth, sometimes right up to the hilt of what must have been at least six inches or more. Bob had moved to a kneeling position alongside her as he leaned over to suck her nipples, whilst, at the same time, he manoeuvred the vibrator, when she exploded with a double orgasm. The first he saw coming but the second was more violent, rocking off her body as her fingers gripped his flesh in a pulling motion. Her grunts and groans were very loud and at times deafening. Withdrawing the dildo, Bob mounted 'Sandy', having moved between her legs, as he clearly was rock hard when he entered her darkened chamber, but then he also moved his hand round her buttocks and began to rim her anus as her actions became more ferocious, as he really had got her rocking in all directions and, at times, felt sea sick with all the ups and downs. He wanted to laugh at the most crucial time for her, so he placed both hands under her buttocks and rode her hard as he gripped her. 'Sandy' was on the crest of the wave and knew she was being well taken care of, as she again exploded, but more sedate as she had multiple orgasms and he also shouted out 'Geronimo', as he too exploded with spurting sperm like a blowing whale coming in for a charge of the Light Brigade as he ran her channel deep as he lifted up her buttocks, as she kicked and bucked like he hadn't seen before and then that moment of silence for both of them. Both were well filled in terms of sexual connotations. Two sweating bodies immersed in their own thoughts of absolute pleasure they shared and experienced with each other.

"Christ, Bob, you really are a true lover. You have vaporised my fanny tonight. I am on fire. Truly, I have never, never had an experience like that. My husband has never managed to electrify me and take me to where you have, it was awesome. It was like a train thundering through my body. God! It was intense for me," said 'Sandy', as she lifted herself up to kiss and hug the man beside her.

"I can't express myself. You really have taken my breath away. I didn't think you would be interested in the toys and gel. I made a desirable choice in that car park that day," said 'Sandy'. She was all smiles and giggles as she cuddled up to him.

In the early hours of the morning, Bob stirred from his sleep, having felt himself being touched in the groin area, not realising that 'Sandy' had aroused him and was sat astride with his penis inside of her. She was a real smooth operator, as Bob had been in a deep sleep up and to that point, when he felt the smooth warmth of skin to skin. 'Sandy' was gently moving back and forth like a well-oiled piston. She had leaned well forward across his torso, her breasts pressed against his chest and her face was buried into the side of his neck as she planted and moved her lips in tiny soft pecks of his skin. With his penis now cradled in her silky chamber, he felt the tension as she squeezed her muscles and the tightness of his fit was slipping back and forth in her juices. She had the control of his head above all other heads that she had experienced in her sexual life. His foreskin was pushed back on the stem and remained like a thick wrap around muff. Still sleepy, and by his own natural instincts, Bob's hands went back and forth over her back and shoulders, even to the point of his fingers reaching her anus, as from time to time, he rimmed her as she let out sequels of delight, as he made her jump forward as he touched on the sensitive nature of her parts that responded to his stroking.

There was no rush of madness between them this early morning hour with pulsating bucking movements. 'Sandy' had taken a more sedate approach in the gentle way she had manipulated her approach to occupying his penis for her own ends of fulfilment. She found it easy to accommodate his penis within her well-lubricated vagina and it was Bob's own sexual feelings that roused and stirred him from his sleep but made no comment or excuse to end her sexual excursion at such an hour, as he let 'Sandy' orgasm quietly, as she whispered in his ear that she had come and was he going to join her. But, obviously, he didn't on this occasion. The two figures remained locked together until his hardness slackened and slipped from her, bringing forth a trickle of seeping juices that moistened and became tacky to their flesh as she rolled off him as they both kissed and cuddled, with arms wrapped around each other.

It was late morning by the time the two of them woke and showered, before sharing a breakfast in the laziest of fashionable ways by not dressing but remaining naked with only towels tied round their waists.

CHAPTER EIGHT
PC Benyon Chasing Shadows

The following Thursday, Bob was working a two-ten late shift. In the meantime, the cardboard box had been returned to him via the internal dispatch from 'Scenes of Crime' Office. The content of the box was required to be entered into the miscellaneous Property Register for safe keeping. At the same time, the accompanying envelope was the biggest surprise of all, as Bob sat down to digest the contents, it being a reply confirming that fingerprints found at 'Marshall Green', and those on the items from the cardboard box were one of the same, identifying a 'Thomas Sands from London'. Details also included his 'Criminal Record Number' and a request had been made on behalf of PC Bob Benyon for his full file correspondence to be forwarded to him via his Force Intelligence Office. Bob sat and read the information three times before he thumped hard his desk top, with a real vocal shout of expression that he had finally had success to his long and protracted inquiries over many weeks of hard graft, and now he had tangible proof to produce to Sgt Anderson that now they can start formulating a synopsis of facts for senior officers to digest and consider the circumstances to the destruction of 'Marshalls Green' and how outside influences were greatly involved in violence, arson and burglary.

Into late evening, Bob received a radio call to attend as backup at 'Wickens Scrap Yard', an isolated business some miles from the village. He was given a rendezvous point to meet up with another mobile who was double-crewed. Another Sergeant had been dropped off minutes earlier by the double crew at a picnic area where a couple out walking their dog had seen five scruffy individuals leave a vehicle hidden on a farm track and walk off into the adjacent woodland.

It wasn't until the couple returning, walked past the parked vehicle and realised that it was near the scrap yard. It was then voices could be heard along with occasional bursts of laughter and, of course, that time of an evening was odd, as darkness was closing in and the gate of the scrap yard was still padlocked. The couple on their return home telephoned the Police Station.

Together, the three officers walked slowly along the grass verge, hankies wrapped round the loose change in their pockets, hats discarded as they reached the perimeter of the scrap yard and quietly listened to signs of life coming from the yard.

"Looks like we are going to have to climb over," said one officer.

"We need to find the skipper. What side of the yard do you think he is on?" asked Bob. "We can't climb over like this, we are likely to break our fucking necks, barbed wire is strung along the top and look at that glinting on the wall over there, (pointing), that is broken glass set in cement on the top of that wall, you'll be cut to pieces trying that."

"Is that what is glinting?" said the young officer. "Glass?"

"The yard has been here donkey's years, it's an old practice to safeguard property, so be warned for the future, never rush in anywhere until you know what you are doing," said Bob, as the other officer agreed with him.

It was then that another approaching police vehicle was sighted with a Blue light flashing.

"Fucking hell. What is wrong with these young ones? Go down there and stop them coming up here and get them to turn the fucking blue light off," said Bob, directing the younger officer to quickly meet the approaching vehicle. "Whilst there, see if they have brought the orchestra with them and what music are they going to play next?"

Bob was livid at the stupidity of fellow officers. The remaining colleague with Bob was laughing at his last comment about the orchestra.

"I bet he will ask about the orchestra when he stops them," said the colleague, as Bob was also smiling as he sat down on his haunches and waited for the new arrivals to join them.

"I just don't fucking believe it," said Bob whispering. "What's your crew mate called?" asked Bob.

"That's young Chris, probationer," said Peter, the driver of the first Police car.

"We need to find the skipper, he's here somewhere, probably watching us make a pig's ear of this, I bet," said Bob.

Anxious to get this job sorted, when eventually, from behind, the other crew and Chris, the skipper, was seen to appear behind them on the track. The six officers now engaged in a plan of action, as noises could be heard coming from within the scrap yard, then a scrapping noise as if something large was being dragged over what seemed a concrete surface outside.

"They're making a lot of bloody noise, sounds like a pantomime in their Bob," said Peter, as he sounded dismayed by the antics taking place, as they all started to chuckle quietly among themselves.

"Are we waiting for the key holder Sarge?" asked Bob.

“Do we know if they have been called out?” asked the Sergeant. “Well, we can’t wait all night, we need to get this sorted quickly.”

The Sergeant directed the last two officers to arrive to work their way down the side of the fencing and to see if they can find a way into the yard.

“That voice I know,” said Bob. “That is young ‘Leafy’, Old Teddy’s boy from off the top lane, so the others must be as well,” said Bo, as he further said, “Fucking crazy lot, I bet they have all been on the cider tonight.”

PC Chris, the young Probationary Officer decided to go and climb over the front gates. Having placed a heavy blanket taken from one of the police vehicles, he climbed and straddled the main wooden gate, and confronted by a gypsy youth climbing from the other side and he, too, was perched and straddled the main gate, as both figures clapped eyes on each other. The young officer, shocked by his encounter, disappeared over the gate into the main compound of the scrap yard. By his lack of concentration, rather than on purpose, he fell to the ground. The gypsy youth was pulled to the ground by Bob and the waiting Sergeant grabbing his leg as he came crashing and shouting ‘POLICE’ into the custody of the two police officers outside the gates. The youth was now handcuffed and placed alone in a nearby Police car. At the same time, all hell had erupted inside the compound. Noise and shouting was plentiful, as it was obvious the remaining gypsies were now trying to escape. Chris, the young officer who fell over the gates into the compound, could be heard tapping on the gates to attract attention.

“Sergeant, are you there?” asked Chris.

Facing rather a dilemma now, having now attracted the attention of the other gypsies who were now trying to escape, as each created a chaotic scene of pandemonium in their panic.

"Chris, where are you?" asked Bob.

"I am here," said Chris, in a whisper of a voice as he tapped on the gate from inside the compound.

"Chris. What the fuck are you whispering for? Are you with anybody?" asked the Sergeant.

"No Sarge," said Chris, in another whispering voice.

"Then why are you fucking whispering?" asked the Sergeant, as he threw his flat cap to the ground in frustration.

"Have you seen the other two PC's yet?"

"I don't know why I am fucking whispering, and, no, I haven't seen the other two," said Chris in one almighty voice.

Bob started to laugh out loud as he looked at the Sergeant's face as they heard Chris reply to the Sergeant's earlier call. The skipper was muttering two to the dozen, not knowing whether to laugh or cry, when without warning, two figures approached from behind the parked police vehicles.

The moments had become hilarious. As the Sergeant was unaware of the key holder's arrival, he was peering through a crack in the wooden gate to observe any signs of movement on the other side. It was also a frustration for the Sergeant, as he could not understand why his eye was reflecting and why as he moved up and down the crack, the reflection followed him. When he stopped, so did the reflection.

"It didn't make sense," said the muttering Sergeant, and then stepped back and looked towards the top of the gates. He was puzzled by the eye reflection.

"Skipper key holders are here," said Bob.

"Right, let's get these gates unlocked shall we," said the Sergeant.

The gates were unlocked and opened wide as the headlights from the Police car were turned on full beam to floodlight the compound of the yard. At the far end, movement could be seen, and eyes seen in the darkness.

Finally, the six officers arrested three gypsy youths inside the compound of the scrap yard, even to the point of them having dragged the safe outside, having forced the main outer door and inner office door to remove the safe into the yard, and was the scraping noise the officers heard earlier.

It was then, a noise was heard as Police and gypsies stood silent listening to squelching sounds, as to what appeared to be, the sounds of feet moving in sync to the sounds. It was like walking in a bog that made the suction noise each time there was movement, but from where were the sounds coming from?

"You hear that skipper," said Bob rather bewildered, "We must have another adrift somewhere. We were originally told five youths. We have 'Leafy' and his two mates and the one we arrested earlier, that makes four, so where is the fifth one?"

The squelching noise continued as officers were becoming bemused as the gypsy youths began to laugh and smirk among them, and for no apparent reason that could be explained at the time.

"It sounds as if someone is treading water," said Pete. "Listen up everybody. Why are they bloody laughing to themselves?"

"I'll fetch the key holder," said Bob. "This is getting stupid, we need to get them in the cars or is the van coming up for them?"

Returning with the key holder, Bob explained the noise best he could, as all ears were straining to the now feint noises that sounded like running water. Even the key holder was stumped for an answer. Then, Steve, another young police officer stumbled over a concrete slab with the beam of his torch and soon realised that the slab had been covering a large hole in the ground supported by large pieces of timber. It was then that the dangers were pointed out to the other officers, when the penny dropped for the key holder.

"That shouldn't be like that. That slab has been moved. It covers the cesspit," said the key holder.

"Oh! fucking hell, I bet the fifth one has fallen in there. Jesus Christ, we are going to be here all bloody night if we don't get a lid on this," said the Sergeant, in a pissed off voice.

"We better get some light on this hole and see if this missing one is in there. Christ, it stinks," said Pete laughing. "What if he is in there? How are we going to get him out? He will be covered head to toe in shit."

The last remark set everyone off laughing, as torches were switched on in a blaze of glare searching the interior of the cesspit. Then it was discovered, a pair of staring eyes caught in the beam of a torch.

"There he is, he's sitting down in all that shit. Unbelievable, he looks pissed. Look at his eyes all glaring," said Bob.

As laughter continued among them, he was now the butt of everybody's banter. Even the key holder was savouring the moment with a face full of smiles.

"We are going to need the Fire Service for this one," said the Sergeant. "Look, the prisoner van is here, let's get this lot away first."

Eventually, with the assistance of the Fire Service, the fifth gypsy was extracted from the cesspit in a distressing state, covered in human waste and smelling to high heavens, as no-one wanted to go near him, when a sudden burst of water thundered across the ground whacking into the youth with such force, it knocked him backwards. This, again, left one and all present in fits of hilarious laughter. There did not seem to be an end to his demise and suffering. The water pressure was greatly reduced, and a long-handled broom was used to try and shrub some of the waste from his clothing as he was in an awful mess. The most surprising was how quickly he sobered up in the circumstances in which he found himself. Eventually, it was agreed to transfer him standing up in the prison van, which meant the driver needed to be especially careful with his driving and great care was given to how he was transferred to the Police station without there being another ridiculous situation. Back at the police station, the youth was taken into the exercise yard and stripped naked, his spoiled clothing bagged up and ready for disposal. The youth was then taken to the prisoner shower block and blessed with soap and hot water and issued with clean clothing.

The officers involved in the incident had congregated in the custody suite, to follow up with the induction of the other prisoners in at the reception desk. Once booked in, it was time for their paperwork to be completed, as one by one, they drifted off to the canteen for tea and coffee refreshments.

(It was only later, after speaking with Chris the Probationer, did the Sergeant realise that it was the young officer's eye reflections that he saw through the crack in the gate that followed him with his movements. Both were using the same crack at the same time to keep track of the events that were happening in the yard and outside the gates. It was a touché moment of the ridiculous kind, to say the least, as the Sergeant could not believe what he had heard from the young Constable. It sounded more like a scene from a 'Carry on film,' than Police officers doing their jobs).

The Sergeant was eyeing up the room, which included other officers listening to the melee of conversations as he looked over the rim of the coffee mug held to his lips, to gauge the reaction of those present to young Chris's tale of woes at the scrap yard and the cringing embarrassment of a superior.

"Skipper, have you seen the 'Special Supplement Notice'?" said the Station Duty Officer. Express Warning to all shifts before going off duty. Everybody needs to endorse the notice on the briefing board as read.

(Attention is drawn to a crime spree that involves twenty gypsies living in the Home Counties and is actively engaged in theft of high powered motor vehicles and the burglary of Post Offices, Clubs and dwelling houses. In small numbers, they leave their respective sites in the early evening and to avoid identification, they wear full-face balaclava helmets. They select isolated premises, which they enter by various means, and goods are stolen from within those premises and it is known by Police that they are stealing two or three vehicles per night. They travel the countryside at high-speed, which makes it difficult to mount surveillance against them. It's been proved that their driving is reckless and has resulted in the death of at least one person so far. They have also driven at Police Officers, intending to cause injury and have previously abducted a member of the public, who stopped to give them assistance after they were involved in a serious road traffic accident. It is therefore stressed that 'EXTREME CAUTION SHOULD BE EXERCISED' if contact is made with this group. Details of the offenders are attached – 'END OF NOTICE').

"I am getting sick and tired of hearing the fucking word gypsy. I have had my belly full tonight, it means that we are going to get a right run around until they are captured, it would have to be our areas involved," said the Sergeant,

He beckoned to the officers to follow up and read the notice before going off duty and initial the briefing board to say you've read it.

CHAPTER NINE

The Truth Will Find You Out

Lenny Burns had finally received news from Frank concerning the jewellery find at 'Marshalls Green'. Lenny had been quick to act in chasing old Frank for news on his long-awaited appraisal of Bling found weeks earlier, hidden in the grounds of the property.

1. Guilloche blue diamond-fronted necklet – 43+grm.
2. Three-stone white diamond ring set.
3. Three colour brick style bracelets – 9ct gold.
4. 12-pointed Star Brooch Diamond setting with 37 diamonds white grain.
5. Spray Brooch with 93 cut diamonds.
6. Set of three miniatures set in scroll-shaped wirework boxed surrounds.

Frank continued listing the remainder of their find in pounds sterling.

"At least over one and quarter mill," came Frank's reply.

"Yes, that is nearer the mark, since I have spoken with my sources on the photos you sent me. That is their opinion and markets available should you decide, twenty percent service charge deduction paid on the sterling, should you want to proceed Lenny."

"Alright, Frank now going, get back to you soon," said Lenny.

Now in a rush to move his position, as he wrapped his mobile heavily in tinfoil before driving away, although, ecstatic at Frank's news and the big profits to be had on his find to share with Tommy.

"Tommy, Tommy where are you brother?" asked Lenny.

Muttering to himself and puzzled still by his absence and that of Toni's whereabouts, needed to start looking for answers, he thought.

Neither Frank nor Lenny were aware of the growing presence and continued gypsy problem in the country lanes around the Manor House, or the depth of their involvement regarding the house fire and it's raising to the ground. Lenny realised that what he had found came from a big job, a big burglary. This is not from a smash and grab, he thought, that stuff was well chosen and the owner's a big-time loser.

An hour before duty time on Friday mid-morning, Bob had met with Sgt Anderson in the station canteen at Sub-Division. Bob provided real facts of his findings and the results of the fingerprint examination was the result he had long hoped for, explaining that he was waiting on the Criminal Record file to be forwarded to him and hoped that a reasonably updated photograph will be attached to confirm the man in the pub was the man he had met.

"If I can confirm from a photograph that the fellow is one of the same, then we have a positive ID (identity) and something to work with. I've placed all the items from the cardboard box in the Mis: Register for safe keeping. Also, 'Leafy' the young gypsy, is still in custody from last night," said Bob.

"Yes, I heard about last night, bit of a fiasco I hear," said Sgt Anderson.

"Well 'Leafy' was the one mentioned on the night of the

house fire. He was soaked in petrol and got taken away. Another had a leg broken. What do you think about chatting to 'Leafy'? What worries me, is if he dumps it all in my lap, then that means CID having a big moan about interfering," said Bob, frowning and frustrated as he spoke.

"You know what it will be like Sarge? How'd think we ought to play this?" asked Bob.

"You are right, we need to gather what we can and then go for a paper exercise detailing the facts we've obtained and, to some degree, as to how we obtained the info. We dump it right in their lap and send a copy to the Chief Super to cover our arses," said the Sergeant. "We best be going, it's near two o'clock start."

Elsewhere, Lenny and Karen had returned after a long spell in the Lake District and returned to their hideaway, but not a hideaway really, as neither was of Police interest. It was more of the silliness and conscience on their part and not compromise as one would have thought. However, Lenny had been in touch with Frank and received a good thumbs up on the jewellery after it was given a good going over by the real experts and better from the initial reports he had been given weeks ago.

Karen's relationship with Lenny had grown in stature as they were very much a 24/7 couple with only the three dogs to worry about. Time for them as a couple was plentiful with hugs and kisses, and moreover, the endless touches and gropes between them put yards of smiles on their faces. They had fucked outdoors in the garden, kitchen, lounge and bedrooms, even when Karen had leaned into the boot of the car; Lenny was soon behind her as he prised her legs apart and mounted her from behind. He had lifted her dress up and over her head, as she used both hands to stop and support herself from falling into the car boot completely. Karen was more mystified, as she whimpered in between her laughter, as she could not believe that Lenny had knobbled her in this way.

"Lenny. Lenny, bloody hell, where did this come from, (pausing and laughing) you sod, why couldn't you have waited?" said Karen, as she tried to push herself upright from her dogging position, but Lenny was standing and holding fast against her bare arse as he thrust and thrust deep into her.

He listened to her whimpers and whispers of her groans, as she still fought against the position she had found herself in, as Lenny began to grip her breasts, fumbling the material to find her nipples in the process, and then that moment Lenny burst into final spurts, as he shot his load in one fucking movement, standing back with one hand holding his bedraggled penis that was still dripping stickiness, when Karen was able to extract herself from the car boot as she turned and faced Lenny, who was holding his dick in his hands, and trousers round his ankles, and grinning (like the cat who got the cream). Karen with hand on forehead, was bewildered as to what had just occurred, as she stood with her legs apart asking Lenny for a tissue. Thankfully, she had not worn any knickers at such a juggernaut approach of shock at Lenny's actions.

"Bloody hell, where the hell did that come from, boyo', boyo'? Why couldn't you have waited until I came in, then throw me over the table and fuck my arse, that's the way to treat a lady," said Karen with bursts of laughter. "What has come over you, you randy bloody git?"

"Well it was one of those moments we men have from time to time, and the opportunity was offering itself, and seeing your dress with lots of loose material at the hem, was ideal for me to jump in quick and up end you at such a sexy sight. You have such a tight arse on you," said Lenny, grinning.

"I am all hot and bothered, so you can come and have a shower with me and finish me off, now you have done yourself," said Karen.

"Come on then, I'll race to upstairs," said Lenny, as he continued to giggle in the frolics of their joyous antics together.

Obviously, neither was aware that PC Bob Benyon from the local constabulary was slowly closing his net on identifying Tommy Sands as one of the occupiers of 'Marshalls Green', and soon the paper trail PC Bob was following would lead him to discover Lenny's details and existence as a criminal associate of Tommy's past, which they have shared since their teenage years together and their crisscross family lives they shared in the East End of London.

Bob had been extremely busy all week and Monday was the last time he had had contact with 'Sandy', but then realising that, she had been house sitting for a friend. Nearing the weekend, his thoughts had turned to her. Would she be contacting him and whether his prowess would be in demand, as he grinned to himself,

"Bloody stupid. I must be crazy, am I the only one?" he muttered, as the thought had crossed his mind several times since their affair began with such gusto. She had an insatiable appetite for sex, no wonder her husband was never around. Perhaps he knew that he couldn't cope with her and hoped she would find someone like me. Perhaps it is their arrangement that they have an open marriage, that he was the playmate and that her husband was for siring their children of the future. Whatever, it was none of his business but just curious thoughts, more about being nosey, but why spoil a great fuck with silly thoughts when it was laid on a plate for him and a woman with great energy and free of inhibitions.

It was around eight o'clock, when the balloon went up. All hell broke out on the Police radio. Call after call was made to various patrols and an indication that it would be his turn soon. He guessed right, as he answered his radio call. He was being directed to the gypsy camp near 'Marshalls Green' – "Injury RTA" came the voice of the radio operator, "Ambulance on route." Bob acknowledged the message and made his way up to the gypsy camp. It was only on arrival did he realise how serious the incident was. Pulling the police vehicle onto the verge, he was met by a gathering of travellers, all shouting and screaming. He was led to the body of a youth lying on the steps of a caravan, his condition was obviously serious. To Bob, the youth was dead, he couldn't find a pulse. Bob knew that he needed to keep the lid on this situation, as it would soon turn ugly. The Ambulance soon arrived, and Bob conversed with the crew and got the youth into the ambulance as soon as was possible, otherwise we could have a riot on our hands as more travellers converged and the number swelled. Bob radioed in the serious nature of the incident, requesting further assistance and that the attendance of the Duty Inspector would be required at the location. Sgt Anderson realised Bob's situation was precarious, to say the least, as some of the young were clearly a load of hotheads and this would be disastrous for everybody. Bob kept an eye out for Old Ben Witney, in the hope he could add more information than what Bob had obtained. The crying and screaming was becoming ridiculous and frightening at the same time as some travellers were shouting for revenge, and yet Bob was clueless as to what they were referring too. Was this an RTA or something more sinister? Bob did his utmost to preserve the scene, but still none the wiser as to where this occurred, when finally, Old Ben stepped out from the gathering and explained that the gypsy youth's body was thrown and dumped from a large black vehicle that sped off towards the next village.

Bob entered the ambulance as the paramedics were trying to resuscitate the youth, but then realised that he was already dead when he was thrown from the offending vehicle. Bob was informed of the many injuries the youth had on his body. He was beaten, and this is not an RTA said one of the ambulance crew. Bob insisted that they leave the scene for their own safety sake and he would deal with the aftermath as some had been drinking and were getting rather angry. So, it was decided to take the youth to hospital and he would bring his parent(s), if there were any, present on the site, rather than have them in the ambulance. By the time the ambulance had left, more Police Officers arrived in support of Bob. Sgt Anderson had arrived with the Duty Inspector. Bob joined them in conference at their police car and explained the situation.

"I would like the family members taken down to the hospital by us, rather than them going down mob-handed, as the youth is dead, although, I have not told any of them that he is. I need to find out who he is first. Can we get transport down to the hospital ASAP before they kick off and give us a load of aggro," said Bob to the Duty Inspector?

"I agree with what you have said. Skipper, get a Panda to take family members down to the hospital. So, you don't think this is a fatal accident then?" asked the Inspector.

"The ambulance crew reckon he had suffered a right beating, rather than the result of a vehicle accident. Apparently, a large black vehicle appeared at speed and the youth was thrown and dumped on the doorstep of one of the caravans. The vehicle then left at speed heading towards the next village," said Bob.

He remained silent, just thinking through the events as he saw them appear to him. Large black vehicle - could that be the Russians now lashing out for answers as to their troubles? Are they muscling? Could it be revenge for the alleged burglary committed against them?

"Skipper, what about 'Scenes of Crime'?" asked Bob.

"That's already been done by the Inspector. We need to get this examined and quickly get out of here and decide on what has taken place. Are there any witnesses to this?" asked Sgt Anderson.

"No, not at the moment. I am waiting to chat with Old Ben, but as it stands, the vehicle just appeared, and the lad was dumped like a sack of coal," said Bob.

"Fucking hell, this is going to be a nightmare. How many family members taken down to the hospital?" asked the Sergeant.

"Just Mother and Father. Old Ben pointed them out and I got them away in the Panda. We just need to be careful about what we say here at the moment. Some have been on the drink for hours, I suspect and one or two are looking for an excuse to kick off," said Bob rather anxiously.

"Yeah, I guessed that when we first arrived. We ought to make tracks ourselves. 'SOCO' done their bit and gone and the Inspector's left in another vehicle. I'll come back with you Bob," said the Sergeant.

"Have all our lot left then?" asked Bob.

"Yeah, what you are thinking then Bob?" asked the Sergeant.

"I wanna get Old Ben to one side for a chat. I was thinking about saying he is wanted by the parents at hospital. I mean, he does know the family and he would be a help to them, being older and wiser," said Bob, as he remained in deep thought for answers.

"Try it, see if it will work for us," said Sgt Anderson.

"Ben, can we give you a lift down to the hospital? You will be a big help to the parent's old mate," said Bob, appealing for Old Ben's help.

Finally, Sgt Anderson, Bob and Old Ben Witney left the scene to return to the village. On the drive back, about a mile from the caravan site, Old Ben requested that Bob take the next turn left; he had something to show them both. Further along the side lane, having turned off the main route, Ben urged Bob to stop the Police car and to get out and follow him into a nearby field. Doing this, Old Ben stopped by a large tree. Nailed to it was a 'T' shirt laid over the surface of the trunk. Dead centre of the garment was a series of holes. Old Ben told both Police officers to look for themselves. Seeing and touching shocked both officers as they turned to Ben.

“Fucking hell, Ben. Who has been taking pot shots? Who is using shotguns for target practice?” asked Bob.

Alarmed at what they had discovered, both officers stood in silence as both, in turn, looked over the ground for traces of evidence that might have been discarded.

“Young ones using four ten shotguns, rabbit guns they got,” said Old Ben. “They hide them in the hedgerows along the lane.”

“This makes it a different ball game for us mate. This is sinister, to say the least. A really frightening turn of events and in view of the ‘Special Supplement Notice’ that’s just been circulated, we are looking at big numbers here, not one or two gypsies out of control,” said Sgt Anderson.

Bob agreed at the Sergeants findings. Old Ben had stood away from the officers as he chewed on the end of his pipe, as he focused on the lights of moving traffic going up and down the main road. Bob realised that Old Ben was a bit fidgety, and instincts told Bob to get back in the police car and drive, drive, drive well away from this location, as he couldn't put Old Bob at risk from his own people, as he knew how hard the fraternities can be on their own people.

Old Ben Witney was escorted into the hospital by Bob and the Sergeant and left in the company of the gypsy youth's parents, who clearly were inconsolable at the loss of their son. Both officers joined other Police Officers who had brought the parents to the hospital and this coincided with the arrival of CID Officers. So now, a growing contingent of Police officers was present. It was apparent from the medical information supplied, that the youth was dead on arrival at the hospital and that close examination of his body showed he had been violently beaten, as his injuries were not consistent with a Road Traffic Accident. After much discussion among CID and the numerous phone calls made that this was now going to be a Murder Investigation and a Major Incident room was going to be established on Division. At the same time, 'SOCO' were required to attend the hospital for evidence gathering, including details of the youth's injuries. Two local officers were detailed to remain at the hospital to preserve and safeguard the crime scene and evidence tampering until they would be relieved later by other officers, especially not wanting fraternity members coming to the hospital and making a big scene over the youth's death and interfering with the Police investigation, as the body was going to be removed to the mortuary as soon as 'SOCO' had completed their evidence gathering.

The nature of the incident was wicked and evil that was indescribable to throw a dead body from a moving vehicle on to the near doorstep of the youth's parents. It was sickening beyond belief. The action of which was a turning point in how the Police would approach this incident as a major concern for their sub-division and the safety of Police Officers was going to be a primary factor in briefing all officers and of all ranks.

The youth's parents, along with Old Ben Witney, were removed to the Police Station for preliminary enquiries in establishing the youth's identity and obviously to record personal details of the family. Bob found this a golden opportunity to take Old Ben out of the way for a coffee and a chat about the events as he saw them. Bob's thoughts had turned to the tree and how sinister that looked in the early evening night sky, situated a few yards from a broken gate, fencing, and a short distance from the lane that is probably not used that often as it wasn't one of those short cuts that linked to any major thoroughfare, so the location was isolated and certainly not near any occupied property. But for Bob, it was more the silhouette of the tree itself that made the landmark a very eerie place. It was a morbid place for some reason and held a strong interest for Bob, although he was unable to explain his premonitions, but he felt that the location played a bigger role in his enquiries.

(Bob was unaware that this was the entrance which provided access to where the vehicles had been brought and buried on the land that belonged to 'Marshalls Green').

It was clear from the information Bob gleamed from Old Ben, that the offending vehicle was one of the same, that had been driving around for some weeks and was not local but belonged to the alleged foreigners. So where did they or who was it who found the gypsy youth? Where was he when he was caught? Was he out doing burglaries, or had he been seen somewhere, kidnapped and beaten? So how many foreigners are we talking about, thought Bob, and were they possibly Russian as earlier believed, and, most importantly, where was he murdered and the time it happened was the immediate focus of the enquiry.

Bob had sought assurances from the night Duty Sergeant that Old Ben, along with the dead youth's parents would be escorted back to the caravan site when the interviews had been completed, as he wanted to finish at ten o'clock and get off home, albeit, to an empty house. Bob was beginning to feel as if his brains had been scrambled with so many incidents and conjectures occurring around him, he needed time alone to think this through in a more orderly fashion.

A house in darkness and a wife away with family was another uncomfortable feeling as he felt like stranger entering his own home. The warming atmosphere that once existed had long gone. It felt drab and dreary, just a place to crash out and sleep and store his things. But again, Bob had to make do with his situation for the time being. Once indoors, he settled down to re-examine the information he had acquired and how it was likely to affect his working area and his colleagues at the Police station.

Bob took pen to paper and listed the facts as he saw them.

- 'Marshalls Green' destroyed by fire?
- Occupants unknown at time of fire?
- One occupier now identified – Tommy Sands (criminal)?

• He was still waiting for his criminal record file to arrive with photograph for identification. (Was he the man in the pub?)

• Who were the other occupier and resident of the property?

• It's known that the property is owned by an off-shore company.

• Commercial Law firm officiates over the affairs of the property, which remain confidential to UK sources.

• Estate agents acting for the Commercial Law firm and liaising with Local authority and Police.

• Stolen Petrol tanker crashed into building? (Deliberate or accident? – Question remains unanswered).

• Unidentified dead body found in cab of Petrol tanker. (No missing person report, not even from the travelling communities themselves).

• It is known that 'Leafy' gypsy youth was involved with tanker and that another gypsy received a broken leg when the vehicle rolled into building.

• Finding the underground construction and array of several types of equipment and technology items.

• Finding underground the black Range Rover without registration plates (VIN – Vehicle Identification Number) enquiries continue as to the history of vehicle.

• Where is the alleged jewellery once hidden in the grounds of 'Marshalls Green'?

• Who hid the jewellery in the grounds?

- Where was the jewellery stolen from?
- Jewellery alleged to have been stolen from foreigners.
- Who are the foreigners?
- Where do the foreigners reside (Police district)?
- Are the alleged foreigners using large Black foreigner vehicles?
- How have these alleged foreigners found their way to our Police area?
- Were these foreigners responsible for discharging shotguns and causing damage to caravans at the site some nights ago?
- Use of shotgun on 'T' shirt (practice shooting or actions of someone's anger). Is this auctioned by gypsies?
- Where did the weapons come from?
- Murder of gypsy youth (beaten and not RTA victim).

Need to know answers, missing links, and are these links part of a bigger picture that identifies major flaws in the current Police investigation. Is there a lack of knowledge and understanding, or is it simply that two and two does not add up and involves other unidentified Police districts? Bob realised that the true nature of the dangers exists for all officers and is real and not a fabrication, or an overkill, on the conjecture, simply because no tangible evidence was available. Are we again dealing with the bullshit of being Politically Correct by those who have short arses, the real 'Pinkies' who run around with their own sad agendas for quick-fired promotion, who walks over all and sundry to climb that ladder in the big blue sky. Bob then looked at the obvious and it was clear to him that this was an open book and the story line was dysfunctional, to say the least.

- Nothing criminal involving Tommy Sands and 'Marshalls Green' was found, including the vehicle and it was all legit with Police alarms now protecting the vehicle and the underground construction.
- Petrol Tanker was stolen for unknown reasons that involved members of the gypsy fraternity. It also appears that the dead body found in the cab of a vehicle was a tragic accident which involved sheer panic on the part of the deceased and the injuries sustained by two other gypsies at the time were self-inflicted by lack of knowledge and lack of action by the victims.
- Unknown gypsies, whether local, or from elsewhere, have caused a situation to occur between themselves, and alleged foreigners being the other party concerned over an alleged high value jewellery burglary details remain unknown to local Police.
- Is the troubling presence of a large black foreign vehicle seen in the area on numerous occasions by travelling folk, responsible for the shotgun discharge causing criminal damage to many gypsy caravans, and the vehicle being one of the same who dumped the dead body in the camp?
- Are the many vehicle thefts and burglaries locally attributed to local gypsies or outsiders? Could any of these offences be caused by those mentioned on the 'Special Supplement Bulletin?'

- What connection does the 'T' Shirt have? Is there any significance to the recent troubles, or is this just an added coincidence and detraction to the main incidents?
- The alleged stolen jewellery supposedly hidden in the grounds of 'Marshalls Green'?
- (Q) Who hid the property there?
- (Q) Who originally stole the alleged property?
- (Q) Stolen from where?
- (Q) Has the jewellery been found and re-stolen?

Bob realised that the visiting black vehicle was a priority and obviously this would be dealt with by the Murder Incident Room in tracing it. So, he decided to continue his enquiries on the second occupier of 'Marshalls Green' and to see where this might take him.

He hoped that personal information on the crime file of Tommy Sands would help him to understand his background and associates who may be mentioned on the paperwork.

So, as matters stand, the Petrol Tanker was a separate incident and was one of theft and criminal damage. Whether the house fire was arson or caused by other means, involved known named gypsies, some already in custody.

CHAPTER TEN

A Long Weekend – Monday Come Quick

More gypsy incidents continued to be the nuisance call over the Saturday late turn shift, patrols appearing to be all over the place, answering distressed and harassed calls from the public. It seemed to Bob that the lid cannot be contained any longer on the gypsy problem that clearly was escalating, and it appeared that Bob's policing area was taking the brunt of complaints from the public. Senior Officers need to be listening, as they clearly aren't at the moment, as the gypsy subject was a political hot potato and management were scared to get their fingers burnt, career-wise that is. But sadly, it was a lazy indicator as to how junior ranks were exposed to the continuance and obvious dangers of high speed vehicle chases, especially through narrow country lanes.

It was late afternoon when the call was received at sub-division about a body having been found on farmland belonging to Derek Adkins of 'Mantles Green Farm'. By the time Bob arrived simultaneously with another double-crewed Police vehicle, an ambulance was already on the scene at the farm.

A gypsy youth had been nailed by the hands to fencing. Although unconscious, he was alive. The scene was horrendous, as it was clear that the Fire Service were going to be needed to remove him safely and a trauma Doctor was called to attend the farm. The paramedics were able to do as much as they could without interfering with the hand injuries, as they were more concerned about the bloodletting, as the flow had been restricted by the nails fixed to the wooden fencing.

"Oh! My God," were the first words Bob uttered on

seeing the youth nailed to the fencing. "Christ, what bastards have done this?" as he gestured to the Derek Adkins, the farmer whose land the youth was found on.

"It was our farm dogs that raised the alarm. They were barking for ages. So, after my coffee, I came out to shut them up, but they ran off as if I should follow them and, of course, I did and found the lad like this. He was unconscious when I found him. Looking at the injuries, the blood had dried, so I suppose he has been here sometime," said Derek, who clearly himself was in shock at having found the youth. As he stood shaking on the spot, one of the paramedics insisted that he go indoors and make himself a steaming sweet drink and to wrap up warm. Bob realised that Derek had been well and truly shaken by the incident and decided that the other two officers make a good search of the farm buildings.

Eventually, with the presence of the trauma Doctor and Firemen present, the unconscious youth had been sedated by the doctor before his hands were freed from the fencing. It was also established that he had been badly beaten on each side of body, as skin abrasions and bruising were found just above the waistline.

Bob remained bewildered by what he was seeing, as he radioed into control room with an update of the incident, as clarity was needed for the controller to fully understand the principal injury to the youth and that he was still alive with a doctor present. It was whilst the doctor was still attending to the youth, one of the other Police officers returned with further news that another body had been located behind one of the farm buildings. You could cut the atmosphere with a knife. Aghast at what had been discovered, the news was shattering, as everyone present stood in shocked silence as to what had been unearthed at the farm.

Bob went with paramedic and police colleague to where the body was found. It was sad news to be told by the paramedic that the youth was dead. The four attendees stood back in absolute shock at the dreadful news and the doctor's presence was required to certify death. It was in disbelief, as no-one had an answer to what had taken place.

The doctor certified the youth's death in the presence of others present and it was clear that the youth had met a violent death and was probably murdered in situ to where he was found. The ambulance left the farm with the first youth for hospital, whilst the doctor looked in on Derek the farmer. At the same time, Derek was informed of the other youth found dead. Derek was beside himself at such shocking news, as his wife too, became hysterical and screaming on hearing the news.

Bob called in the update and the shocking news of a second body being found, with a request for the appropriate departments to be informed and their attendance, including CID and Senior Officers.

Bob telephoned Sgt Anderson with the news that what they both feared would happen one day, and now all hell had broken out and it could only get worse as the day wore on.

Sgt Anderson was quick to respond, by driving out to the farm. Bob requested that dog handlers be called out, including a dog that searched for firearms. The farm needed to be searched thoroughly and would require more officers to do the groundwork with much farmland to be covered.

During this time, Bob received a tinkle on his private mobile. It was a picture of a pair of briefs and thumbs up. Knowing this had been sent by 'Sandy' as the message read briefly, 'Back home later', it was her cheer up to him, unaware of the incident Bob was now involved in. It did bring a smile of relief to his face, as he wished he could change places at this very moment, although, it did help to focus on more endearing times with her.

Within hours of the incident, a 'Major Incident Room' had been established at the farm, with considerable activity taking place from ground searches, SOCO search for evidence and the use of a drone used for the very first time in a major incident. Senior officers had been and gone from the farm, although it was agreed that an armed guard was now necessary to protect the caravan remainders in the lane. As word soon spread to the fraternities, as many travellers were uprooting and leaving the area as quickly as they can hitch up and hit the road. Bob was desperate to gather as much detail on the families as possible before they left the area. The identities again remained unidentified. No traveller was revealing names of the two youths found today at the farm. It was left to Bob to try and prise snippets from Old Ben with a cash incentive in the palm of the hand. Old Ben provided the names, one was a Loveridge, the other a Smith. Neither were local travellers.

"They were brought here as a message by the foreigners in the night, they were kept in the boot. Tied up they were. The travellers had big arguments with the three foreigners and they had gun. They left quickly when they saw the traveller's shotguns," said Ben.

"I can't get over the savagery of this attack. One has been nailed to the fence and the other is dead. What evil is this? Do you have any idea as to where these people are coming from?" asked Bob, appealing to Ben's conscience. “This is becoming a killing spree on travellers. We have got to stop them Ben, before they kill again.”

“Young Leafy, he knows governor, he’s seen the big house. They live many miles away, but it was ‘Leafy’ and others who got chased off,” said Old Ben, still sucking on the end of his pipe.

Bob knew that ‘Leafy’ was still in custody, although, unaware of the latest incident, perhaps he might give up the location of these people and let’s find out and identify who they really are, they must be stopped. Bob returned to the Police Station for his meal break and at the same time informing CID at Sub-Division of the information he had gleamed from the traveller’s camp.

“Leafy, the one in custody, has the knowledge as to where these foreigners are living. His backside will probably go, once he knows of the killings,” said Bob.

Bob carried on with his meal break and texted a few times to ‘Sandy’. It was nearly a week since he spent the night with her. Now she was back in her own home, perhaps she was feeling sexually peckish tonight, thought Bob sporting a self-proclaimed big grin of satisfaction and hoped she was.

Before leaving the Police Station at ten o’clock, Bob walked out into the street and hoped that perhaps ‘Sandy’ might be parked up nearby. His instincts were on the ball, as he saw the headlights flash a couple of times on a vehicle parked along the street. It was ‘Sandy’. Bob raised his hand twice to indicate to her ten minutes and he would be out of the station. Greeting her with a kiss of sorts, as he didn’t want to be found that close to the station, he decided that perhaps a drink up at the local village pub might be more suitable around other people, until they decided on how they were going to spend the next few hours together. 'Sandy' looked every bit the one with the bit between her teeth, eager and restless to cuddle up and touch Bob with real genuine friendship that was well and truly developing between them. An hour later, Bob decided that he would leave his vehicle at the police station and return with 'Sandy' to her home.

It didn't take them long to stand cuddling in the shower, once arriving back at 'Sandy's', naked and dripping wet by the time the couple entered the bedroom to towel themselves dry. She looked gorgeous in the warm glow of the sidelights, as she rolled down the duvet as they both climbed on to the bed and rolled into each other's arms with a long lingering kiss for starters. Passion was racing, as 'Sandy' fingered his wet hair, as she kissed and kissed every part of his face. Eventually, she settled down with a long cuddle from Bob, as he explained the day's events and why the area was becoming rather dangerous out there and it was better to fuck together in the house than in the open. 'Sandy' giggled at his remark as being funny in a kind of way, more about where to fuck, but to her, it didn't matter, so long as she was with him to enjoy his company. 'Sandy' didn't question once his work or ask uncomfortable questions. For her, it was taboo. Why spoil their time together? It was about them and the fun they shared in their love making, as sex was sex. Bob was delivering and injecting real quality into their affair and for her, it was a beautiful thing to happen, as once again, she compared him to her husband and Bob was far superior the better lover as they have fucked well together. She has experienced multiple orgasms for the first time in many a long time.

'Sandy' had reached down and took hold of Bob's penis. She fondled and played gently with a hint of masturbation, as Bob pushed up against her hand. It was then that 'Sandy' slipped down the bed and laid her head on his tummy as she moved her hand back and forth, as she felt him begin to rise to her touches. Then, her head moved right down into his groin area as she placed his penis into her mouth and began a slow sucking motion on the stem of all stems that had come alive with her lips gripping his girth and her tongue teasing inside her mouth. As she focused on his tip, at the same time, she moved her body in between his legs, as she was kneeling like a curled-up ball, as her hands rested on his thighs, as she moved her mouth up and down on his penis. His hands had clasped the back of her head, as he encouraged her rhythm. Then, he pulled back and turned her on to her tummy, as he knelt between her legs. At the same time, he placed pillows underneath her tummy as he went down on her, with fingers rimming her anus at the same time as he was placing his tongue inside her, occasionally taking her clitoris between his lips and sucked, and gently pulled, as she began to twist and wriggle. Bob realised how moist she had become, when he moved closer as he held his penis and slowly teased her vagina lips. First, a small entry, then withdrew several times, but each time he went deeper into her, until he injected the whole of his penetration, so that both pubic bones were rubbing against each other, with both hands on her haunches, as he pulled 'Sandy' back to him and held her tight, as she squeezed him time and again. He felt the internal pressure from her as her thigh and leg muscles tightened with her movements. It was one of those fucking moments. In fact, it was more than a moment, as they both remained in this position, skin to skin, bone to bone, rubbing hard as 'Sandy' was clearly having small orgasms as Bob felt those small quivers ripple through her body. 'Sandy' was taking herself right to the edge and then controlling that final moment, so as not to tip over the edge. She was on a roll, saving something big for herself. As Bob began to buck and withdraw, in and out, in and out, and as his pace gathered a forceful momentum of energy as he was fucking her as hard as he could possibly manage. 'Sandy' had gripped the under sheet with both hands, as she buried her face into the mattress, groaning and whimpering, with every one of Bob's strokes that entered her with such speed. She really was very vocal tonight, as she was well and truly away with the fairies, as she, too, had gathered her torso to work with Bob on his final strokes, as her orgasmic sized orgasm had blown her away, exhausted and still whimpering and now dripping in perspiration, as Bob had hit that big moment that many women dream about and it happened tonight of all nights, as she conceded this was the fuck of all fucks that she had ever experienced, when she rolled on to her back, her face flushed, as she wiped her hands over her cheeks and down over her breasts, with her hands coming to rest between her legs, cupping her pubic bone, as she withdrew back, her legs with knees bent. Bob provided the tissues. He knew the routine, as 'Sandy' wiped herself from the trickle of seepage from her vulva lips that were warm to touch. 'Sandy' crawled to her sleeping position, with tissues stuffed between her legs. Bob followed as they both laid side by side with only their heart beats ringing in their ears. It was clear from their earlier comments and past performances up to now, that neither had fucked their own partners with such consistency as they had shared together, and none were failures, they remained equal to the feelings they experienced.

Whilst sharing breakfast together, Bob's mobile sounded and on answering, it was Sgt Anderson requiring a change of duty time, to start at ten o'clock this morning and not for him to do a late shift. This suited Bob, as his day meant an early finish and arranged with 'Sandy' a visit to the cinema, and cinema it was to be for both later.

Bob's day was mostly spent as a run-around in holding the fort together. With so much pressure unfolding, management had not yet agreed to extra officers being drawn in from other divisions. But later in the day, Bob realised that the despatch had arrived overnight, and the contents had been dispersed in various dockets of the officers and, of course, he saw that he was included, as he fondled the package that had arrived addressed to him from the National Criminal Records Office. At last, he hoped he was about to find the truth to all his recent enquiries to do with 'Tommy Sands' and 'Marshalls Green'. The attached photograph confirmed that the man in the pub, the man who had left the cardboard box, was one of the same who lived at the Manor House; it was indeed 'Tommy Sands'. At last, Bob's hunch had paid off. Seated, he pawed over the assortment of attached pages, from convictions, antecedents and family history, to associates. Associates was the most important for Bob to browse and scrutinise. He knew that he would find the second man among the list of associates, the second man who lived at the Manor House, the man of mystery.

Bob's first task was to find Tommy's last conviction and

it was clear from the information he read, that it was nearly six years ago when he was last convicted for a series of non-violent crimes, along with another – 'Lenny Burns'. Going back over their history, it was clear that they were together on most of the crimes they were convicted of.

Bob made a telephone request to his own Force's Criminal Record Office, with a request of obtaining 'Lenny Burns' criminal record and any current photographs to be added to the request. At last, Bob felt vindicated that he had at last solved the mystery of the two occupants of 'Marshalls Green'. Now, he could start putting together a solid argument of identification, but at the same time, he realised that neither men had, or were involved in, further criminal activity since residing at the Manor House. There simply was no evidence to substantiate his thinking. What Bob found underground, including a high specification vehicle housed within the construction, did not constitute criminality, but more of a hobbyist. It also made sense as to why the cardboard box and items left for him at the pub, it was simply to help him do his job, as the gypsy subject on the night was very prominent in their conversations, including the statement he made about there being a negligence and a political correctness that had hampered many an investigation concerning the gypsy and travelling folk, by bad Police management that had provided a blank cheque for them to commit and continue their many criminal activities, because of the lack of interest and action by Senior Officers, and now, sadly, it was all coming home to roost and the consequences are now greater than anyone ever considered with two murders, violent assaults and a mandate of rampage through the surrounding villages that remains unabated.

During meal break time at the station, Bob caught up with Sgt Anderson and briefed him on the news. You could see in the faces of both officers, that their persistence was achievable in following their noses like all good coppers are taught in the good old days of policing, when joining the service for the long haul of a police career.

Bob had already outlined his next enquiry, by going back to Bill Sheffield at the Local Authority with a request for help in assisting further his enquiry, by use of their Drone being flown over a square mile radius around 'Marshalls Green' and the adjacent woodland areas belonging to the Forestry Commission. Bob explained that there had to be several abandoned stolen vehicles somewhere on their police area. It doesn't make sense, as few stolen vehicles are turning up and of course once they had little use for the vehicle, they burn them, and I feel that we will find several hidden and burnt out vehicles local to us. Remembering over many months of the reports we received from the public of fires being seen and yet never located, and I feel that those fires could be vehicles being burnt out by the travellers.

Bob and the Sergeant sat with younger officers taking their meal breaks and it was with idle chat that both officers were asked by the Probationary Officers as to how diverse policing was, and how the adrenalin soon rushes through the veins and the many strange stories told. It was then, Bob mentioned of one story that stuck in his mind, as to how strange people can be even with their own siblings.

Bob went on to tell the story of a young boy and only child who, during the Second World War, saw this man occasionally in his mother's house dressed in Army uniform. The man wore a flat cap and wore insignias on his shoulders and lapels. The man came and went at odd times and had little to do with him when visiting, but there were also times of long absences in between his visits, before the man reappeared at the house. It was a most odd relationship, as the boy was eventually told that the man in uniform was his father. All the boy could do, was to stand and gawp at the uniformed figure in the house, as often from his bedroom, he would hear the front door close and footsteps on the path outside. The boy would peek from the window to see the figure disappear into the night.

Coming to present day, the boy was now an adult of middle age who was found wandering around a small village early one evening, when he stopped and spoke with a patrolling Police Officer who so happened to have been in the area. It transpired that the man's mother had recently died, and she was a crossword compiler for a national newspaper and that in her Will she had left him details of a crossword to be solved. By solving the crossword, the man would know where his father was buried. His father was a member of the 'Special Operations Executive' (SOE) during the war and was killed and buried in France. His mother never made mention of his father whilst growing up, and he is the only child, accepted the fact that he lived with his mother and she never talked about his father. Now, he was left with this riddle and old memories came flooding back to the man in uniform, but sadly a man he never knew, but why was his mother so cruel in doing what she did by leaving a crossword puzzle to be solved and for him to find the grave of his father. The events are true, as the man travelled from another Continent to finally discover the missing link in his life and that of his father and who his father's family were and are there any present-day relatives alive, hence his visit to the village to pursue answers to his many questions that are foremost in his mind.

Bob's story had left the conversation among his colleague's stone cold and much reflection on what Policing was all about. Never can it be taken for granted, there was always another side to the coin and that Police Officers must do their jobs with open minds and never to be the judge and jury that befalls their work. The story was a tragic tale of selfishness but also outlined the difference between the years and the upbringing of those older generations and how they behaved by the standards and etiquette of the day, and in modern times for us to digest as to how any parent, albeit a mother, could behave towards a sibling.

Indeed, the story was most shocking, and all agreed the anger they felt towards the mother was real and personal to them, but they were Police Officers and should reflect the office of Constable. It was only human to have feelings and an opinion of the mother and it leaves a bad taste in the mouth nevertheless.

Bob's day finally came to an end at six o'clock. It was for him, a complete change and rather relaxing, as work goes without having to drive here and there throughout his tour of duty and now, he was off home to change and off for a meal and the cinema with 'Sandy'. He also felt obliged to stay overnight and engage in more sexual activity that was now becoming more of a hobby which they both enjoyed, rather than it being a one-way ticket for him and a partner left frustrated. Between them, they have experimented, as 'Sandy' had hoped and expected of him. Bob had taken his task like a duck to water, having done their utmost to fuck each other silly and in every conceivable way possible, but for both was the growing trust between them and how inhibitions were never ever a concern to either, both being free as a bird in their ideology of their sexual preferences.

As expected, having arrived home to 'Sandy's' house, no sooner were they through the door and rushing up the stairs, when Bob grabbed her ankle and held her fast on the stairs, bending forwards with both hands supporting her position. Bob, once again, upended her clothing and tried to mount her from a dogging position. He was so excited and stiff that he coaxed her to bend her knees a little so that he could enter her, as his penis was throbbing and raring to go. When he entered her from the rear, they both were sharing the hysterics of what they were performing. Bob humped and humped, and she remained bent over with her knees weakened from the excitement, as Bob was in full flight of his thrusting. He was well and truly fucking her hard as she let out loud cries of her delights with groaning whimpers that echoed round the house. For 'Sandy' to be taken like this was unexpected, but the thrill was a dream, a desire she had hoped for in their experimenting ways of sexual gratification, without asking or encouraging him to fuck her like that. Not from their first time together has she not had an orgasm. In fact, it has been more multiples for her, as Bob certainly was able to control himself, clearly an experienced lover, who was conscious of a woman's emotional stimulus and he was giving her good service every time they have been together. But she had kept her words and thoughts to herself; it was more of him delivering by his own initiatives than pretty words from her and enlarging an ego that didn't need any encouragement from her as Bob was most comfortable in his own skin and the great lover he was.

Finally, sharing a shower together with their clothes strewn all over the stairs and landing, for them, it was not a night to care, but a night to share as they kissed long and passionate as Bob's fingers of one hand tweaked her nipples as they faced each other and a finger of the other hand was rubbing her clitoris, when her orgasm began to explode as she jumped up and placed her legs round Bob's waist and her arms wrapped round his neck, as she began to cry for the first time. Bob felt her uncontrollable movement of the orgasm that shook every muscle in her body, as she tightened her grip on him, as he turned and carried her into the bedroom where they remained for the rest of the night, tightly cuddled up. It was a first for Bob to hear her openly cry from their love making. He was now more in control than 'Sandy'. He felt, perhaps, it was mostly a charade on her part in the beginning and now he had hit a nerve that took her on a journey to another emotional level of their love making. It was intense, to say the least, but so enjoyable to be free and flying high to fuck as they like, as neither could get any closer together than skin to skin and minds that think alike.

CHAPTER ELEVEN

The Hunt is On – Who are the Killers

On Monday morning, Bob on Rest day, popped down to the Local Authority office to meet with Bill Sheffield, the Planning Officer. Bob's request was for the use of the Drone by his staff to provide him with some Aerial detail of the landscape around 'Marshalls Green' and the woodlands that bordered along the property and way beyond the gipsy encampment. Bob provided a video card to retain copyright and avoid any compromise to unauthorised use of Local Authority property, being so aware of the stupidity of some individuals who were brainwashed into being politically correct. Bill agreed to assist, as he also needed details of the underground construction on the property of 'Marshalls Green' and whether any planning laws had been broken. But, of course, it was hidden from public view and remained as part of the landscape and, furthermore, when was it constructed in part or whole, was another burning question as Bob arranged for Bill to come and have a look for himself. Extraordinary as to how this was constructed, and nobody complained. If it weren't for Police interest, the Local Authority would be none the wiser. Indeed, there is no monetary loss to the Council, the revenue of the property has always been paid and is up to date on our records as,

"I did check the last time you were here," said Bill Sheffield.

Bob spent the rest of the day just relaxing and browsing family history matters and photos of the past. He had considered visiting relatives but decided to remain local and visit a coffee bar. It was surprising, just by a few minutes alone and watching the world go by, how much he took in of the world around him. The people that he sees often shopping while on patrol, mothers chastising children, the elderly struggling to walk or carrying shopping. Life in any community was the hustle and bustle of people doing many things. For Bob, he found this fascinating. He could sit all day long and merely watch as the day goes by, people's behaviour towards each other, body language, arguments occurring in the street or greetings of pleasantries; you could recognise those who were genuine and those who were not.

You had to laugh at some of the moments he had witnessed as he sat sipping coffee above the noises that echoed around him from loud voices, crying children and, of course, the banging and the brewing of the coffee machines that operated in the cafe. It did make one feel relaxed by not clock watching or having to rush away for some unexplained reason. Sometimes, he was recognised and sometimes he received a wave of friendship, but always he sat alone. Even with 'Sandy' present, it was nigh on impossible to display any attachment, as people were never that stupid, as it would have been interpreted differently by the wagging tongues and gossips. Although, unwittingly this time, they all would have been right in guessing the kind of friendship that existed between them, and it was a sexual one.

By early evening, at home, Bob settled back to re-examine two areas of his enquiry that had been niggling and eating away at him. He could not shake from his mind the silhouette of the tree with a 'T' shirt nailed for target practice. Beyond doubt, a somewhat sinister discovery; it was his gut instincts that told him to return and take another look at the area. Being drawn to this location was unexplained, although. Old tyre impressions could be seen on the ground, indicating considerable vehicle movement having accessed and passed over the field for some reason. But evidently not all at once, as some impressions were laid over other tyre tracks and, in fact, some width of tyres were either heavy goods or farm machines, it was a right mismatch picture of intrigue.

(The tree reminded him of that lonesome eerie picture of windswept moors with rain lashing down and wind howling, while a shadowy figure was seen standing offset to the tree when with, in the blink of an eye, the character disappeared, leaving an untold mystery).

Bob also remembered a past comment that was remarked upon by the Bull & Butcher's pub landlady, Judy, when he had mentioned four dogs had been seen on many occasions at the Manor House. Then the story told by the Firemen who used the pub as a watering hole for refreshments, that one dog was seen ghost-like in the burning debris which was stomach-churning to watch the animal suffer, before finally being succumbed by the fire. He remembered Judy commenting on a couple who sat in the bay window of the pub later that day, and both were upset and fidgety. They weren't sat there for very long, for when they left, they were seen getting into a small car that was parked near the refreshment table outside, and three dogs are seen in the back of the vehicle. Bob recalled, from what was described at the time, that they appeared to be the same breed of animal as those up at the 'Manor House'. Someone remarked later to Judy as to how attractive they were and an unusual breed and colour. It was not like seeing a regular breed, if that makes sense, as Bob recalled her last words and at the time had no meaning. It was only now, by churning over the events in his mind and drawing on his past knowledge of what Old Ben had told him, it made sense to his now reasoning of who the second occupant of the 'Manor House' could be.

Was it 'Lenny Burns', who sat in the pub that day? Was it him that found and retrieved the three remaining animals?

"One dog died in the fire, and the other three were never found," said Bob deep in thought. "Those animals ought to have shown up by now if they were still on the loose. Someone would have seen them running around."

Bob now felt he had found something significant, a missing link in the chain of events. Could that have been 'Lenny Burns', as, according to 'Tommy Sands'' rap sheet, they were inseparable in life and crime? Bob was playing a hunch of a lifetime. "It just had to be," muttering to himself, as he flicked through his notes. Then remembering a further detail from his previous conversations with Old Ben. He mentioned that there was a Jaguar at the 'Manor House' and used regularly, often seen in the village and, of course, the village had only one petrol station. Otherwise, it meant travelling extra miles to fill up, and that was unlikely when living a legit lifestyle.

Bob sat for ages mulling over and analysing his questions as he sipped on his whisky to hand from time to time. He felt the rush of adrenalin as the excitement within him began to paint a clearer picture of his thoughts.

"Right, two vehicles and two men occupants of the house; Range Rover, we have that, where is the Jaguar? (Pause). Now Judy said the couple were in a small car, so if it was 'Lenny Burns', where is the Jaguar? And whose small car was it they were using?" asked Bob.

Fiddling and spinning the whisky glass round in his hand. You could cut his concentration with a knife; it was so intense and focused at this time. Bob was well aware of making something fit when the shape of the piece didn't fit the puzzle.

"So, what is different before the house fire and the couple seen in the pub? – The Jaguar was never found in the debris of the fire, no other vehicle was discovered, so where is the Jaguar? And why the small car, could it be a rental model from somewhere?"

Bob muttered to himself as his thoughts were ahead of his words going two to the dozen at this time. In between times, it had gone two o'clock in the early hours of the morning when Bob stirred and woke, realising that he had fallen asleep in the chair, as he made a move to climb the stairs and reach out for his bed and not that of another, as he grinned to himself when finally undressing and settling under his duvet to finish off the night.

By nine o'clock the next morning and another rest day, Tuesday, to enjoy, Bob was ready to leave the house with his first stop in the village to be the local bakery for fresh bread and a bag full of jam doughnuts. As he stood at the counter and waited for his order, he decides to sit with a coffee and let the shop staff deal with the queue first. It was a chance meeting that 'Sandy' saw him sat in the coffee bar of the Bakers when she joined him with a smile a mile wide if that were possible.

"I have written a verse for you all at the police station. An innovative word for Police Officer; saves me dropping it into the police station," said 'Sandy', out loud for all to hear.

Still laughing, as she handed him an envelope and then left the shop, Bob opened the envelope and read the verse. His raised eyebrows approved her words, and others in the shop were itching to know what she had written, as he was goaded into reading aloud the verse to a baker's audience.

BOBBYJAC

Here comes the 'Bobbyjac.'
Walking down the street
Here comes the 'Bobbyjac.'
Pounding out his beat

Past the jeweller's window
Crammed with antique clocks
Checking the shop doorway
Trying all the locks

Moving on the Wino
In the Market Square
"Come along old son you can't
Spend the night there."
Nodding to the cabbie
Out on his last call
Ginger, Tom and Tabby
Prowl along the wall

Lonely footsteps echo
Through the silent streets
"Glad to get these boots off
And ease my aching feet."

Sometimes it's a lonely job
A 'Bobbyjac' must do
Worst of all its foot patrol
'Especially 10 pm until two.'

Who'd be out on such a night?
Only the insane
Villains tucked up in their beds
Me out in the rain

There goes the 'Bobbyjac.'
Walking down the street
Back towards the station
Finishing his beat

That's slightly clever of her, came a voice; others clapped and laughed. The reaction of those present showed their approval of 'Sandy's' verse very much. "She has got it right", said another voice from the waiting customers, then Bob was given his order and left the shop with a big grin and a moment when his heart missed a beat on seeing 'Sandy' appear like that. He was chuffed that she had gone to such an effort to write the verse, it broke up the monotony of the morning.

"The lads will be interested in reading that, 'BOBBYJAC', a name to remember 'Sandy' by," he muttered.

Hearing the toot of a car horn and looking around, as he saw 'Sandy' waving as she was driving off, Bob grinned and waved back as he, too, walked towards his car, heading for the lane and the strange tree that haunts him.

Reaching the side lane and the location, Bob parked up and walked the open ground through the broken gate and continued to follow some of the tyre impressions in the ground. Eventually, he came to fresh territory that had apparently been recently landscaped for some reason, although, one could see depressions appearing in the field from where the changeable weather had caused the earth to be slightly sodden in places. Bob had no inkling that he was standing on the buried vehicles from Tommy's Crime operation. It merely was an inquisitive mind trying to understand the reasoning behind the work that had landscaped the ground as it remained earth bare and not covered in grass as one would have expected, being part of a grazing field for animals. For Bob, it was to set his mind at rest by visiting today. It helped him understand more of the layout below the 'Manor House', as clearly, the land was part of the estate and realised why the ground remained like it was because the occupants were no longer present, whereabouts unknown?

Bob decided on revisiting the Bull & Butcher pub to have a further chat with Judy, the Licensee's wife, realising too, that he could have lunch, as it was still early afternoon and the kitchen may well still be open for orders.

“Judy, your Dan, how long does he keep the security tapes before he wipes them clean?” asked Bob.

"I'll get Dan for you, and you can chat with him," said Judy.

Dan came and joined him at his table and explained his reasons for asking about the security camera and the tapes.

“I keep them up to six months. Well, I started to do that because of the Irish travellers we had in here,” said Dan.

"Yeah (grinning), Judy did tell me about that, and you were flooding the place," said Bob.

“Well, the problem for us, they came back months later to give us some aggravation one afternoon, so I decided I would keep the tapes for a longer period. Why do you ask?" asked Dan.

"Well, on the day of the house fire, your car park was used by the emergency services because of the road being shut off. Well, at the same time, a couple in a small car arrived and came and sat in your bay window of the pub for a short while. It appeared that both were upset at the time, but it was the comments after they left the pub. There was the talk of three dogs being in the vehicle, and the Manor House had four dogs, but one died in the fire, so where are the other three dogs? That's why I am asking whether they might be a couple I am looking for and were those dogs the same missing dogs from the Manor House?" said Bob anxiously, hoping that Dan can help him.

“Well, I can have a look for you. Can you remember the date it happened?” asked Dan.

Bob’s order came to his table; his meal was ready to eat as Dan left him to eat his lunch in peace. At the same time, Bob rang the station and spoke with one of his colleagues. He requested the date of the house fire. This, he gave to Dan as he continued eating his meal.

“How much time do you have Bob?” asked Dan, “only I have found the day; it will take some time to whizz through it,” said Dan.

"I am okay for a time, I am on a rest day," said Bob, now eager to get started.

Dan took Bob into a secluded area of the pub, enabling him to view the tape without interruptions. From time to time, Judy looked in on him to see how he was doing and bringing a fresh coffee with her. It was probably four hours later when Bob surfaced with a face full of delight. He had found what he had been looking for; a couple entering the pub which appeared to be distressed. Now, to roll back the tape machine to see their car. Bob sat, after some minutes, transfixed on who he believed was the couple. From then, he gently moved on the video until he had a better look at their faces. But it was the dogs he needed to find first to establish the higher probability that this was the right couple. Eventually, he managed to confirm the outline of the animals in the vehicle, and he would stake his life on the fact that this was the couple he had been searching for. He now had Lenny Burns in his sights, so the photograph from the Criminal Record office remains the most crucial piece of the puzzle in his enquiries to date. Focusing on the female, Bob realised there was an age difference, but she was a beautiful woman. Sadly, at times, the videotape was grainy and did a disservice to her, but he felt assured that he would recognise her, aware now, having seen her full face as she entered the pub, so at last, he was moving in the right direction. Bob was anxious to see if the vehicle registration plate was visible, even rewinding to when the vehicle first appeared from the roadway. Fortunately, he was able to make out sufficient detail to play with the digits and hopefully identify the owner of the car. For Bob, it was a day to remember as he returned to the bar with one of the happiest faces one could wish for and full of praise for Dan and Judy's help. It appeared that Bob's continued tenacity was paying off, as clearly, patience for him was a virtue that he would long remember in his service, with so much time and energy spent on gut instinct and a hunch was finally paying off for him. By the time he got home, he was genuinely whacked out and ready for bed, when his private mobile went off. It was 'Sandy' contacting him. Having thanked her for the verse, he requested that she come to him for cuddles only night and no fucking, as he was well and truly exhausted.

'Sandy' agreed and that is what happened. She spent the night at his house, and they behaved themselves, other than passionate kisses, cuddles and no fucking. As both had a good night's sleep, waking more refreshed than they both expected. As their sexual urges were, for them, intense, as they lay skin to skin and Bob was shockingly piss-proud, and his movements were admired and greatly eyed by 'Sandy', but, as agreed, she would have to refrain from any sexual contact. But their urges got the better of them down in the kitchen, as Bob upended her borrowed housecoat, exposing her naked arse, and before she had time to blink. Had penetrated her over the kitchen table and was fucking with all his might. As if there was some urgency in his fucking, as his hands found her naked breasts among the material, as he fondled and caressed her nipples, and no sooner had he started fucking her, he withdrew squirting over her backside and lower back.

“Oh! My God, where did that come from?” asked ‘Sandy’.

As she stood and kissed him with one long lingering passionate moment, Bob clung on, as his hands tried to finger masturbate her while they held together. She eased her legs apart, as Bob continued to manipulate and eventually entered her vagina. As ‘Sandy' closed her legs and taut her thigh muscles tight grasping his finger inside her vagina, working herself off until she reached orgasm.

"Bloody hell, I can't believe it. You are magic Bob, we can fuck anywhere, and you still manage to give me an orgasm. God almighty, I can't believe you are real at times. You are the best fucking partner I have ever had the pleasure of inside of me," said ‘Sandy'.

As she stroked his face gently, her eyes were transfixed on his face as if searching for something, but more mesmerised at just what happened in the kitchen and before breakfast – touché, as their faces broke into smiles for each other.

"I wished we had met in another time, for our lives to begin together Bob. You fascinate me; we are good for each other, fuck buddies are not the icing on the cake, our friendship is the true buddy and the trust we have to share, and that is special for me," said ‘Sandy'.

As she once again cuddled up to him for reassurance, as she was naked under the housecoat and Bob saw just how beautiful she was. Makeup was not necessary, as she held her beauty, a real ‘English Rose'. Bob admitted to her that he could fuck her all day long and not let her out of his sight, as he wanted more and more of her juices and touches that flowed from her. They indeed had a kindred spirit to ride and share.

Wednesday morning, ten o'clock start for Bob, saw him team up with Sgt Anderson by eleven o'clock. Bob's exciting news about the video security tape was hopefully the break they had been seeking. Arriving at the prearranged meeting at the Bull & Butcher pub was a sobering moment. While he sat sipping coffee and spending many minutes playing the tape back and forth, it was clear that the couple seen on the tape could well be 'Lenny Burns'. The woman remained unknown, but clearly of younger age to the accompanying man with her. More time was spent on re-examining the tape to identify the animals in the vehicle and, in fact, the tape revealed the arrival of the vehicle entering the field used as a temporary car park that day, as many more vehicles came and went. It was a good job the pub was situated on higher ground to that of the roadway. It meant that all floors of the public-house overlooked much of the opposite farmland. Again, by careful monitoring, second by second movements could be seen in the same field as parked vehicles at the top of the field heading towards the hedgerow. Two figures could be seen, but identification was impossible. Playing the tape at normal speed the couple is not picked up due to the camera changing positions around the pub. So, the figures going towards the hedgerow means access to the lower fields adjacent to 'Marshalls Green'. For both officers, it was a near-impossible job to pick-up the return of the figures seen on the tape. Again, a slight movement could be seen elsewhere at the top of the field, but appeared smaller than the data seen; could they be the dogs?

"Could they be the dogs?" asked Bob, as he pointed to the monitor screen. "Fuck me, that is a dog moving around, it is a dog. See how it is weaving around."

Sgt Anderson just stared and stared at the monitor and then stood up and walked away from the screen,

"I need a break for a moment, but I am sure you are right Bob. It's convincing, I'll give you that old mate," said the Sergeant.

Both were now in deep thought, as Judy brought fresh coffee.

"How are you getting on, any luck with what you are looking for?" asked Judy, anxious to be of service to the officers.

"Could be Judy; would you remember that couple we talked about if you saw them on the film? I know you mentioned that others remarked on them both being upset at the time," said Bob.

"I don't know. I suppose, if I was to see the film and their movements, it might ring bells for me. I can vaguely picture the couple, but I would not be able to recognise them," said Judy.

"I was hoping that perhaps you might remember more of the woman. She appears very attractive and well-dressed from the video," said Bob. "She's a real looker on the video."

"What I do remember about her now, was that she didn't wear a lot of makeup. That's right, they sat huddled up at the table by the window, and the next thing they had left," said Judy. "God! you have stretched my mind on this, Bob. I am sure it was one of the young girls who were here at the time, who waited on tables at lunchtimes, she mentioned them being upset and she was crying. I am sure that was it and why they left the pub because of it," said Judy.

Sgt Anderson asked Judy's husband, Dan, to keep the tape for them.

"It's not for court or anything like that," said the Sergeant. "It's that we are waiting for some photographs to arrive and we want to make a comparison to the man, that's all."

"That's not a problem. I am not about to reuse them anyway," said Dan, as he left their company to open up the beer cellar, as the delivery lorry was reversing into the yard behind the pub.

Finally, both officers finished their coffees and bid farewell to Judy, as they left to re-visit the Local Authority Planning office. Bob had received word from Bill Sheffield, his contact at the Authority that his errand had been completed and was ready for him to collect. Both officers felt jubilant and hoped the Planning Office would also have good news for them.

An hour later, both officers left the Planning Office, having got the answers they sought. Bill Sheffield's staff had done a fantastic service, by using the Drone to film the landscape and, in doing so, were able to identify three burnt-out shells of vehicles hidden in the dell of a woodland that belonged to Dan Adkins, the farmer. So, the next part of their enquiry took them to 'Mantles Green Farm', to speak with Dan, the farmer. Engaging with Dan, for permission to search his woodland, was a godsend on his part as he was still beside himself from the recent attack on the gipsy youth and murder victim found behind one of his buildings.

From finding and detailing the three vehicles in the Dell, it was clear that the cars had been used like dodgem cars. All three had extensive damage to the bodywork, and this goes back to Bob's earlier brush with travellers he saw on Forestry land when another vehicle was set ablaze by gipsy youths. Deciding that the cars would remain and not be recovered by Police. As the Division would incur the cost to the public purse, it was determined to identify each of the vehicles from the information they had found in the Dell and inform the respective owners of the finds and where located for their insurers to decide to recover the vehicle shells from Dan's farmland.

At the same time, Dan informed the officers that it had been agreed between his senior officers and local authority to move the travellers of the lane on to one of his fields, as it had been decided that it would be much safer for them and your lads looking after them. The council is going to put some concrete blocks along that section of the lane to deter any other travellers parking up, as there is no street lighting on any parts of the roads. It's all dark country areas that make life more dangerous at night if you are on foot. Dan pointed out that the travellers are still coming to the farm for their regular water supplies and the fence section has been repaired and made right. At the same time, more security lighting had been added to the buildings, and it was very noticeable that the hedgerow had been cut right back to expose more of the buildings and not provide excellent cover for intruders.

Sgt Anderson informed Dan the police patrols had been increased in the area and, of course, armed officers were protecting the traveller's camp. So, we hope that matters will settle down and we can get on with our investigations. Dan informed them both that 'Old Ben Witney' was spending more time at the farm to show willing on the part of the gipsies as Dan and his family had been kind to the fraternities over the past years, and they respected and admired him for his troubles.

Bob realised that, while at the farm, he would find Old Ben and have a quick natter with him. Dan informed Bob that Ben was down in the sheep pens to the left of the property. Bob laughed, as it was easy to find Old Ben; merely follow the sweet-smelling aroma of pipe tobacco, and that will lead you straight to him.

Old Ben volunteered details of a farmer who was making guns.

“He had one of those turning machines to make barrels and bits for the guns. That is where they've been getting the four-tens from, they break down and stick them down the legs to hide them,” said Old Ben. “This is a bad do governor. Nasty people they are, they ain't yet found out who the young one was that be murdered here.”

"No, we are still searching for the foreigners. We are here today about the burnt-out vehicles in the Dell in the woods on the other side of the field," said Bob, pointing in a direction for Old Ben to grasp.

“That be our youngest on the camp. They go off in the night and chore the vehicles and drive back to the fields. They're mad, drinking cider all night and racing around the field. Some have been hurt," said Old Ben.

“Tell me more about the farmer making the guns, Ben,” said Bob, anxious to get details from him.

"Well, they call him the ‘G' man. He has machines that make the traveller guns; he makes good money; the farms by the river and uses a boat to come and go at times. He is receiving antiques and garden stuff, but they come by the river – see who's gonna catch him, no vehicles come and go in the night," said Old Ben,

Always remained to suck the end of his pipe when he spoke to you, it also hid his lip movements at times when he whispered near the other travellers, them being none the wiser.

Bob managed finally to get more details of the farm's location from Ben. At the same time, he slipped him more money for his troubles.

"When all this is sorted Ben, I'll see you properly rewarded for your troubles. I have my Sergeant with me today, and he will cover for me, and we will see you all right mate," said Bob, as he patted Ben on the shoulders. "I am most grateful for your troubles, Ben. I appreciate what you have done for me."

Leaving Ben to get on with his work, he returned to Dan's kitchen door and knocked. He entered, and Sgt Anderson was sipping tea by the glow of a warm fire, like still in the old days of cooking, it all looked inviting to sit and chat all day, when life was life and, in a tick, over and not everybody in a mad rush. Mrs Adkins lifted the lid on the warmer and Bob saw the larger than life scones she had baked earlier. Mrs Adkins looked at Bob.

"I suppose you would like one of my scones before you leave," she said.

Bob's face lit up at the invitation, and with a very hearty, "Yes please" reply, the smell was how baking ought to be, with wafting smells hanging in the air that made one's mouth water and that came with childhood memories. "Those were the days," he thought, "Nothing like it Missus 'A'" said Bob, as he was handed the warm scone to take with him.

Eventually, leaving the Adkins farm for the village, Bob

explained the information he had gleaned from Old Ben.

“I slipped him another twenty pounds,” said Bob. “I am not putting this down on paper, I have already forgotten about the money. Anyway, we are not using him for court or evidence, are we, so I am going to let it roll to keep him happy. When this is all over, Sarge, you could help me apply to HQ for a little sweetener for him, that will stand us in good stead for the next time we need help,” said Bob. “Are you okay with that? I haven’t mentioned payment to anyone else, only you.”

"Yeah, that's okay. What about this gun making farmer? He sounds a crafty bastard. Who would have thought the travellers are visiting in boats by night, that is a new one on me? Can any of them swim and where do the boats come from? We have not had any stolen,” said Sgt Anderson.

“Well, no, they are probably just borrowing them as and when and then returning them to where they have taken the boats in the first place, and all this under cover of darkness. I like it. That is a new one for me. Crafty bastards, they know every trick in the fucking book, don't they," said Bob laughing. "You have got to hand it to them; we need them on our side, should we ever go to war again."

Both were laughing on the drive back to the village,

"Time for meal breaks Bob anyway," said the Sergeant.

“Have you got your grub with you, Sarge? I am going to stop off at the Bakers first,” said Bob. “I’ve got the scone in my flat cap; I am going to need a knob of butter for that."

He smacked his lips together at the thought of eating it, as the Sergeant laughed out loud at his mouthing antics.

By the end of duty, at 6 o'clock, Bob had provided a substantial report for his force intelligence office to action, with regards to the farmer and firearms information. Details of the three vehicles found in the woodland had been passed to the late shift to follow up, as Bob was unable to provide Crime report numbers, as none of the vehicles had been identified as stolen at this time. Bob took home the USB (Universal Serial Bus) storage device to examine further the Drone footage of the area and to be clear in his mind that he had covered every angle of the ground that most interested him.

By nine o'clock, it was somewhat laughable, as Bob three times attempted to dial 'Sandy's' mobile and three times he cancelled. He couldn't make up his mind as to whether he wanted to see her or not, but did she want to see him, that was the question. As two minds think alike, she rang him just after ten o'clock, and that forced his hand about wasting time on the phone when they could sit and talk somewhere.

Both agreed, the late evening was too warm and muggy for sleeping. Instead, decided to meet and drive to the highest point locally that looked down over the valley. Parking up, the couple walked hand in hand to the War Memorial that had stood for a hundred years and seen for miles from the valley below. Even the granite steps felt warm as they sat close together. But more importantly, it was the view below, with such a bright starry night. Above and below, thousands of lights dotted all over the landscape, and at times, the headlights of moving vehicles could be seen.

'Sandy' was plugged into her iPod as she hummed a tune, as Bob listened, and he was fascinated by the sights below. Lights in some areas disappeared as the night wore on. The night air to breathe was becoming heavy and still, at times claustrophobic, without a breeze, it felt uncomfortable.

It was when 'Sandy' stood and faced Bob with swaying dance movements, her body obviously in tune with what she was listening too, looked good with the valley lights behind her. As from Bob's position, he recognised that something was different about her tonight. Her skin was more toned and shiny; she seemed more relaxed, as her movements flowed, and her femininity was hot and glowing, as she moved and twirled in front of him as if to tease him to his feet.

Instead, 'Sandy' in a button-fronted one-piece dress which made her femininity more outstanding and inviting. Bob would have fucked her then and there if he wasn't in control of himself, but it was her who took the lead, by showing her back to him, then turning around to reveal her dress unbuttoned at the front as it slipped from her shoulders to the ground. Her nakedness bloomed under the stars, her breasts full and firm as her lithe figure appeared impressive. Bob lay back on his elbows and looked up from his position on the steps of the monument and grinned at what she had done by undressing and no underwear either. Wearing only a belt around her waist, holding her iPod and cable leading to her earpieces, she moved and danced in front of him. She encouraged him to stand and join her, handing him one of the earpieces. It was a waltz, and a waltz at midnight was appropriate as the two figures gelled together in a dance as she took hold of him.

'Sandy' had an ulterior motive on this night, as she slid a hand inside his Joggings, tugging on the garment several times, it was her desired fantasy to dance naked under the stars, and now she had her opportunity, as Bob followed her directions, as he stepped out of his joggings. 'Sandy' put her hand to her mouth in astonishment. He neither was wearing underwear. He remained bollock naked from the waist down, showing his 'fiddling stick and two balls of lust'. Her desire was for them to be skin to skin while dancing under the stars. She then pointed to his top to remove.

Now, both naked continued to dance together; it was one of those romantic moments as each shared an earpiece as they waltzed together. It was graceful; it was elegant as their movements swept across the grass with dotted lights in the background below and a sky full of shining stars that looked down on them. No woman could ask for a better setting to her desired fantasy. Bob had got behind her imagination as they danced and danced and laughed together. At the same time, he recognised the softness of her skin had become smooth and shiny to touch but tanned. She had got herself an all over tan that was the difference to the way she was acting out her fantasy. Her bush had been trimmed and shaped, having ignored this in the beginning, as he was more focused on the full package and the way she moved her body. Had she dancing skills and training, he thought, she was so light on her feet. He felt bewitched by her sudden talents. He just stared and stared into her face as the whites of her eyes were bright and bright which made her all the more striking.

It was when the dancing stopped, and 'Sandy' bent over and touched her toes in front him, he saw the outline of nature's fruit, shaped peach-like but could he fuck her in this position; would she last; would she ache; would she let him? That was the question. He could try, stand behind her and hold on to her waist, as he fucked her in this position. Was this her fantasy? Was she telling him something, by bending over and offering herself to him? Her peach looked impressive in the night light, as nature cast a shadow between her thighs, that he felt he needed to lick and kiss and show more sustenance in dealing with her sexual demands. She was demanding, but not requiring, in the real sense of the word, goading and bullying. She was subtle in her approach; she was street-wise in knowing the many signs of man, and it was nice to be touched and loved in this way by such a gentleman as Bob.

Bob knelt behind her as she remained bent over double, pushing out her swollen peach between her thighs for him to lick and kiss, as Bob's hands held her haunches as he pushed his lips into hers. She needed a good tonguing, which had not been achieved before; so much was to be served on her plate tonight. It wasn't long before he felt her shudder and quiver with the first tremors of her orgasm, as she let out a right shrill and banshee cry of delight. Bob stood up and placed his arms underneath her weight in steading her. As she appeared to go weak at the knees, he felt her tremors, while he carried her back to the monument steps and cuddled her tight, as she looked right out of it with eyes closed and lips pouting and purring.

“Oh! My God that was so nice, Bob. You have left me weak at the knees,” said ‘Sandy’.

As she sat up with her hands pushing against his chest, she looked into his face and smiled.

"You are my gotcha man, my very own fuck buddy. I am so lucky to have found you, Bob, I am," said ‘Sandy', in a low whispering voice, accompanied by gentle pecking kisses all over his face.

"I can't get enough of you my darling, you are all things nice," said Bob, "What more can I say?"

"No other man has spent so much time inside my vagina as you have Bob. Not even my husband has managed that I have been married to him longer than I have known you, (chuckles expressed), and I doubt if ever there is likely to be another to match you as my lover," said 'Sandy', as she snuggled up close, as her hands gripped his arm at her side.

"My, my, that is some compliment to live up to my girl," said Bob.

"You deserve it, and more, I am so happy around you, we make a good team you and me. You are such a relaxing man, and I love every minute of it," said 'Sandy'.

"Anyway, tell me about the change I see in you tonight," said Bob.

"You have noticed then. I did wonder at first," said 'Sandy', teasing him with a kiss on the nose and sucking and nibbling his earlobe.

"Yes, I noticed, your skin is so smooth, you have obviously had a work out since I last saw you and that is what, all of two days is it?" said Bob, as he began to giggle in hysterics.

"I had a makeover, waxed and trimmed and was well pampered the other afternoon, most enjoyable, and the oils they used were so perfect when I had that massage. You noticed I got trimmed at the same time," said 'Sandy' grinning to herself. "Well you never said you wanted to, so I had it done for you. No more hairs between the teeth Bob, just a straight run for home," said 'Sandy'.

With a loud vocal laugh, Bob laughed at the same time as she.

"Yes, I have experienced hairs stuck between the teeth before. We all love to nibble from time to time," said Bob.

"Variety is the spice of life, and many women do want to experience new things in a sexual relationship, but sadly, it always seems to be the same old thing every time she gets laid. The old man climbs on and humps her then rolls off and goes to sleep. No foreplay, no thought to our emotional values, only his lusting to fuck the brains out of us women in ten minutes, no that's a lie in five minutes. We want to try various positions and make the relationship more exciting, but sadly, so many men don't try. Look, when we all start out in a new relationship, we can't get enough of each other. Then, as time goes by, men ease back on the throttle as they have caught us women in their web, then they switch off and take us for granted after that. So, what happens? We, women, have to go off and find it somewhere else. We need the loving, we need the fucking and be fucked, I mean not just standing on the doorstep and stroking the letterbox," said 'Sandy' (pause).

As she looked into his face with such a smiley look, Bob got the message and laughed at how vocal she had become for women's rights.

"We women want to be fucked by our chosen man; we don't want to be a second-hand Rose waiting to be pricked by the next dick available," said 'Sandy'.

"Oh, Bloody hell, you are so funny with your words 'Sandy', Yes, I know what you are referring to, but I am me, and I like being me and what I get for being me is a fuck buddy like you, so I have no complaints," said Bob.

"No, I don't have any complaints, just admiration for what you have shared with me. I never thought for one minute, back in the car park when we first met, that you had such a wonderful thing between your legs and your control is incredible," said 'Sandy'.

"Well, I was a toy boy in my younger years, and the same problem existed then as it does today for many women, men lose interest. In fact, that is why many men go to prostitutes because they can do the business and get laid and walk away afterwards without any commitment. That is what many are scared off by, commitment," said Bob, "It's the responsibility they don't want. You see this on a Friday and Saturday night when I am working. Girls promised the earth when they are full of drink and going home with a new boyfriend; they get laid with stars in their eyes, having been well fucked in the back of a car, in the cemetery, bent over a brick wall or laid on their backs in the local recreation park. Come the next day, they can't get hold of the bloke, and the mobile number he leaves is a duffer. It happens all the time, and the girls don't learn from it. Then, they wonder why they get labelled slags and whores. They fall in love over a belly full of drink and wonder why they must leave the area for a new life, as no man wants them in their town," said Bob.

"Yes, you are right. Some of my girlfriends would go bonkers if they knew you existed and could last the distance. Well, on average, it's about forty-five minutes to get us on the boil – give or take a few minutes either way," said 'Sandy', laughing her head off. "Men - it also surprises the number of men who haven't a clue about where to put it and what to do with it. Why? Because as soon as you touch them, you are covered with manmade glue, and it goes all over the place. I remember once, having a face full of the stuff. He was a good shooter in the spurting sense, as sadly many are, but they don't bother to take aim or tell you when the train is coming down the line until it's too late," said 'Sandy'. The younger men have got worse over recent years and why the older man, if you can find the older man who has the experience, is the 'Prince of fuck-ability' and very much in demand," said 'Sandy'.

She turned and gave Bob one hell of a cuddle, followed up with one long passionate kiss that seemed to linger. As Bob's hand touched one of her breasts as he felt the firmness and the hardness of her nipple, he bent down and took the other nipple between his lips and gently sucked and sucked as 'Sandy' felt his tongue stroke her nipple in his mouth. This made her feel aroused, as her head rolled sideways, as she felt the thrill of her nipple being sucked as she drew back from his touch.

"God, you could fuck me all day long, and that would not be enough for me. I suppose I am what many men would call a nymphomaniac. I can't get enough of the right stuff (laughing). I enjoy my freedom as a woman and more ought to follow and enjoy what nature provides us all, and it's free. You know, I can't understand some of the tales my friends tell me about their menfolk. Not all are married, but the ones that do have a moan now and then about not getting laid that often. Why don't they get their husbands to go sick one day and spend the time in bed fucking? Once in a while is not going to hurt anybody. Who is going to know, unless the wife has a noticed pinned on her back saying 'Just Laid'. You know, you mention about drink and attitudes, a friend of mine was like that for months, always with a different bloke, then one morning she woke to find the bottle still between her legs. The bloke used a bottle on her. As she said, there wasn't any sperm coming seeping out; she was dry and sore below. She learnt a hard lesson and has changed her life around, thank goodness. But how disgusting, that a guy can do that to a woman, really shocking," said 'Sandy'.

"Many women have these kinds of experiences and secrets from their past in the way they have been used and abused by fellows. Some learn the hard way, others sadly don't, and it leaves them scarred for life mentally and physically. We get to know these stories at times from the domestics we go to or by other means, through friends and family, or the girls themselves who decide to trust somebody. If girls are going out over a weekend to be stupid, then they will pay the price. Look, when the clubs turn out, girls are so drunk, they are falling all over the place, but then there are those who bare their fat arses, showing off their thongs, big thighs. Christ, it's horrible to see them laying and crying on the pavement with mascara smudged and running down their faces. I shudder when I think about it," said Bob. "Anyway, come here, I want a cuddle and not on the steps of the monument."

The couple moved off the steps and walked to a grassier area that appeared comfortable as the lay together, still naked, side by side while gazing up at the stars. Eventually, 'Sandy' turned on her side and kissed Bob, as her hand reached down and took charge of the 'Pinkie' that lay dormant on the mat. 'Sandy' showed her expertise in the way she touched and handled Bob's strong attachment with such care and attention. When finally, she slid down over his body and took his penis between her lips with such tenderness, as she used her lips to push back his foreskin, exposing a more darkened coloured shaft that needed a place to stay and, more or less, regarded it is a home from home. 'Sandy' rolled on to her back as Bob reinforced her gateway by introducing a widening of her thighs, as he placed his hands under her buttocks as he pulled her to him. Finally, he was inside of her, and she could feel his pulsating throbs. He was working his old fellow in the joys of joyful comforts for her, as he pushed gently back and forth in a prolonged and deliberate manner, that took even 'Sandy' by surprise as to how different his techniques can be in making love by the real quality of what he had introduced into her silky lining and that spoke volumes, as he went deep, deep right into her, as their pubic lines touched and rubbed. This was the night of nights for 'Sandy, a fantasy that came alive under the stars, which brought to her door the satisfaction she knew she would receive from her partner who fucked her well, in her being serviced up to the hilt.

CHAPTER TWELVE
Money for the Boys

Frank Boxer had been expecting news from abroad but not the news he received, it was a shock to find that One hundred and seventy thousand pounds sterling had appeared in a private Bank account that had been specially set up for him before Tommy's crime spree occurred.

Frank contacted Tim at the Corporate law firm to establish the credence of the monies; he was informed that it was kosher money,

"It was fucking genuine," he screamed out to Primmy,

"If I have my money, then Tommy is alive somewhere and hold up, otherwise how could my share of the money be paid into the account, only Tommy and Tim would have known about it, so Tommy has come through by the look of it, what a fucking boy is our Tommy,"

Frank's thoughts turned to Lenny and Karen, not able to reach either of them he knew that he would have to wait until Lenny called him, but the news seemed unbelievable, worrying one minute then great news the next, so now he needed to decide on placing the money elsewhere and make it disappear and no questions asked, with an older family to look after now was the time to sort out his three siblings and get them settled and he and Primmy could end up being grandparents to the children. Over the coming days Frank was able to check on the others and found they each received good settlements for their participation and already some of those had closed their accounts and got cash in their hands.

Frank and the others had not visited 'Marshalls Green' after the fire all had been told to stay away and never come back to the area, point taken by all as nothing would be achieved by visiting, only to make others suspicious as there were still no leads from Frank's thinking, no visits, no turnovers as Tommy had maintained that he would make sure that none of this would happen and if by chance there was a 'cock-up' along the way then Tim was there to handle matters he also received a very nice retainer to keep his services alive.

Early turn six o'clock Saturday morning saw Bob arrive for his morning duty, within minutes Bob had opened the waiting envelope addressed to him and immediately saw the picture of Lenny Burns for the first time and now he can confirm that the couple in the security video at the 'Bull & Butcher' pub was one of the same he had finally established without doubt the two male occupants of 'Marshalls Green', after all the hard work had now finally paid off and he felt ecstatic at the result. Having identified 'Tommy Sands' and 'Lenny Burns' both former East End London Criminals, both residing and living at the 'Manor House' for the past five years, knowingly without incident and clearly not of Police interest today. So now the hunt was on for the two girls who were they and where do they come from, having a picture of one who clearly is associated with Lenny and extremely attractive appearing to be younger than him, but too old to be his daughter, probably his girlfriend.

Bob was beside himself when over the radio he heard a great deal of chatter indicating that some incident had sprung into life and required further support on the ground by mobile officers. Bob was unaware that it was the 'Gunmakers' farm and buildings that had been subject of a Police search and due to the circumstances of the property an obvious danger had been exposed at the property that required the Dept.: for Environment, Food and Rural Affairs (DEFRA) and the Bomb squad to attend the property and now officers were having to cordon off the area including door knocking on houses nearby to evacuate local residents.

Bob listened intently when he received a phone call from another officer who filled him in with details of why the area was going to be evacuated. It appears that one of the farm buildings contained many tons of farm fertilizer that had been stacked to the roof and so compact was the products that no ventilation had been provided and unfortunately it was discovered that a time bomb existed as the fertilizer was weeping and seeping from its packaging and had the potential of acting like a bomb that would flatten the surrounding area for some considerable distance and this was on the advice of the Fire Service who also has attended and advised the Police and local authority of the dangers to life should an explosion occur. Panic had set in as knocking door to door advising people to decide and leave their properties ASAP. A reception hall in the nearby town had been opened to receive those who wish to be catered for with food and drink organised by a local woman's charity and paramedics had been retained at the centre along with the services of a local Doctor concerning existing medical conditions and prescriptions that may be required. The build-up in numbers was increasing by the minute as people left their homes for the centre, another location had been opened at the local Rugby club and the same applied there with food and drink being supplied.

Coming off the phone Bob took the first opportunity to telephone Sgt Anderson with the news and details of the events occurring at this time, Bob needed to pinch himself with two strikes out of three at the moment, he needed to find out about the three burnt out vehicles in the woods, were they stolen and where from he needed answers to his thoughts and the growing knowledge he had acquired made his quest all the more personal in knowing the truth.

He had also been left a note in his docket concerning the release from hospital of the gypsy youth who had been nailed to the wooden fence. He had been requested to pay attention to the area, although, the gypsy site still retained Police firearm officers who patrolled the area, Bob would be an extra security layer to cover the surrounding lanes and isolated areas where vehicles can be off road and hidden. As the post mortem results of the murdered gypsy youth revealed that he had in fact died from a violent beating with many broken bones and the damage caused to his throat and larynx which choked him to death along with so many contusions and bruising found on his body. It was a very sad picture of an evil and a brutality the likes that had not been seen before in subjecting the youth to a sustained period of beating, meaning that he was held captive somewhere other than the farm and that like the other youth made to be an example, a warning to the other travellers that this war of revenge was not over as there would be others.

One of Bob's contentions about the way information was disseminated and passed around the stations was minimal and was worrying when there are such dangerous people around, albeit, anonymous they may be but surely somewhere these suspects are known to the police. Once briefing boards were top heavy with snippets of updated information that kept everybody on their toes, but sadly we must endure the new broom that clean, no matter the effectiveness there were too many entrants who lacked real personal skills and failed in themselves with the basics of streetwise common-sense values. Some management appeared to be deliberately destroying the morale of officers for their own lack of knowledge in not understanding the basic principles of Policing. Individuals who farm and cultivate a uselessness for their own silly purposes of climbing the promotion ladder in the true belief that faking and covering up the issues to appease a higher authority was socially acceptable and was neither corrupt in so many ways of short changing the public in their basic rights of consent given to a civil Police force acting as agents of the people and the crown. Such people were now becoming a social disease in Policing with such intense naivety in believing that they know better than those doing the real principles of Policing, as those of greater service were now political pawns as simply many knew more than those in many roles of management and that in its self was an embarrassing scenario that couldn't remain it had to change to avoid conflict and argument so that management is made to look good.

Sunday morning just after seven o'clock Bob teamed up again with Sgt Anderson, Bob had already spoken with the Sergeant about the need for him to view the drone video that Bob acquired from the local planning office.

"Have a look at this and tell me what you see Sarge," said Bob,

The video watched by the mystified Sergeant as he saw

nothing that appeared to be unusual to him, then it came to the tree that had the 'T' shirt attached.

"Right see those vehicle tracks, where do they do Sarge," said Bob.

"Well they lead across the field and stop at the edge of that earth line," said the Sergeant.

"Right now if we go and walk the ground shortly you don' notice the tracks they are so feint, but from the air it shows the tracks by the colour change of the ground, it's like the archaeologists who use that ground scanning equipment to trace outlines underground and of course the helicopter shows the indents in the ground from the air which provides more clues to the changing landscape," said Bob.

"Yeah, I am with you on that, so what do you think has happened here, if those tracks stop at the edge you are referring to, then what is underneath, what is the reason for covering over those tracks, let's go and have a look and see if we can follow those tracks ourselves," said the Sergeant.

"I have no idea but I need to check on the maps again, I need to see if any changes have been made in that area, it's a grazing field for cattle and not a ploughed field for crops, that is the difference, I also found different tyre impressions and some were wider than others, so big vehicles have used that field in recent times," said Bob.

Later that morning both officers arrived at the location of the tree and broken gate, the gate posts were examined, and it was clear that chunks of wood had been gouged out as if the entrance wasn't wide enough in the beginning and whatever it was, was driven through creating the marks and forcing the posts over at an angle.

“See the marks are about two feet from the ground and it had to be a heavy vehicle to have pushed over the posts, they are really deep in the ground and had to be, to hold such a solid gate on its hinges like this, you try lifting the gate, it’s bloody heavy skipper,” said Bob.

“Yeah, I can see that, so we appear to have vehicle movement, a ‘T’ shirt full of shotgun pellets and a location well off the beaten track,” said the Sergeant, “I see where you are coming from but is it anything to do with our current crime spree,” said Sgt Anderson.

“I am playing on a hunch that all what we have found knits together, but how that happens I don’t have an answer, we now have the two old villains in the Manor House and of course the traveller situation and burnt out vehicles left all over the place,” said Bob, “That’s why I need your opinion on what you see here.”

“Fair enough let’s follow these impressions and see what we can find,” said the Sergeant.

Following the tyre impressions, it was clear that more than two vehicles were involved due to the distinctive markings of the tyre treads, Bob measured the width of the impressions and realised that these treads were too shallow for farm machinery. Tractors, Combines and other like equipment had very deep treads for agricultural usage in gripping the ground surfaces the machines would encounter. Finally, at the edge of the darkened soil it was clear that new soil had been dumped. Again, the colour change of the ground was obvious to the type of soil of the field, so why the imported soil, what is underneath as the tyre impressions can be clearly seen when searched for and where they disappeared. Walking over the open ground other depressions in the soil could be seen as the soil was newly placed and settlement of the ground had not stopped nor compacted to be solid enough to walk on. Grass had tiny shoots of life protruding through in places; weeds were plentiful again in some places and had grown aggressively.

"Well I don't know what to make of it Bob, it's certainly new groundwork, the way those impressions run as if this was a hole that's been filled in and of course it gets to the level of the field, hence the tyre impressions stop, but those tyre marks don't lead elsewhere, you are right Bob, something is buried under there," said the Sergeant.

"That's right if those tyre marks belonged to a machine that was used to cover the ground then those tyre marks should also lead back to the gate and it's obvious they don't, they stop here, so where is the vehicle that was used to cover the ground, it had to be a 'JCB' type of machine with a bucket attachment and those tyre markings would be big and clearly seen in the soil, what if the machine was used to just fill in a hole, it wouldn't need to leave tyre marks in the new landscape it would have been working round the edges on solid ground otherwise it would get bogged down, so those impressions that disappear belong to another vehicle, that is the only logic to this," said Bob.

He was excited by his findings it was the only answer he could envisage at this time and the Sergeant had come around to Bob's thinking, there had to be more than one vehicle used and what significance did the tree and 'T' shirt play or could this be two separate scenarios and both unrelated.

"You are becoming a real Crime fighter Bob," said the

Sergeant laughing his head off, "Everything you've touched appears to be turning to gold for you my son."

They stood together laughing and in jest as to what they may have discovered on the property of the 'Manor House' and whether it was related to the fire or had some other connections to the occupants themselves as owners of the land.

"The picture being painted concerned all of this area in that Policing has been neglected over a period and now it is going to take a lot of man hours to put things right. I can understand why the local Parish Council is always having a dig when we go to these meetings, management comes down from division and gives some assurance that this will change in due course when you know it's not going to happen, government cutbacks fucks all this up, it can only get worse, politicians have chandeliers up their own arses as that is the only place they see the light shining in abundance for their future whether in or out of politics, they don't give a fuck about the communities, no logic and no fucking common sense." Said Sgt Anderson in an angry and frustrating voice, "The problem never goes away, hoping the problem flies away with the Cuckoo's of this world society has become fucking lazy."

"This is what fascinates me about the States, if it moves and law enforcement don't like it they shoot it, can you imagine that happening over here, parts of London and some of the inner cities up north is like living in the wild west when you listen to the news, shootings, stabbings and killings are regular incidents today," said Bob, "Politicians blame their, there are too many wankers in public life today, fucking useless, but we the English let them get away with it, these celebrities who hang on to their little corners of the public life suddenly for whatever reason become experts on our lives, they are nothing people, we make them and put them in the public eye, so we ought to be taking it away from them to shut them up, but we don't, the English are their own worst enemy, we don't work together, we spend most of our waking hours whingeing and moaning about this and that and we love it, we lap it up like the cat who goy the fucking cream, we are a switch off society, how many times do we witness all these wonderful schemes, the organisers are all there to get their pictures in the media and months later they have all disappeared bar the one who is running whatever the organisation represents. We love bull shit by the bucket load, we shame ourselves and we all agree so long as it's not in my backyard," said Sgt Anderson.

His voice echoing and vibrating out loud, it was obvious he was angry and frustrated by the way of the world and the back sliding in the Police today.

"You are right, but who is listening, the celeb's only get involved when it suits their criteria or when it affects or a member of their family and yet the problem they raise awareness of has existed for years run by real holy anonymous Saints, then the celebs selfishness takes over as they set up a foundation or some charity and off they go on a whistle tour of self-righteousness. It's more about their conscience, at times I wonder why they don't simply join and provide the support of established charities or whatever, it makes me laugh when the local media hail them as the Holy Saints on white chargers and much of the media air time they get on television can be phenomenal at times, ordinary folk wouldn't get it and all the arse licking that goes on among the television presenters, some of them are a bit dumb when you listen to their questions, some of which makes great comedy on air." Said Bob.

Agreeing and sounding off like the Sergeant expressing a vocal frustration at the way Policing has become. A victim of the media and the nasty culture that is expressed by those who want to control the lives of others to their extremes and if you don't tor the line you are hounded into the ground by those bastards who express a narcissistic streak and shows little empathy to others and society stands back and simply lets it happen.

"My opinions are strong Sarge for me Ted Heath, Doctor Beeching and Harold Wilson sold this country short and especially the English and the Welsh allowed this to happen. We are taken into what we believe a Common Market for trade and 'Heath' sold out the nation he was an out and out liar, the Conservatives will defend him to the hilt but the man was a Judas for this country, deals under the table as to the political map and future of Britain which was handpicked and assured to the French and the Germans and that is why we are so lacking in the will to fight back, the English especially have been muted and financially Britain has been blead dry over many years, this happened after the Second World War, we gave enormous financial aid to rebuild Europe at the expense of our own Country and we are still paying through the nose to those arseholes in the Europe that is why they are so desperate to keep us in their political club because of the money we hand out, weak and porous, unlike our forefathers who had real true grit and gumption and Britain would never, never be slaves and yet we are today, we are slaves to Europe and a nation without any real skills, politicians have socially engineered our society over decades to support their political sickness that we all endure," said Bob.

Now really going for it gunning for the extremists who have fucked up the nation and our young who lack or have no skills or training, only to be told how useless they are as foreigners are needed to come to Britain to run the economy on our own money and to save Britain from self- destruction.

Sgt Anderson realised that he had touched on a raw nerve for both as it appeared to be the same elsewhere among other Police colleagues, enough is enough and morale now in the gutters of the service with so many wanting to leave the service for a better life than the one they have at the present.

"Right we have put the world to rights Bob, so what now my old China, we all think alike today, and it will only get worse with the kind of bad politics we have today, we have a job to do mate and we need to focus on getting the results expected of us, so far so good, we have done fucking marvellous up to now. When we get back you need to start shaping and drafting an interim report on where we are now and the findings and facts we can now prove, I will give a copy to the governor and keep him up to speed first and see if he wants to add any comments to your draft, at the same time we also are covering our arses," said the Sergeant

With a big laughing grin as both officers returned to their Police vehicle to make up their pocket books before returning to the Police station. On their journey back to the station Sgt Anderson reminisced about the past and remembers an incident which involved Bob.

"Can you remember crossing swords with a former Prime

Minister and the aggravation that caused among senior officers," said the Sergeant laughing loud, "Arseholes went that day." Still laughing!

"As if it was yesterday Sarge, (pause sound of giggling) nothing has bloody changed in the last twenty or thirty years, boy that was a morning that was. Of all the days it happened I was on a Sunday early turn, I am sent out to his place at seven o'clock when I arrived he was standing in his driveway in a fucking Chinese dressing gown, before I am even out of the vehicle he is on me like a 'Rottweiler' moaning and whingeing because there is not a Police presence at his house, it had been withdrawn as he was not a politician at that time. It hit the fan when I told him he was a 'Joe Blogs' and not the Prime Minister (ha.ha.ha) and that he was not entitled to a Police presence. I was pissed off with him as Sunday early turn was the only time I would return home for an English breakfast, so his attitude fucked me up as I was still there at eleven o'clock as management was having a meeting and headless chickens couldn't sort themselves out as to who made the decision to withdraw the Police presence, it was gone twelve o'clock by the time a group of lower management came out from division to sort things and appease him so I was allowed to leave thank Christ, next day on the Monday he is re-elected as an MP and again becomes Prime Minister, what a right fucking balls up, I was angry believe as I never got my bloody breakfast, as it was I had to write up the incident over a cup of coffee by which time it was two o'clock and off duty," said Bob – Still laughing to himself about the incident.

"I remember that story everybody couldn't stop laughing, especially when he said you said he was only 'Joe Blogs' and the Prime Minister, it went around the whole force at the time, lots of funny comments," said the Sergeant.

"Well I told him the truth that day and he didn't want to listen, he was a 'Joe Blogs' end of story," said Bob as they both continued laughing together, "The governors knew I was right, they caused the aggro not me, what happened after I left I have no idea."

"It still brings tears to my eyes, it could only happen to you Bob," said the Sergeant still tickled pink with laughter.

Bob just looked across at his Skipper with a big grin of satisfaction both remembering that day in the past and the laughter it raised between them.

"Did you hear about the time when I knocked him over at his breakfast table and spilt his orange juice, the lady who sat opposite was aghast as he went flying," said Bob (pausing and laughing) "What happened was, I had to shoulder charge a heavy Oak door that wouldn't open in the proper way, when I forced it – it shot back like a rocket and hit the back of his chair and that sent him flying," said Bob.

The laughter between them was electrifying as they continued their journey to the Police station. It was an hour after arriving back at the station Sgt Anderson closed the door of his office and took a phone call from the Divisional HQ. It was a good ten minutes before he came looking for Bob, the Chief Super has been on the blower mate, apparently that 'G' man farmer has coughed his heart up now he is in the bag, arrested and charged and will be appearing shortly in court for a remand back into Police custody.

"Bob, you have hit the jackpot my old son, he has

dropped a lot of shit in all directions and includes local dignitaries and more on his customers and how they use the river at night to come and go. The fertilizer is the worry, evacuations have been taking place and the Ministry staff are there taking care of the situation, place would drop off the planet if it exploded, so you have one big pat on the back mate, job well done from the Chief Super himself mate," said the Sergeant.

"Back into our custody that's interesting he must have a good story to tell, be nice to know who the travellers are with the shotguns and whether they are from around here, the bloody problem is they run on nicknames they don't bother with real details of people so long as the cash is there they will do business, so I hope he has a good memory for what he is about to receive, that's fucking naughty about the fertilizer someone is not doing their job properly someone in authority needs a kick up the arse over this, poor management again we seem to employ chancer's, because for three hundred and fifty-two days of the year nothing happens and then the next day they take liberties and it hits the fucking fan," said Bob exasperated.

"Well at least that has been tidied up and now we can see what comes out of the pot concerning intelligence, with him being closed this is not just about the gun making there's more to this, didn't you say that there was a false wall made of straw bales in one of the barns," said Sgt Anderson.

"Yeah, I did didn't I – I forgot all about that, that must be the reason he's being held in custody, stolen property and more turnovers to be done, I bet. Yeah, Old Ben said that this straw wall had been used for years, no one bothers, who is going to climb or pull bales around, bloody dangerous if you get it wrong and the whole lot collapses on you, it will kill you, they weigh a ton, our problem is that not many would realise on a search that this could happen, we need to be a bit more savvy at times when dealing with such people and property searches, as they are streetwise and way ahead of us in their thinking, we have a lot to learn from them, real foxy people to deal with as I have said before," said Bob.

"If you let me have that interim report in the meantime to keep others up to date in what we know and what we are doing then we can't be blamed if the wheels come off, only thinking about the bigger picture, there is a lot on here and we could lose ourselves in the quagmire if we aren't careful, it's too busy all of this, we need more prisoners to calm things," Sgt Anderson.

CHAPTER THIRTEEN

Romance is Still Alive

Tuesday early turn for Bob had seen the previous day an extremely busy one with extra Police patrols arriving at various times throughout the day. It seemed that the current gipsy problem had forced the hand of management to increase patrols in the area, so double crews overlapped each other throughout the day and so would continue until further notice.

Bob had completed the interim report for Sgt Anderson who was due duty at eight o'clock this very morning, having spent a restless night with so going through his mind Bob realised that there had to be more than he had acquired. (Old Ben Witney had been Godsend to him being able to identify people, places and to find the underground construction), But for Bob there still much to gain as he expressed his feelings to Sgt Anderson as there were aspects still missing. Even without information forthcoming from the Murder Incident Room, as the enquiry appears to have stalled with the little update being released to officers on outstations. Bob decided that he needed quiet time alone to think things through on station and hoped that he would be given the opportunity to work through in a more rational way for others to consider a more visual approach to what he wanted to do and explain in detail.

Meeting later with Sgt Anderson and requesting the time and the use of the briefing pin board in the Sergeants office, he was able to convince they were on catch-up all the time and never making arrests with what they were finding at the time of crimes being committed and no prisoners,

Over the next couple of hours, Bob laid out the 'Pin board' with pictures and written information that explained specific individuals, including the murder victims, and the mysterious foreigners who came and went leaving murder and destruction in their wake. Joined later by Sgt Anderson and from time to time other officers popped in and saw much and impressed at what Bob had found adding their thoughts and left notes on the board for Bob to consider the picture that was now beginning to emerge for all to see and understand how dangerous and dangerous the situation had become.

The absence of Bob's four weeks away was evident to see as to what was missing from the briefing board, what had been the reason for the fire at 'Marshalls Green', it all points to gipsies seeking revenge, the revenge alleged to be missing jewellery stolen from foreigners.

Bob needed to find Old Ben for another chat, he needed to know just how long the travellers had been using the grounds of the 'Manor House' and whether their paths had crossed by being seen or caught by the occupants of the house, which had to be the starter for Bob.

At the same time, Bob arranged with his force Intelligence departments to send him details of crime events of some substance occurring in the four weeks that covered his absence. He also remembered the major crime spree that occurred in Bristol about that time and was a significant media news story and that to have gone stone cold with little or no mention since by the media and yet involved enormous sums of money and property.

Bob couldn't stop shaking his head; he just could not believe that such crimes of substance and magnitude now appeared on the back burner, albeit, committed in another Police Force area, it didn't make any sense that so little information was being released right across the board.

With coffees in hands some of the local colleagues appeared in the Sergeants office to browse over Bob's work shown on the briefing board, the atmosphere was quiet and studious on the part of his colleagues as it apparently got the ‘Old Grey Matter' thinking among them. The information was beginning to come alive, and now some was making sense as to what may be missing and what was needed to bring this all together. His colleagues left rather impressed with his efforts, as it meant they now had a route and inputted themselves by leaving Bob notes in a purpose placed tray for them to use. Sgt Anderson had copied Bob's interim report and placed on the pin board for routine use of staff; he realised from a stand back viewing position when gazing at the board, where the gaps in their enquiries appeared and where sections needed to be acquired and upgraded.

It was that moment of inspiration, the eureka moment that sent Bob into a right old spin, when he added times and dates of the various crimes occurring in his absence a pattern emerged, but he had focused concentrated on the ‘Manor House’ as the central piece to his puzzle, the fire occurred on a Saturday night going into Sunday morning, it was the later time on Sunday when Lenny Burns was seen at the pub with three dogs and woman with him. Bob believed that the couple were arriving back at the ‘Manor House' from somewhere? – Unaware of the tragic events that were to greet them later.

Which meant that no contact prior, was made between Lenny and Tommy. Everybody has a mobile phone today, so why didn't the couple appear to know, surely Tommy would have made an urgent call at the beginning of the house fire to warn and inform Lenny.

Bob was in full flight of his thoughts, excited most about what he may have discovered. As he quickly jotted down his discovery, heading this up as a possible first link as to why no bodies were found in the debris of the fire – 'THE HOUSE WAS UNOCCUPIED' it had to be. That had to be the answer as to why the couple were so shocked when learning of the fire; they had been out of contact for some reason. But then the dogs – four dogs left in the house and kennels, so had they been fed, watered and exercised before the fire. Could it mean that the animals having been looked after by Tommy before leaving the property unoccupied? Knowing that Lenny was returning later to the house with his female companion, had the friends prior arranged this and why it would explain why no bodies were found in the fire, only the dead body in the Tanker vehicle was located.

Bob sought a second opinion from colleagues while a number were on a meal break at the time, requesting their presence in the Sergeants office, he explained his findings as they appeared to him: -

- Lenny and his female companion were distraught and distressed on Sunday when caught on the video security camera of a local pub.
- I suspect that the couple were absent for reasons unknown from the 'Manor House' that night or longer period away.
- They had not been informed prior – 'Meaning at the time of the fire' – as one would have expected his friend Tommy Sands to have made contact and warned him.
- I believe that sometime prior Tommy and a

second person left the house on Saturday, possibly early evening having settled the four dogs before leaving the property.

• Knowing that Lenny was returning on Sunday morning

• Tommy and his companion would not be aware of the house fire if they left the property on Saturday evening. They would have been elsewhere and asleep at the time of the fire and the reason why Lenny and his female companion were found to be beside themselves on Sunday that they were clueless about the fire.

• Lenny and his companion appeared to have been in the area early on the Sunday morning obviously on their way back to the 'Manor House' when they became aware of the destruction of the house. Unaware of the house being unoccupied at the time of the fire, they believed that Tommy and another were in the house at the time and perished in the fire.

• (Furthermore, because of their no-contact policy, agreed prior to their organised 'Crime Spree' all parties continued to follow these arrangements no matter how frustrating and angry others might have felt as it was the need for safety on all their parts in protecting each other from detection and arrest and thus avoiding mistakes that would put them at risk)

Bob made it clear to the small group present that any information no matter how little and it is felt it belongs on the briefing board then please leave in the tray provided and it will be added to the growing tree enquiry. Sgt Anderson was the first to comment as to how good the briefing board looked, seeing it all come together and linking in parts made more sense in understanding the full extent of what was at stake.

It was at that moment the Sergeant took a phone call from the downstairs front office; Bob saw how concerned he looked,

"You need your hat and tunic Bob, I need to get the others off their meal breaks we have a vehicle chase going on, and we need to go up to the forestry land to meet a couple. Apparently, they want to see Police urgently, they won't say what it is over the phone, beats me why not, so anyway we need to do that job first, and the others can get mobile and see what this vehicle runner is all about," said Sgt Anderson.

It was clear that the vehicle chase involved gypsies with two stolen vehicles, with numerous Police vehicles engaged in the pursuit including traffic officers from other stations, the dangers were evident as the roads were busy at this time of day (12.30pm) as many of the public would be out and about taking their lunch breaks. The vehicles were heading towards Sgt Andersons policing area and listening to the force radio controller, near collisions and dangerous driving was eyeballing to eyeball for the police crews, adrenalin high and intense, driver's concentrations was paramount to be well focused and were being advised by the controller for safe driving and no risk takers.

Finally, Bob and Sgt Anderson found the earlier informant on Forestry land who had required Police attendance. It happened to be a couple out walking their dog, and more significantly it was a retired Police Officer known personally to the Sergeant. The news that greeted them was frighteningly familiar and appeared sinister at the time, as the couple led the way, the informant's wife stood back and away from her husband and both officers as all three disappeared into a hedge thicket about two hundred yards from the road.

The bodies of the two young males appeared to have been laid deliberately on their backs side by side; both seemed to have a single bullet hole each to their foreheads. Their dress and style of clothing indicated to the officers that they were more than likely to be from the gipsy fraternity.

All three remained in close conversation with each other, already Sgt Anderson's alarm bells were ringing as this was catastrophic and the worst possible news to be told to senior officers.

"Two young lives wasted, for what, revenge. But who the fucking hell is responsible for this, our area is becoming like a bloody cemetery," Sgt Anderson.

The retired Police Officer was right not to call this one in; it needed a more private approach to stop the media rush which would be clamouring for a story. The Sergeant thanked his old colleague for his discretion and not losing sight of one's past discipline. Retired copper, and a judgement call on his part as he returned to re-join his wife, who had remained patient in those moments of her dress as she had felt the eerie impact of being so close to what now appears to be a murder scene. She and her husband bid farewell and went on their way leaving both officers transfixed on what their eyes were able to view and witness without walking and trampling all over the ground and contaminating the crime scene.

"This is a mobile call, Bob, lest we forget the radio and do this contact on a need to know basis first, I'll get CID up here first and alert the Scenes of Crime dept. To be on standby, Christ! This is all we need now, and we are taking the hit on this," said Sgt Anderson he spoke more in a faint voice to Bob.

"It's so shocking; you couldn't write this as fiction. Why are we missing this, is it the foreigners? Could it be someone local who hates travellers, four dead bodies and no answers, I'm fucked on this I just cannot get my head around this for a small country station like ours, this is big time crime for the city," said Bob.

Somewhat anguished and angry to think that this is happening right under their noses and no results from the increased number of mobile patrols. At the same time, other Police patrols remain chasing two stolen vehicles in their area and were clear listening to the ongoing broadcasts over their vehicle radio that the vehicle chase was close to their positions. Dangerous driving was happening by the information being passed over the radio, listening to the noisy vocal clutter it was apparent that the drivers of these two vehicles were now ramming and forcing other cars off the road, doing their utmost to avoid capture, but apparently prepared to risk life and limb in doing so.

"Bloody hell listen to all that noise, Christ! They are some bastards they don't give a fucking toss about anybody," said Bob.

Now fidgeting and impatient as to their long wait for CID to arrive at their location as Bob wanted to get involved in the vehicle chase, as they indeed will not be included at this time in the murder enquiry. Bob had turned up the volume on the radio as he returned to Sgt Anderson's position standing some yards away from the vehicle in open ground; the echo of the surroundings broadcast the events second by second. Bob could feel the adrenalin building inside of him, wanting to get on with the job and to get involved in the next vehicle chase. Which was still ongoing close to their positions, engines could be heard roaring in the distance, and police sirens could be heard. Across the lower valley below their area, apparently, the vehicles were heading towards them through the narrow back lanes of the countryside. Gipsies love these country lanes as it only allows the width of only one car to travel and no overtaking is possible, but the dangers are evident by suddenly stopping and abandoning the vehicle is often their chosen choice of escape as any vehicle following is more than likely going to ram and collide with the abandoned car. This more than happens in sharp bends where one is not able to see the imminent danger that befalls the oncoming vehicle in taking avoiding action when travelling at speed. The gipsies are surely having this in mind by using the narrow lanes, to a point where the traveller may even detour by gate crashing into a field and using the open ground to escape into surrounding landscapes, with hedgerows and woodland available to hide in evading capture.

With CID colleagues now having arrived on scene with Sgt Anderson bringing up to speed those present and showing where the two bodies lie, as neither officer had previously scoured or disturbed the crime scene unnecessarily other than examining the two figures for signs of life.

Continuity was established between the uniform section and the CID department on their handover in reassuring that no further contamination had occurred at the scene since Bob and Sgt Anderson's arrival. Bob remained listening, quietly chomping at the bit wanting to get back on the road to join the vehicle chase that was heading in their direction.

When finally, both officers became mobile again their force radio was still blaring with so much background clutter. It became difficult to determine the direction of travel of the offending vehicles, although, they were somewhere in their police district and Bob's need to get stuck in and not miss out was growing by each yard of travel as neither officer could decide in what direction to go. With so much continuous commentary directed at the force radio controller from the chase vehicles, both officers agreed on their plan of action and went in another direction in the hope of foreseeing and anticipating where the gipsies were likely to stop and do a runner across the fields.

It was while slowly driving through one of the narrow lanes they came upon a darkened coloured Land Rover parked on the brow of the hill of the road. It appeared sinister not resembling a standard looking vehicle, its shape menacing as it looked down on them approaching. Both officers then realised why the car seemed to be different as they drove closer towards it. Fixed to the front of the vehicle was the outline of what appeared to be two steel ‘RSJ’s’, indicating another purpose for the vehicle’s use as the hallmarks gave the impression of an armoured vehicle that looked down on them from the brow. Across the windscreen it looked as though some changes had been made with viewing slits in what could only be described as steel plating, but what was the reason, why had it been positioned on the brow of the hill blocking vehicle movement from either direction. Bob saw exhaust fumes omitting from the vehicle, realising the engine was running, although, not able to see if the vehicle was occupied. Bob realised that this was more than sinister at this time, especially with stolen vehicles being pursued in the area, his thoughts were recognised by Sgt Anderson as Bob placed the vehicle in reverse and slowly moved backwards putting more distance between themselves and the Land Rover ahead of them Sgt Anderson saw the Land Rover creep forward and stop on several occasions, like a game of 'Cat and Mouse' and who was going to make the final move, Bob began to reverse with purpose and the momentum needed to be greater on acceleration as he was using the interior mirror as his focal point of steering the vehicle aided by the wing mirrors. It was clear that the officers were at the mercy of any vehicle travelling towards them as there were no turning points in the immediate vicinity ad the width of the country lane could only take one vehicle at a time with no passing places provided. Bob picked up speed accelerating back at least hundred yards when Sgt Anderson called out the alarm,

"The vehicle is coming at us Bob, step on it old mate, it's going to ram us."

Bob lost no time in turning in his seat and grabbing the back of the passenger seat to anchor his grip as he put his foot on the floor. As the Police vehicle roared back down the lane pursued by the Land Rover when Bob saw the break he needed a gap in the hedgerow, small enough to force the Police car up the slight bank as Bob aimed and propelled the vehicle towards the deficit. The car went crashing back through the gap, the noise was ferocious as the bottom of the scrapped the ground and felt by both officers inside. It bounced, it smoked, it sounded awful as at speed it shot into the field at such a rate of knots that Bob still had his foot pressing down hard on the accelerator. It was then that Bob released his foot as the vehicle spun on the grassy elements of the field, and then rocked sideways several times before coming to a halt. Sgt Anderson had banged his head as the peak of his car had collided with the windscreen of the vehicle as it spun around forcing his forehead to be jolted backwards several times before it came to rest.

The offending Land Rover was not to be seen from their position as Bob left the vehicle and raced back to the hedgerow and the gap they travelled through. The Land Rover was not to be seen but could be heard in the distance as Bob listened to the roar of a racy engine. The vehicle's driver was deliberately intent on ramming the Police vehicle, and now the stakes were high and had been increased as to the potential dangers they soon found themselves facing. It was clear to Bob the car had been designed to maximise as much damage as possible as a ram raider to any motorist on the road let alone a Police vehicle, it was more of it being a mobile can opener as no vehicle could stand the impact with 'RSJ's' girders being fixed to the front of the Land Rover, it was nothing more than looking like a real mean machine on wheels. Bob thought, "Why." As he returned to Sgt Anderson who apparently sat in pain from the jolt he received to his head and neck, it was more of a whiplash. Bob drove the vehicle further down the field in search of a gate entrance, in doing so was then able to park up and call for the assistance of a traffic vehicle examiner to aid the worthiness of their vehicle and whether able to drive back to the Police station.

Sgt Anderson had already decided he would wait for treatment and stay with the vehicle until assistance arrived from other offences. It was whilst during their wait they both reflected on how close they had come to being seriously hurt or even killed as the Land Rover was a foreboding sight and one of heavyweight able and capable of crushing the Police vehicle with one blow, especially with the driving momentum of the car travelling downhill and the gravity behind it.

Eventually, assistance came, and the officers returned to the Police station, Sgt Anderson was conveyed to the local hospital for a check-up, and their Police vehicle was removed for further examination and roadworthiness.

Bob sat with his coffee for a good half hour in silence ignoring other colleagues around him, he needed to gather his thoughts at this time, and instead of his mind being cluttered he needed to be focused before he started to write up the events for senior officers. Details had already been passed to their headquarters control for a force full broadcast of the description of the vehicle.

It was some hours later that Bob received word that the Land Rover was designed to be more of a weapon and the occupants were travellers who remained for much of their time hidden in the woodland of the Forestry Commission, the vehicle just bulldozed merely a path from one field to another instead of using the roads, it cut across country at will of the driver. Bob's information comes from other Police sources. Apparently, this vehicle has been roaming for some months. Disappears and then reappears weeks later, strange events as the car has no index number displayed. Due to the way the car has been designed it appears that the doors on the vehicle are welded, and that access for the driver is by climbing through the driver's window, so it becomes more of a mobile fortress and will take some stopping and most certainly not a vehicle to tangle with. The information broadcast was reiterated at numerous times during Bob's shift as he could hear the wireless echoes from the front office all the way up to the canteen. Bob was nearing six o'clock time and well over his formal finish time of two o'clock as there was still much to clear up before he left for home, when minutes later Sgt Anderson arrived back at the Police station now earring a neck brace for a whiplash injury, so clearly, he will soon be on sick leave for an unspecified time. As he was greeted by Bob who also showed some concerns for his injury when the call came from downstairs that the two stolen vehicles had been located and in the area of where they met the Land Rover, it appears from the Radio comments that one car has been abandoned in a field, and the occupants have decamped, the other vehicle had ploughed through the hedgerow, across the country lane where the front of the car came to land on the part of the opposite bank. The vehicle was now broadside across the road, the weight of the car had now compressed front and back into the earth banks and suspended over the lane. The force of the impact had stalled the engine, however, when Police arrived it was apparent that the accelerator had been jammed to the floor by bricks and the vehicle set off in motion driverless and purposely aimed at the hedgerow for maximum disruption by blocking, either way, the lane to traffic, this apparently had been achieved by the travellers to escape the closing Police presence. It was clear that a Jib crane was going to be needed to lift and remove the stolen vehicle from its present position.

“The bastards have done it again, they have escaped, what the fucking hell is all this about, why have we ended up with all this shit on our doorstep Sarge,” said

Bob.

You could feel the anger and frustration in his voice as he punched the air with his grievance, Sgt Anderson also looked bewildered at hearing the depressing news as it was all happening in real time and was relentless by the way the gypsies appeared to be on a course of self-destruction by the way they were challenging the authorities as if it was social game to them. It was apparently all the young ones involved. Which was significant in its self in the way the older traveller was beside themselves in the way their own young were acting bringing so much distress to the fraternities in general.

CHAPTER FOURTEEN
Crime Goes Unabated

Lenny and Karen left their hideaway for the long drive, eventually reaching an ideal location in the open countryside for Lenny to decide on making his unregulated stop to telephone big Frank. Lenny unwrapped the tinfoil from around his mobile before use; he remained very conscious of his call being traced that he went to great lengths to avoid being identified, it meant his method of security could omit no signal.

Having parked up, he left the vehicle to make the London call to Frank. Karen saw him pace up and down from the front passenger seat, she watched him through the windscreen and saw how his facial expressions changed from a downbeat look, from frowning to one of what seemed pure joy as Lenny raised his arms and punched the air. With what could only be described as excitement on his part accompanied by a roaring loud vocal cry that echoed in their surroundings, Karen was bewildered as to why his self-expression, leaving the car to join him. Lenny grabbed hold of her and whisked her off her feet with such a robust spin of their bodies, round, round, and round he spun them, parting with a kiss he stood back and held her shoulders as he spoke directly into her face with blurting news of Tommy? (However, no mention of Toni).

“Frank has been paid out, Frank has been paid," Lenny cried out in excitement.

As again he kissed Karen full on the lips as he grabbed hold of her and gave an almighty cuddle that she wrestled against as she gasped for air, breaking free Karen too took hold of the moment to enjoy the exciting news that Lenny was expressing. Their relief at the story of Tommy as it had to be him who had paid Frank and the others out, Frank explained his surprise to realise just how much had been paid into his account. It was more than he had expected, so it was Lenny's turn to find out if monies had been spent on their account by making a few enquiries himself later that day.

The signs that Lenny received from his maze of enquiries were electrifying it was clear that he had realised more than one million and now safely tucked away. He at one point panicked at so much money and whether this was genuine. As he was shocked that in his absence from the operation itself on the night and the events that have since followed. He had questions, many, many questions to ask of Tommy and the whereabouts of Toni, where the hell was she as the whereabouts of both remained a mystery, but at least by knowing that the money had been paid out told him that he was alive out there somewhere.

Lenny had run and exercised the three dogs leaving Karen alone in the car. On his return, Karen realised the good news had made him chattier and somewhat frisky, at a glance once he was back in the car it was apparent to her that he was becoming horny as his hand fidgeted and pulled on his trousers in the crutch area.

"Excuse me, old girl, it's a bit tight down there now and it ain't the underpants," said Lenny.

"No, I didn't think it was," said Karen,

Realising how much stress had gone from Lenny in such a brief time since speaking with Frank, this had uncorked his long, deep-seated feelings, bottled up since the House fire. Karen reflected on the most recent time when he became sexually active. Having caught her bent over while reaching into the boot of the car and that came out of nowhere, so spontaneous it caught her unawares as he fucked her, but not one of his lasting fucks, perhaps shorter lived for her and now she saw her man wriggling in his pants.

It could only be all good if Lenny had finally found a reason to believe that

Tommy was at least alive somewhere and bring more of the old Lenny back out of the closet and perhaps now to start living their lives together. There was another part to this story that Lenny had told her. Frank had his sources ferret with their Policing contacts, and it appears that no enquiries were being made about him. His name had not come into the frame for any reason other, as Tim explained as one of the owners of 'Marshalls Green' so what was going through Lenny's mind was fictitious, it was all in his head he had nothing to be concerned about. Tim had stood in and dealt with all the matters concerning the house through Estate Agents, so it was well covered without the need for him to be drawn into any Police enquiry.

On the drive home Karen kept an eye on his crutch and occasionally grinned to herself, it is evident that Lenny was very much his old self as Karen could see that he had a hard-on, the stress and worry had been lifted. Karen slid her hand down between his legs and teased him as they laughed together,

"You sod, is this what you have been hiding from me Lenny," said Karen as they both continued to smile.

"Yeah, it's woken up mate, it's come alive since Frank gave me the good news and being very rich in the meantime, what a weight off my shoulders, good old

Tommy he certainly came through for us," said Lenny,

Still grinning as he felt Karen's hand rubbing gently over the material of his trousers. Her gentle touches made him reach a point where he pleaded for her to stop, as she saw how big he had grown. He was struggling in his seat to contain himself trying not to get overexcited and mess in his trousers. It was a time for him being mind over matter and drive safely as they would soon be home and finally relax from their earlier excitement.

Having settled the dogs, Lenny made his excuses to Karen and left the kitchen, still wearing the outer coat she had remained in the kitchen while making their coffee's but also with one eye on the door and a cocked ear listening for Lenny's movements. Feeling confident Karen quickly removed her skirt and panties, now naked from the waist down, she undid her bra and tugged the garment from under her clothing as she wrapped the discarded items and tucked them in the washing machine away from Lenny's eyes.

She concealed her nakedness under her buttoned coat that she was still wearing and continued to stand at the worktop while making the coffee; she remained busy when she heard Lenny's return to the kitchen. Karen had an inkling of what Lenny had in mind when he left the kitchen and the real reason as to why she removed her clothes and kept her now unbuttoned coat on. With both coffee's she turned the opposite way to Lenny's approach and placed the coffee onto the kitchen table, at the same time from the waist up she laid herself across the table surface, her legs apart with her face turned away.

When Lenny entered the kitchen, he was stark naked showing a massive hard-on as Karen suspected that she was about to get laid at sometime within the hour, but the kitchen had not been her first place of choice to do it. She had surmised his craftiness in wanting sex especially seeing and feeling his crutch on the drive home. He was ready alright, and in her mind, she wanted him to fuck her, to fuck her the right way of being wanted and not as an excuse to relieve himself just like taking a man's piss then walking off. Having anticipated his thoughts and the reason why she undressed and remained wearing her coat as concealment in wanting him to take her, to fuck her, she wanted him inside her, and now she prepared her moment of desire for him to take her. To fill and spurt into her silky lining in the only way how, by good old man's penetration, like a sword being sheathed in its scabbard she couldn't be more explicit in her needs by laying across the table.

Lenny soon took the bait as his hands ran down over her coat and buttocks feeling and gently squeezing as he moved. As he saw fit, then standing directly behind her with both hands placed around her waist he drew back and down over her lower body, at the same time he began to pull up the coat bit by bit from the hem as he slowly exposed her naked thighs and more as he continued. He then apparently realised that she was naked under the coat as he pulled her upright and removed it from her shoulders. Karen laid back down on the table waiting for Lenny to touch her, to stroke her. To be gentle with her as she was beginning to feel herself moisten and now at the mercy of her partner and his throbbing slightly bent penis that she imagined was now turning purple from the rush of blood that kept it stiff and hard.

If only a penis could talk, can you imagine what tales it could tell (giggling to herself) she thought? Such a dark place to enter and yet what thrills and excitement its entrance can bring to a woman (still laughing to herself) with such strange thoughts, she longed to be touched by him, as she waited for that first touch upon her flesh.

Lenny stood directly behind her naked buttocks as he leaned forward and began to massage her back from the shoulders, at the same time she felt his hardness brush and stab her flesh from time to time as he leant over.

Then finally his hands reached her arse as he fondled more of her roundness, her legs already apart as he placed one hand between her legs and cupped her vagina, it was evident to Lenny that Karen was ready as she was dripping wet to his touch. When his finger reached into her, Karen's reflexes jumped a little acknowledging his presence inside her as he pushed his finger up pressing on her flesh towards her anus.

This made her squirm and moan, then a long throaty groan and grunt echoed in the kitchen, as the dogs became restless at the noise and inquisitive as to what the pair were doing on the kitchen table, as Lenny told them to lay down and be quiet.

(Karen in between her groans, giggled to herself about the dog's interests - Bloody hell! - She thought) Karen had chosen the place of a deed from her previous encounter with Lenny when he fucked her while she was bending over at the car; then she told him to wait and fuck her over the kitchen table, now the fantasy was a reality on the promise and suggestion she made at that time. Her novel idea was now working her into a small frenzy, as he was pressing hard inside, as she felt the spasms take hold in her excitement as he was only using one finger. He took her to the plateau of tease then eased the tension on her muscle, then again, and again he made her high with her emotions as he saw her hands turn into fists as she continued to groan and whimper, her sounds were like that of a mating stag real sounding voracious appetite as her body shook and shuddered to his touch, then she shouted out,

"Cor, you fucking men are awkward, Lenny fuck me for Christ sake, I am blowing like a sperm whale, fuck me Lenny I want to feel you inside, stop teasing me and get on with it for fuck's sake, fuck me,"

As she roared and blurted out her words of frustration, Lenny also saw the benefits dripping from her. As he withdrew his finger and held his penis up against her front door, it was already ajar. So, there was no bell to ring as he entered with one hard push, which made Karen give out a deep throaty gasp of appreciation, as he was in over her doormat and now was wiping his feet in her hallway. That needed decorating to her specifications as his purple penis was straining at the bit to get going and to change her wallpaper. He bucked and thrust deep into her vagina, by this time Karen had grasped the edges of the table from the force of Lenny's pushing. He was fucking her; this perhaps was the arduous fuck from recent memory, he was going it, as she felt her insides pummelled to sexual fulfilment that was genuinely blasting her silky lining in the right fashion of what she had hoped for.

Then she became overcome by her virtues as her mind and soul thundered through her body in a mass of orgasms that didn't seem to stop. Her noise was exhilarating but also frightening to Lenny as he had never heard sounds like it before with any woman, this was real cave man stuff and boy. Was she going for it when she finally screamed out as they both came on the same explosive journey that floated them on another orbit, now physically drained and covered in dripping sweat and perspiration?

As he withdrew from her, his fingers ran down over her flesh which made her shiver and goose pimple. As he stood back from her, his penis dripped and looked forlorn at such a unique experience it had gone through. Lenny laughed and giggled as he helped Karen back onto her feet, the edge of the table could be seen imprinted across her waistline, at the same time Lenny had to steady her on her feet as her legs were so weak from exhaustion she could hardly move, as they both laughed and cuddled together. Lenny sat Karen on the edge of the table as he removed her top and left her completely naked, he bent down and kissed her nipples one by one and caressed each breast. Karen kissed the nape of his neck as her hands stroked his back as he continued to kiss her breasts and at times his lips took hold and sucked each one in turn. When Karen pulled away and laid on her back across the table. She realised another orgasm sensation, Lenny just watched her body buck and shudder as she came, but also Lenny saw for the first time from her lower torso a squirting liquid seeping from her vagina, it was enough for him to notice and experience as he cupped the palm of his hand over her vagina as his fingers reached underneath and pressed against her anus which again, brought further excitement and movement from Karen. Still not finished she pressed her pubic-line hard against his palm and wriggled at the same time,

“OH! God,” she cried, sounding loud groans and

whimpers.

Karen reached down and grabbed his arm with both hands as she pushed and pushed against the palm of his hand. She was masturbating as she felt that warm rush and feelings that struck a chord with emotions, it was intense. It was electrifying as the thrill remained constant and exhausting as she went into a prolonged spasm of orgasms as she continued to hold his arm and when finally, she let go and burst into tears. She was sobbing her heart out when Lenny took hold of her with an intense cuddle that held her tight against him.

Karen reciprocated and placed her arms around him as she lay with her head on his shoulder as she felt a feeling of great calm and relaxation, something she had never experienced in any relationship of hers. Lenny remained a soothing pillar as he continued to cradle and cuddle her as they finally stood together.

It was awhile for both to climb the stairs together and shower, as their physical exploits were far more draining and tiring than either could have imagined.

It was around teatime when Lenny and Karen roused from their sleep and one by one showered for the second time to refresh. They both felt like jelly and weak at the knees from the muscle effects to their legs, and of course, this generated the laughter between them as neither was entirely in control of their bodies.

It was only later that Karen pointed out the time to Lenny as their fucking had almost lasted one hour. For most of that time, she was laid over the kitchen table throughout and held by his firm penetration that bound them together like super glue. Neither wanting to let go, now realising the energy and the marathon performance by them both, exhilarating beyond anything she had shared with any lover before and it was their lack of power that continued to make them giggle at their weakness.

Having later eaten and the dogs fed it was more of a chilled-out evening, not even the television could hold their attention as they both continued to periodically nod off, struggling to stay awake, when finally, they called time and headed off to bed and a house left in darkness.

It was late morning when they both decided on their day's agenda, now knowing from Frank that neither, especially Lenny was of no interest to the authorities. They agreed to revisit the area of 'Marshalls Green' and to see if any changes had been made and whether debris had been removed and the site tidied up.

Lenny had never made Karen aware of the underground construction that housed Tommy's Black Range Rover and much more besides that was kept underground, it just never had been up for discussion before, and it was a fact that existed in his knowledge only at the time.

So, it was they drove back to the village and up into the surrounding country lanes, just a slow drive to take in the best part of the day weather-wise. Then finally driving down to the entrance of the Manor House and parked up at the front gates. Indeed, the debris had been cleared, and the site was made suitable only the floor remained as you could trace the outline of the building that framed the concrete base. Nothing remained just a safety cordoned, and warning notices displayed on the site.

It was then that Lenny began to describe the mound that overlooked the original house to Karen, indicating specific points and very in-depth conversation followed as Lenny was keen to get into their underground mancave, and check on things. Lenny was not to know that the construction had been police alarmed to safeguard the property, although, he had not made up his mind to enter that day or wait for a more organised time that would suit them both on another day.

Eventually, the couple stopped off at the local pub; the dogs were left in the car as they decided on a meal before heading back home. Judy Stokes the licensee's wife of the Bull & Butcher was the first to speak to Lenny, as he gave his order from the menu and waited for their coffees to be served. The couple occupied the same table as they did on their first visit the day after the house fire when they found the dogs.

It was a pub regular that referred to Judy about the dogs left in the vehicle outside, which drew her interest to the couple and the mention of unusual dogs. It made her think as she slipped out the side door on a pretext of an errand by staying close to the walls of the pub she was able to see from her position the mentioned dogs. But realised the vehicle this time was much more prominent, in fact, it was an estate car and not a small saloon as before. But this time she had the vehicle details on a security camera, and that also meant the registration number, although, she did manage to get her husband Dan to take a wander and mentally make a note of the vehicle's name as he passed.

Minutes later Judy telephoned the Police Station to speak with Bob (PC Benyon) hopefully; unfortunately, he was not on duty. Explaining the reason for her call, and the officer informed her that there was no longer an interest in the individual as matters had been resolved by official business parties connected to the individual and the Estate Agents who represent 'Marshalls Green'. Although, Judy requested that note is left for Bob to call on her when he was next available as she had more information to digest and consider.

It was a good half hour before the couple finally left the pub and disappeared, Lenny had decided to let the dogs have a run before returning home so driving out to the countryside and a location that would suit him and the dogs. It was more of a wooded area he chose as Karen decided to remain with the vehicle as Lenny walked over open ground in full view of her. By which time all three dogs had disappeared noses to the land as they ran like 'Hoovers' across the ground sniffing all in sundry as they ran along the hedgerows one after the other. Lenny realised just how exciting it was to see his dogs working the ground and showing their natural instincts in their behaviour as hunting dogs. It was for him a lovely sight to reminisce old memories when he had the four dogs together, especially when they sounded off with such deep baying sounds. Loud and eerie sending shivers down the spine and never knowing where they were going to appear from, they were described as the ghost dogs and an appropriate description of the breed. (Weimaraner's)

The time now was pressing for Lenny the dogs had not returned at the same time he kept Karen in view. Realising that he was going to have to look for them, he returned to the vehicle and encouraged Karen to join him; he felt happier that she was with him, instead alone in the car in such an isolated area. Walking off into the wooded area, Lenny also carried with him a sonic whistle that was ideal for signalling dogs and this he used, at the same time they walked further and deeper into the woods, thick forestation was everywhere making the interior a right place to hide, the couple kept to a small track that weaved its way through the woodland, when Lenny alert to danger stopped and listened as he pulled Karen off the road into a dense part of the wood. Someone or persons could be heard on the track but not from what direction, as the couple paused and remained concealed, the voices belonged to three youths who were following behind them, now Lenny let them past undisturbed as the three were far ahead of them. Lenny recognised them as young gipsies, probably up to no good, it was some minutes later that the couple heard the roar of an engine. Lenny pressed forward in the undergrowth to a position where he was able to see, seeking out the direction of the engine noise. It was then about a hundred yards further in that Lenny saw the darkened shape of a Land Rover, with windows covered, the vehicle was in a recess in the ground. It appeared to Lenny that the car was purposely hidden for some reason and that curious as he was to know why the windows were covered over with slits in the material. It was the clanking and the banging that gave the game away; it was plated up in steel panels that protected the windows. Even more astonishing when he saw one of the youths climb out of the vehicle via the passenger door window, he realised whatever the purpose it was sinister and eerie to be in the position he was as the dangers were obvious. Then bang, bang, bang, the sounds of a shotgun blast could be heard, and later much laughter echoed out among the trees. Lenny made his way back to Karen only to find the three dogs had returned to her and lay at her feet exhausted, with tongues hanging out the side of their mouths.

"Come on mate let's get back to the car, it's not safe down there, did you hear the bangs, they are using a shotgun, and there is also a vehicle hidden in the undergrowth, so they are not up to any fucking good, they are fucking trouble mate," said Lenny,

Somewhat concerned even with the dogs present their position was precarious should they be discovered as he had no idea as to how many of them were about in the woods. Instead of walking back on the track the couple worked their way through the trees, it was slower but gave them protection in the shadows as they moved as fast as they could without causing alarm to the dogs. Eventually reaching their car and ushering the dogs into the back they were soon off to find a more public place to rest and water the animals.

It was the local garage where they took refuge to rest and water the dogs, Lenny watched Karen walk to the kiosk, she later returned with two coffees and the local paper.

“Lenny this will interest you, read this story," said Karen.

"Fucking hell, that is the vehicle I saw back in the woods, it's the same one that chased the Police, fucking hell. It says here that the vehicle has a frontal design that could be used for ramming, it appears that RSJ's are fitted to the vehicle. Sounds more like a fucking tank, they are fucking this lot mate, remember the run-ins that Tommy had up at the house, probably the same lot from the camp," said Lenny,

With an excited voice of discovery, the Police ought to know what he had seen back there in the woods, he realised this is a bloody dangerous situation, and he wanted none of it, but his conscience was eating at him he had to do something, but what.

There drive home was full of thoughts for both and was disturbing to say the least as they felt fortunate to have found their way back out of the woods without being discovered, it sent shivers down both their spines and them couldn't get into their house quick enough and settle down for the remainder of the night, although, Lenny did on several occasions peek out of the window to be sure of their safety.

Forty-eight hours later Lenny's envelope received in the post at the local Police Station was opened by the Station Duty officer. Enclosed was the article about the Land Rover incident and a map detailing where the vehicle was seen and discovered and at the time accompanied by local gipsies, along with the actual time and date of the encounter, although, sent anonymously it provided sufficient detail for the facts to be established by the Police officers themselves.

The information was placed on the briefing board that Bob had been supervising, what with Sgt Anderson on sick leave it made matters more difficult in being short staffed, with more mobiles being detailed from other policing areas to beef up the lack of manpower on the station.

Within hours of the letter having been received a sub-division Inspector was brought in to supervise a search of the area, but first it was decided to use the new crime weapon, the force drone.

It could send immediate signals back that could be monitored and analysed and whether the vehicle was still concealed in the woodland.

Once this has been achieved the force helicopter could

then be detailed to

survey the area with heat-seeking equipment for possible suspects and whether the vehicle had recently been used. It was going to be a wait operation, the drone made little noise and could come and go without attracting attention, unlike the jet engine of the helicopter. Extra officers were placed on standby as the Inspector decided that time was of the essence, the short delay was for the drone operator to arrive at the station. It was determined to wear civvies than a uniform as the area was so isolated and what with narrow lanes a marked police vehicle would be too conspicuous and would attract the wrong interest.

By late morning the operation was in full swing as other chosen locations around the perimeter of the woods had other officers secreted on local farms that bordered on to the woodland and forestry commissions land.

The dog handlers were kept back at the local station ready to be deployed if the need arose; the long wait was the frustrating part of police work as recognised by the officers themselves.

The drones effectively provided clues that a vehicle had used the narrow track, it was clear that the undergrowth had been flattened on both sides of the path for something much more substantial to have passed over.

Again, the recess on the ground where the vehicle was last located could be seen, as shadows appeared around an object that was depicting an oblong shape. Meaning that the depth of the recess was sufficient for a vehicle to be hidden and undiscovered and from the recess one was able to see a full track that led off the main trail through the woodland, albeit, in parts the road had been widened and reached the entrance to the recess hidden between the canopy of the trees.

The force helicopter was now called upon to go airborne and whether able to detect any heat-seeking movement below, whether by vehicle or person. Officers sat patiently listing to the force radio crackle with other police business being assigned and called upon in other parts of the force area by the force radio controller.

Eventually, the word came through that the vehicle had been in situ of where first discovered in the recess, it also showed the movement of three persons, one inside the car and two outside and close to the vehicle. They also found a further three persons in various parts of the woodland, but still near the car. The Inspector was delighted with the news it was a definite go, go, go as he reorganised his officers, the dog handlers were sent off to be much closer to the location, and two firearm officers had been deployed at the nearest farm to cover the other uniform officers at those locations.

While the preparation was being made to raid the location; word came via the helicopter that the vehicle was on the move and contained only one occupant being the driver. The real concern was now being expressed as to how to stop this vehicle. With so much added protection added to the car and doors welded such regular access wasn't possible, the dangers were evident as the Police could not afford this vehicle reaching the highway, it had to be stopped at all costs while off the road. The adrenalin was building in the waiting officers, not knowing which way the vehicle would emerge or was it an engine warm-up of a few yards with the car remaining at its present location. Either way, the news was not good at this time with so much preparation already in place, it was again a wait and see the moment that was heart stopping to those involved.

The duty Inspector realised that should make the vehicle move off it had one way to reach the highway, it was then that other voices remarked about using a JBC or Bulldozer to challenge the vehicle, we need something of steel to match steel as there was an open discussion by officers trying to alleviate the dangers.

Farm vehicles what about requesting the farmers to park dozens of their massive machines in the lanes around the woodland, block whole roads. Not with one car but with many, should the vehicle make it to the paths, it can't go anywhere, it just would not be able to tackle so many parked machines, even if it rammed the first vehicle it still would not be able to break free, the lanes are too narrow. The Inspector looked amazed at the justification of blocking the roads; the ‘Beat book' would have details of the local farms, so we could quickly make contact including those officers already deployed at the farms.

Within half an hour officers in the area could hear the roar of engines and machines descending on the various lanes and locations around the woodland and over the next thirty minutes farm machines had now been parked and abandoned by their owners. At the same time the drone had been redeployed and flew over the various locations as many as six machines had been parked one after the other at the sites, it was a tremendous response by the farmers to get behind the police. Officers were now at specific traffic junctions to forewarn motorists of the numerous obstructions placed in the lanes which were now temporarily blocked and impassable.

The helicopter was able to detect that the three figures discovered elsewhere in the woodland had come together and were walking away from the others and heading towards the open ground, fields occupied by dairy cattle grazing. It was decided to wait until the three were out in the open and a better of the opportunity of capturing them without warning the others in the woods. One of the dog handlers had been brought to the location to wait on the moment should there be an attempt to escape, a runner who needed to be stopped 'ASAP', it was an arrest waiting to happen, it was imperative that none of the three is allowed back into the woods, two officers were sent from another direction to cut off any attempt of reaching the others with the vehicle.

Finally, it was close enough for the officers to break cover as the three gipsy youths remained together, realising they had nowhere to run they stood still and were quickly captured by the officers. The two officers in the woods were instructed to stay and to move closer to the other group, softly, softly was their order from the Inspector, no heroics were needed, but all officers required patience and personal safety. The dog handler also joined the two officers in the woods, at the same time other officers moved their positions closer to the woodland, remaining unseen and by stealth, it had to be explicit by all involved.

It was then that horrifying moment came blasting over the radio, the Land Rover had broken cover and was on the move, one occupant the driver. The other two companions remained in the recess; it appeared they had lit a fire to warm themselves as they gestured with arms outstretched towards the fire. It meant that officers from all directions could move in and arrest the two who remained by the fire. With three already in custody it was working in favour of the police to capture a further two, then that leaves the one in the vehicle to focus on.

The land Rover finally broke cover; the driver appeared to be unaware of the police interest on him having been discovered along with his associates. The driver just merely drove around the field as if riding the Dodgem Cars at some local fair; he went one way then another all the time practising his skids, twists and turns when eventually the driver decided to leave for the open roads. Reaching the access point that would provide access to public roads, the driver soon realised that he had been rumbled due to the many farm machinery parked up at the exit entrance and that he could not drive either way as the lane was blocked merely by so many farm tractors and appliances. The vehicle turned back and headed for the one track he had driven down, back towards the recess area he thought safe.

When reaching this point, he too became aware of a Police presence. Instead, he drove past the recess entrance and pushed on at high speed, sounding like a thundering tank and weighed as much as a tank, a vehicle that could not be stopped in normal circumstances, a death machine captured with nowhere to run.

Police officers emerged from their hiding places as the Land Rover finally crashed through the undergrowth and came to rest in a grazing field of cattle. The driver did no more than drive at speed first in one direction, then in another. Apparently, the driver did not have the option of escaping with his vehicle; it was make up time for him to stop and make a run for it or use the car as a weapon, he chose the latter as he drove at almighty speed for a hedgerow. The weight of the vehicle forced its self through the hedgerow. As the car came crashing down broadside across the lane, with engine roaring as the vehicle slowly slid down the bank until its tyres touched the road surface, the smell of burning rubber was wafting through the air, as the driver remained desperate to escape with his vehicle.

The noise was deafening as more Police officers arrived and stood to watch. As the driver attempted to turn his vehicle which was now jammed solid into the bank of the hedgerow. The car was certainly not going anywhere; such a sinister looking thing soon stopped on the road to nowhere, it was only a matter of time before the car would run out of fuel. Indeed, the police had plenty of time on their hands and could wait until the engine fell silent without endangering the lives of others in the process.

Eventually, the truth is known as the driver finally surrendered to the Police, by climbing out of the vehicle via the window of the driver's door and was soon taken into custody.

The excitement among officers at the Divisional Headquarters was one of disbelief in realising that the six arrested earlier had been captured with minimum fuss and no injuries to officers, and the sinister vehicle was now

out of action and in police custody and now garaged elsewhere subject to a forensic examination.

Senior officers called a briefing among junior ranks later that day, bringing up to speed the current position of their enquiries along with CID from the ongoing murder enquiry. What with the cells overflowing with prisoners, the six-newbies added further the need to keep them separated and not to converse in their slang tongue of

Romany. It was decided after the initial induction that some would be transferred to other police stations on the division where continuity of police enquiries could continue unabated.

Meanwhile, the captured Land Rover was yielding good evidence apparently, with items found in the vehicle, either used as instruments of crime or the proceeds of crime and of course an abundance of fingerprints

which may well further the enquiry to other potential suspects, Police wise it was looking good in results.

Senior officers were jubilant at the results of the arrests, and it was decided along with CID to consider a mini task force in bringing the whole of the current crime issues together concerning the gipsy fraternity.

CHAPTER FIFTEEN

Sexual Partnerships

On Thursday early turn shift (6am/2pm) Bob read the note left him from Judy Stokes to find time and call in at the pub. By nine o'/clock the same morning Bob arrived at the pub and spoke with Judy, the licenses wife of the Bull & Butcher. Bob was surprised to be told that the couple he sought from the security video had returned to the pub the day before (Wednesday); they came in around midday and had lunch at the same table by the window, this time they appeared more relaxed and cordial.

“Dan managed to get the vehicle number for you,” said Judy, “Only when I called the station I was told there was no further interest in the couple, but anyway just in case we got the couple on film again."

"Oh! you are a beauty, yes I am still interested in them, it's just that Police wise no crimes have been committed to our knowledge, that's why you were given that information," said Bob,

Delighted in being given the index number of the vehicle. Perhaps now this would provide the remaining parts of his jigsaw, as he explained further to Judy that there were riddles to be solved, especially about the man who left the parcel for him weeks earlier and the mystery as to why he left such an array of hi-tech equipment.

Within the hour Bob had established details of the vehicle being a rental estate car on a one year's lease to an address in Gloucestershire. According to the voter's register and enquiries with the local police, the house had been unoccupied for some time, although, the premises did exist and were a dwelling house and not commercial premises. Bob sat for ages just fiddling and going over the information on his briefing board and wondering how he was going to justify an enquiry with another force area when he had the greater need to meet the couple in person physically. The one request he did make to the local station that policed that area was quiet (pass the house visit) to see if they could establish the vehicle being at that address, by two o'/clock finish Bob received the answer he hoped for the car was indeed present at that address.

Bob was now officially on three rest days off and back on duty on Monday working a four (pm) to Midnight shift. With time to think and decide on angle of approach as he had a plan to think through, at the same time, his love life had gone rather quiet due to the rat race of his work that week, it was more than a week since he had contact with 'Sandy', he needed company and the day was still young for socialising.

Heading home to shower and change he hoped that she was around, perhaps she might like a drive out with him, and Gloucestershire had crossed his mind and remained fresh in his mind at the prospect.

An hour later Bob received a return call from 'Sandy', it appeared that her husband was due home earlier in the week, and why she had been absent from calling. She had been busy rearranging her schedule while waiting for her husband providing a return date, only to find that he had now put back his return for another two weeks due to world matters. Bob was confused by the 'World matters' subject but anyway it was none of his business to know more as been their prior agreement between them and their great sexual conquests. He realised that he came on strong when he thought about sex, when doing other things and being busy it never crossed his mind. Now at a loose end for the weekend he felt more relaxed and horny, he needed sexual sustenance to quench the rise of man, he chuckled to himself, crazy thoughts, he could be desperate, but was she, was 'Sandy' feeling sexually neglected by his absence, anyway, it was time for him to put matters right, she needed fucking.

By seven o'/clock Bob had arranged a rendezvous away from her house, having decided to kill two birds with one stone, Gloucester, he was going to look at the house where Lenny Burns resides and at the same time to treat 'Sandy' to a dinner and the splendour of an overnight stay in a luxury hotel where they could merely unwind away from both their homes.

Bob explained the errand he was on and then on to their hotel for the night, 'Sandy' looked stunning on the outside of her dress code. But underneath she was naked, having left off her underwear. How soon was Bob likely to find out, could it be under the table at dinner, walking up the stairs or perhaps taking the lift to their floor, more wildly to put his hand where it shouldn't be at the same time of upholding the hem of her dress to find out. Bob did make the right approach in complimenting her; she looked different in a way that he hadn't noticed before her face was blush as if she had blossomed more in this last week than since first meeting.

It was whilst over dinner that Bob nearly choked on his food, as coming through the hotel lobby towards the restaurant he recognised one of the two people approaching as a couple, it was Lenny Burns, the person he had sought for weeks and whose house he drove past a brief time prior to his arrival in Gloucester. 'Sandy' looked confused as she had no idea as to what was happening with Bob, as he coughed and spluttered. Finally apologising to her for such an outburst to his extraordinary behaviour, when he leant over to whisper some words of explanation to 'Sandy' her facial expressions said it all, first her eyes nearly popped out, then her mouth opened with a gasp then a hand quickly covered her mouth in astonishment at what Bob had whispered, reacting more in shock as she had a mouth full of food at the time. Bob signalled to her not to look round at the entering couple, as even more bizarre the couple are shown to a table close by them, even leading Bob to pull faces as 'Sandy' returned to eating her meal which encouraged Bob to do the same. Bob realised that this was a good opportunity to take photos and capture the couple together at the table. He had one of those new back to front camera phones, and (lens is at the back of the phone, the front appearance is a gimmick) so giving a false sense of security, and not one to raise the suspicion of others. It neither flashed as it appears to be a high-tech appliance using infrared technology, an expensive investment on his part some months before. Bob managed the opportunity in a casual style of taking pictures of 'Sandy'; it was when he had finished he sat staring into her eyes and face, she was blooming her skin looked soft and silky, but so gorgeous to him as he sat and just giggled to himself.

"What's wrong with you, why are you looking at me like that and giggling?" said 'Sandy',

As she began squinting her eyes and frowning at him to respond.

“I just cannot believe at times as to how lucky I have been to have met you, do you realise how gorgeous and beautiful you look, a real English Rose without a shadow of a doubt my girl,” said Bob smiling.

“What has brought that on might I ask, kind sir,” said ‘Sandy’, in somewhat of a surprise at his words.

"Looking through the camera provides a different entity, very different to you in the flesh, it shows more of your inner beauty which you don't normally see, oh! be Jesus me darling what more can I say to convince you," said Bob as he remained smiling at her,

‘Sandy' said no more than to place her foot in between his legs and mouthed her lips with the silent words of ‘Fuck me' - ‘Fuck me now', she smiled and winked as she placed a glass to her lips and sipped wine. Bob remained giggling and hunched his shoulders as he felt her foot right in his crutch which made him fidget even more, his brow was propped up on his hand as his elbow rested on the table, shielding more of his giggling expressions trying not to be too obvious at ‘Sandy's touching momentum, she was toying and playing with his crutch with each twist of the foot, at times she moved forward in her seat as she pressed hard against his penis and wriggled her bare toes to tease him, at the same time she sucked a finger and pouted her lips at him.

“Okay, Okay I get the message," he whispered, “Do you want more wine before we leave, one more glass,” he asked.

“No not for me, but later,"

Her head nodded and indicated with her eyes (to move upstairs) then sideways meaning they leave now. Bob followed her instructions as they both got up to go the restaurant and return to their hotel room. It was the lift chosen by 'Sandy' as she clasped to his arm as they entered, as he spun her around and kissed her, his fingers ran down over her back realising that he could not feel her bra strap, this reminded him of his earlier thoughts that she came without wearing underwear tonight. Just the idea began to raise his strong expectations as he felt the stirring down below grow from the size of a cocktail sausage to a massive right porker, which needed to be in her juices that flowed in the river of life. He was the one with the dam buster to plug and fill her hollow chamber and fill her channel with his seed and leave her with a warm belly that lasts and comforts her days until the next time.

Reaching their hotel room it was only seconds before 'Sandy' stepped up and provided Bob with a long passionate kiss and at the same time she groped and felt for the zip of his trousers as she foraged once opened for his penis, which she pulled unceremoniously over the top of his underpants, he winced at her squeezing hold as she exposed fully the enlarged six inches plus that she had pulled from the depths of his crutch and was to be hers for the night.

They both stood just inside their hotel room when 'Sandy' began to perform on him, kneeling she took hold of his penis and placed between her lips as she gently sucked and moved gently back and forth, Bob's hand was on her shoulders as he leant back and pressed his back against the door of the room.

Looking down he could see 'Sandy' pushing the whole of his penis into her mouth. He was astonished as to why she wasn't gasping for breath as her lips closed around the stem. With her nose buried in his pubic hair, he could feel the movement of her tongue inside of her mouth, that gave him a strange feeling that made his legs go weak, as he pushed back and away as he bent down to lift her back onto her feet, as again their lips met with a final long kiss before he picked her up and carried her to the bed. Now inquisitive as this was the moment he had in mind, as he laid her down on her tummy and lifted up the back of her dress to realise that he had been right, 'Sandy' was without underwear as he bent down and kissed her naked arse, with a tongue running up and down in the crease of her buttocks, at the same time he opened wide her legs in the shape of a gigantic 'V' as he placed his mouth down between her thighs and aimed for her vagina as her lips had slightly opened, and now his approach was to dart and lick with his tongue, and encompass her lips into his mouth as he sucked and sucked and teased as she started to wriggle with each touch, his hands on her waist as he held her too him as he began to taste her juices from the 'River gf life', at the same time there were moments when he saw the lips of her open vagina carp and pout like a fish exposing a milky white membrane around the edges of her silky lining, Bob at that moment knew he was doing it right, 'Sandy' was beginning to work herself off from his touches and kisses, he was really pampering her fanny with all the time in the world, in fact with all the hours they are to share in the night was more of the reality.

He knew not to rush he wanted 'Sandy' to have and enjoy many of orgasms tonight, he already knew that she was biting and filling her mouth with the duvet cover. Hiding her groans and whimpers from neighbours and with her hands grasping and digging into the duvet cover as she squeezed and squeezed as her knuckles turned white from the thrills that flowed through her body in continuous waves of delight, at times he could hear her deep throaty roars as he continued on plying his sexual skills in fulfilling her dreams as lovers should at all times and to understand the emotional highs and lows women experience in their mating and Bob was risking tonight, this was to be the fuck of all fucks as he would grind her pussy on the bone as the two pubes were to meet in the deep passion they were both exploiting.

At the same time Bob lost all track of the couples movements from the restaurant, completely gone from his mind as he worked 'Sandy' into a sexual frenzy with his hardness having well and truly broken cover, but unlike the 7th Cavalry he had no intentions of charging recklessly into unchartered waters, he wanted to drain the ocean before he decided to penetrate from the rear or perhaps to be more dignified and turn her over and take her from the front and fuck for glory, but, but, he realised as he lifted her dress right up over her head, was this the right way, he didn't know until 'Sandy' slipped back onto her knees and tugged the garment over her head and then lay back naked on her tummy leaving herself now totally exposed to man's elements as to how Bob will proceed and take her.

As he pulled her back onto her knees supported by both hands pressed deep into the duvet. Bob on seeing such naked exposure once again parted her legs wide as he reached underneath and cupped one hand over her vagina and the other stroked her back from neck and shoulders down to her inner thighs as he felt her flesh goose bump and flinch as he teased her in so many ways as to his touch. She even leant forward and rested her body with the flat of her arms laid on the bed with her buttocks raised even higher like the masts of a ship waiting to be docked, she wanted to be fucked and not just docked, but Bob had other ideas he was doing her work, he tried to raise her emotions even higher than before, he wanted to provide an instance lesson of his love making and not just counting this as another sexual moment that passes in time, he wanted 'Sandy' to remember how many times he warmed her belly and left her fulfilled and satisfied unlike many women who could only pray that their hour, day and sexual needs would soon be met and not necessarily by the husband or the obvious lover of choice.

(But an awakening that so many long for in their lives as so many men are real failures and so, so selfish in not waiting for that forty-five minutes for her to get warmed up as they rush the moment and blow a gasket in ten minutes and roll off)

Bob himself laid on his back and slipped underneath 'Sandy' as with both hands he opened and exposed her vagina wide as he placed his lips over her opening like a seal of approval as his tongue darted in and out many times as she bobbed up and down with each entry of his touch, it was beginning to build into something rather special as she found herself reaching a point of no return when suddenly she explodes in violent tremors that wracked the whole of her body in a spiritual sense as she let out such a throaty groaning sound it was err, err, err, nonstop, Bob was full of shhhh's to keep her voice down as management would be making a call thinking a murder was taking place, he at times was smiling by his efforts in delivering such a sexual experience for her to enjoy, it was truly mind blowing with the many different noises she made, as he grinned as to how big her repertoire is as this was a new experience for him, not even his wife made such noises like it, she just squirts? Finally the moment had come for the hairy combination to thrill and entertain the principle of love, as our 'Sandy' had been very patient with her arse in the air and an open door policy that provided much inducement for Bob to finally mount her, to ride her bare back as he took hold of her waist and gripped tightly as he pushed deep as a rear guard action into her vagina captivating the moments of her wheezing, grunting and groaning as he was just vibrating his member at the front gates of their pubes, 'Sandy' moved her haunches sideways to get a grip on his penis that just rubbed at the hilt, she also felt the profound throbs that he made as she brought her legs closer together as she applied her inner muscles to hold him firm.

Then Bob withdrew and continued to move with slow thrusts back and forth, then bringing the tip of his penis to her vagina lips. And just merely throbbed and teased until they were both ready and straight into one long fucking motion. That multiplied her orgasms in what seemed tenfold as her body rocked and rocked as he stroked her back gently, and round to her nipples that remained prominent and hard. As he squeezed between his fingers, then she gave a final squeal and collapsed on her tummy in perspiration. As Bob continued in a kneeling position, she had cupped his balls in her hands and had been gently stroking his scrotum. Until his old man had come alive to her touch, and it was this hardness that stirred him from his sleep. He felt her movements upon him as she gave him her oral sex, then she gently eased further over his body and placed her vagina on the tip of his penis. She leant back until the hardness had pierced her lips as she gently lay still with him inside of her, she made no further move other than she used her vagina muscles to capture his shooting moment as she felt his warm sperm tickle her lining. Her face was buried into the side of his neck as she gently kissed and stroked his flesh with her lips. Bob's arms reached out and cuddled her tight as they both lay together with her remaining on top of him and his penis still inside of her as she felt it slowly shrink until it finally slipped out of her vagina bringing forth a dripping damp secretion that oozed from her, sticky and wet.

Even more sexual moments occurred during their time a gooey covered penis that had laboured so hard in pleasing her needs and passions.

Bob left the bed and went and retrieved a warm flannel and gently wiped away the sweat from her back and buttocks, at the same time the cold flannel 'Sandy' took and pressed it against her forehead to cool down her body.

"Bloody hell Bob, that was some feat of yours, oh! My God, you took me somewhere, where I have never, never been before, god I will miss you, Bob, you are a fantastic lover your wife must be proud of you," said 'Sandy' and so full of praise for him.

"Sadly, no our lives are not like that, in fact, they have never been like this ever, not in the way we are together, you are one in a million for me, we gel so well together, fucking is the afterthought," said Bob,

Cracking then a clever joke as he grinned at what they had just achieved.

"Oh!" said 'Sandy', "I wasn't prying just complimenting

your sexual skills and prowess; you are an extraordinary man for me,"

With her a face full of smiles and a gentle hand that rubbed and stroked his face as she relaxed from her encounter with him, as she remained naked on the bed as they talked.

During the early hours of the morning Bob's sleep was disturbed as he realised that 'Sandy' was helping herself to more of the luxury service he provides her, she had cupped his balls in her hands and had been gently stroking his scrotum until his old man had come alive to her touch and it was this hardness that stirred him from his sleep, he felt her movements upon him as she gave him oral seduction, to begin with, then she gently eased further over his body and placed her vagina on the tip of his penis and leant back until the hardness had pierced her lips as she gently lay still with him inside of her, she made no further move other than she used her vagina muscles to capture his shooting moment as she felt his warm sperm tickle her lining. Her face was buried into the side of his neck as she gently kissed and stroked his flesh with her lips. Bob's arms reached out and cuddled her tight as they both lay together with her remaining on top of him and his penis still inside of her as she felt it slowly shrink until it finally slipped out of her vagina bringing forth a dripping damp secretion that oozed from her, sticky and wet.

It was near nine o'/clock when they both stirred from an exhausting night of hot sticky sexual passion that now made them both more tired than when they started on their marathon night of physical endurance. It didn't take them both long to decide on staying another night at the hotel, neither had prior engagements over the weekend and Saturday was another day in just enjoying each other's company.

Reception confirmed Bob was rebooking the room for a further night, which left them free to go down to breakfast and then to return to their bedroom without being chased out by hotel staff at ten-thirty (am).

"I was thinking the other day Bob, do you realise. We have spent more time making love than talking since we met," said 'Sandy' giggling, "You know every inch of my body, not even my husband can say that, strange how life becomes us all in time in not knowing much about our other halves,"

"Well, you are very infectious and irresistible, for me that is. Fate plays a big part in all our lives, but to be honest, things happen for a reason, and we take it for granted, we never really bother to consider the other side of the coin," said Bob, being honest and truthful. Taking another bite of her slice of toast,

"You are so right, we seem to hold back, but whilst we are fucking we really haven't had time to speak to each other, let's be honest, my girl- friends would have kittens if they knew about us, not about our affair, but the sex we are having, but then again it's not sex, sex for the sake of it is it, we are making real love and why we are able so compatible because of the actual time we spend on pleasing each other or don't you agree Bob," said 'Sandy',

Taking another bite of her slice of toast as she continued to chew and munch while looking at Bob hoping for a response from him as he continued to ponder on her words.

"Yeah, I know many fellows love to talk about their

sexual adventures, even what they do with their wives and that I find rather sad. As many women would be up in arms, if they thought, their husbands were talking about them. I can't imagine being in the company of a woman knowing what the husband has revealed about their sex lives," said Bob, "And yes it has happened on occasions, even going to domestics, I can remember on one occasion when a husband pointed to a wet patch on a carpet and kept repeating that is where his wife was fucked by her lover, whatever the reason it is none of our business, we are only interested in there not being a breach of the peace, assault and abuse if you like," said Bob, Sitting back up on the bed as he continued his conversation with 'Sandy',

"The sex part is nothing to do with us, but having said that you then become party to a secret, and when you are working in a small community like ours then you are going to meet at some time one of those women involved, it can be very embarrassing for them, not for me as they know I share a personal secret with them, and that comes down to trust and they will see that in time and they will acknowledge me", said Bob in a soft voice of reply.

"My friends are not as liberated as I am; I have always had good vibes and the good sex that goes with it. I don't have any inhibitions, and I am not embarrassed about my nakedness, I don't like being restricted, I am a free spirit without any hang-ups. Sadly, I have friends who have genuine issues with their love lives, not all are married, some single, but they have issues and find sex painful, cuddles and kisses are alright if it doesn't lead to sex. What makes me so cross with some of them they acknowledge their problems but won't seek bloody help.

It's crazy, but it is an issue on their minds, and the real worry is the breakup of relationships, guys are going to go elsewhere to get it, and who can blame them," said 'Sandy'.

"I know guys can be funny about a man's problem and again I know where some have left things too late. That is not just about being impotent, some of it has more serious repercussions on health issues which they ignore. Like macho man, so sad," said Bob, shrugging his shoulders, "Your friends, these women who have issues with sex. I don't understand with all these agencies and clinics for women why are they not bothering to seek help. Look today we talk openly about a woman's periods and hygiene, and Tampax at one time this was all taboo and stayed in the female market for discussion, now its discussed everywhere publicly. There is no shame attached to the subject, we are at times a strange bloody nation, so hypercritical and we wonder why so many suffer from depression," said Bob in a more frustrating voice.

"I have friends who have tried to have sex, they are not virgins by any stretch of the imagination, but they have reached a point in their careers and found that sex is painful, some can't even get their lips open wide enough to take a cock and that leads to arguments and frustration on their part, but they sit on it and don't seek help from the doctors. They can masturbate, but again there is that discomfort around the pelvic area as some are always running to spend pennies, then, of course, we woman suffer from cystitis and urine infections, and that makes you burn when you have a wee, and that hurts and of course incontinence is another problem. I wonder how many women exercise their pelvic areas, to relax and energise the lower body area. You are told to do that after the birth of a child. I bet not many; it's more about anxiety and how susceptible the woman might be. Being stressed puts pressure on the muscles, and that can repeat its self-down below, and the vagina remains shut no matter what you do to it as the vaginal muscles go into spasms when touched and their partners locked out at the most intimate moment they had hoped to share together. It is so sad, and of course, I have friends who are suffering like this and why I would be the envy of everybody if they knew what I was up to with you," said 'Sandy,'

Lifting her eyebrows and smiling with a hand giving soft strokes to his face, as she snuggled down against him as they continued their conversations, "You are so relaxing to be with, you are so laid back it's unbelievable that any man can be like that, you are so easy to talk to and not end up having issues and arguments, you are my secret in life and never one to be forgotten."

Again, she looked up into his face as her hand continued to stroke his

face.

"Well what a compliment that is, thanking you my princess you deserve all that I can give you sexually and more if I could, but then you really know we have fucked and I have fucked you way beyond your own imagination, I can remember in my teens a girl who wanted sex but I couldn't get it in she had vaginal spasms that made her tense up and here was me holding my dick and prodding her front door that remained shut, she was a virgin at the time, and it never happened with me, because in those days being young you were never given any instructions you found out the hard way, I later became more of a toy boy with older women and I had good mentoring in my younger years being shown how to please a woman sexually, but more importantly about a woman's emotional values and not to leave her hanging on as women take longer than a man and her feelings were not to be ignored as sadly so many men do, they shoot their load and then roll off and zip up," said Bob as he looked down at her as he gestured at his penis.

"Yes, I know that is where many men keep their brains, selfish they don't think about us women, just a leg over and be damned with the consequences is more like it," said Sandy with her strong viewpoint.

Even more sexual moments occurred during their time together at the hotel, but it was not as intense as the Friday night, it became more of cuddles, strokes, pampering and all over hot kisses from tip to toe.

A fantastic weekend of pure sexual indulgence where both bloody near shagged each other silly, but my goodness it was many hours of uninterrupted relaxing fun, where time was unimportant as the hotel suite was ideal as it provided just what any couple could have hoped for privacy and excellent hygiene facilities and no prying neighbours.

On route home, on Sunday morning Bob once again passed the rented house of Lenny Burns to establish that the vehicle was parked up in the driveway. Satisfied that the couple appeared somewhat settled in a routine, Bob decided on another route of contact, one by an official letter concerning the property held in the Miscellaneous Register as a taster to see if he would take the bait and contact him.

CHAPTER SIXTEEN

Police Pursuing the Criminals

PC Bob's (4 pm to midnight shift) meant three days of catching up on criminal matters, scouring through the incoming messages and crime reports showed a continued pattern of criminality occurring mainly in the early evenings. This was understandable as it meant criminals were able to conceal their movements by blending in with the first evening traffic and therefore not being a suspicious vehicle driving around late at night with several young males on board.

Bob was able to draft his letter to Lenny Burns with a request that he attends the Police station to examine property now in police custody and whether the same belonged to him or his associate Tommy Sands (Bob decided to mention his name to indicate the police knew who they were).

He was somewhat relieved that he was able to apply friendliness towards him in the structure of the letter hoping to avoid panic and alarm bells for him to ignore and flee. It was a very cordial letter that he asked colleagues to read and check as he received the thumbs up, before leaving the note in the Sergeants tray for approval, signature and external posting.

He also learnt from the crime prevention office that the police alarm had been removed from the underground construction at 'Marshalls Green' as this was now in the hands of the agents acting for the Business owners. It seemed in the last few days and in Bob's absence from duty that clarification had been made in the arrest of the six gipsies with the Land Rover incident earlier. Three had been released without charge and the three caught with the vehicle were placed on prison remand pending further enquiries concerning recent vehicle thefts and local burglaries.

Circulation had been forwarded to other police forces naming those arrested and their current whereabouts on remand and available for interview on request from the CID investigating officer at Divisional Headquarters.

Around six o'/clock, Bob had decided to patrol the high street for some fresh air. It was while he was ambling on his patrol that he met two of 'Sandy's friends coming out of an Off-licence carrying a 6-ply cardboard box of wine, this started their giggles on seeing Bob, he replied with a wave of pleasantries were exchanged between the three of them. Bob's thoughts in their passing turned to his previous conversation with 'Sandy' about some of her friends. His smiles continued as he moved on and then, of course, other passer bye began to smile, and so it continued for some minutes as Bob was chuckling to himself about these two women he had met and whether the wine would do them any good in their relationships. Bob knew that his thinking was naughty to focus and speculate on the sex lives of these two women as his mind turned to 'Sandy's previous conversation about her friends, but then it was a fact of life, and the mind was a funny old thing and hard to explain one's thoughts at times. That one hour on foot patrol made all the difference in being able to have that freedom away from the recent pressures of the continued saga of the gipsies, being around folk in their everyday lives.

This was when Bob caught sight of a large black foreign vehicle at the local petrol station, which was a gut feeling on his part that made him note the index number of the car out of curiosity. The vehicle gave the appearance of being one of those involved in the earlier conflicts with the local gipsies and the ongoing murder enquiries. He found it hard to believe that whoever these people are they would be utter fools to return at such a time with increased Police patrols or were they of callous minds and not fearful of detection. He established later with the petrol attendant that the driver of the vehicle was a different speaking male; the accent was not identified by the attendant but spoke more in broken English.

Back at the police station PC Bob was unaware at the time that foreign vehicles had been seen many times in the area. But never was there a vehicle index number taken, his was the first and later provided an address with some fifty miles away. In another Police Forces area and was interesting in its self from all the crime bulletins he had read from that area concerning massive burglaries (value of proceeds stolen) which again appeared to have been committed in the early evenings, gipsies, travellers were the suspected offenders for many of their crimes with no arrests made.

Bob also remembered something that Old Ben Witney had told him about Ampthill and a farm near a significant carriageway where stolen property was taken and sold, this Bob decided that this needed to be explored further with Old Ben and slip him a few more quid to keep him happy. After his meal break, he thought about popping up to the gipsy camp and see if he could locate Old Ben and see what he could glean from him, especially since the arrests of the six travellers. Meanwhile, he had asked his colleague on the front desk to pass on the vehicle details to the other force area about the foreign vehicle being seen in the village earlier and request any information they could provide to be faxed over ASAP.

By nine o'/clock and fairly dark Bob decided to drive out to the gipsy camp and try and tie up with Old Ben for a natter. It was on his way up to the camp that Bob passed the foreign vehicle he had seen earlier parked up and off the road, but no driver could be seen at the wheel. Bob continued his drive still very suspicious of the vehicle and who were these people as it had to be more than one of them because of the previous incidents and where at least two vehicles were involved when the traveller's body was thrown to the ground from a moving vehicle. Using the mileage gauge, he checked as to how many tenths of a mile from the foreign vehicle to the traveller's camp, the distance was less than he thought and realised across the country the range was even less if one was able to know the direction of the gipsy camp.

This made Bob very edgy as it may well be somewhere out in the fields there could be the driver and others making their way to the campsite under cover of darkness and was danger lurking or going to be imminent in his presence, he was concerned. As always Old Ben was easy to find as the smoke from his pipe gave the game away as it wafted up in the air in one long trailing spiral before evaporating in the air and leaving a strong-smelling aroma. Having a quick word about his suspicions and whether the danger was lurking. When Old Ben informed Bob that strangers were out on the field and watched for a good half hour. By their young ones, who were courting at the time, and now we're keeping an eye on them, “We know they are still in the field”, said Old Ben as he waited for Bob to speak,

"Right where are your dogs at this time, I have an idea,

let them out in the field, and I'll turn on the blue light and see if we can flush them out, what do you think Ben", said Bob.

Laughing, Old Ben liked the idea and went to find the dog owners, on their eventual return they went into the adjacent field as Bob turned on the blue light and listened out, the adult males had gone into the area and followed the trail of their dogs. Word came back that the idea appeared to have worked and panicked the intruders to the point of them breaking cover and ran back down towards the area of the parked vehicle. Bob felt relieved as he used his car radio and passed details to his controller to broadcast to all cars to be on the lookout for this vehicle and caution should be exercised as occupants could be armed and believed to be of foreign descent. Bob knew this would make everybody sit up and take notice by throwing a spanner in the works; it was needed in the hope that one of the armed response units may pick up the trail and give some attention to this vehicle.

This one moment changed the gipsies attitude towards PC Bob as others left their caravans and began to form a crowd around him expressing their thanks for his intervention, at the same time he was being called 'Sir and Governor' in their appreciation. It was Old Ben who again led him away from the assembling crowd to a higher point where one could look back down the valley towards the village. Headlights could be seen in the distance, but then again it could be any vehicle heading in that direction, there were no guarantees that it was the one Bob had seen earlier parked

up.

"Governor", said Old Ben, "What did they do to the gun

maker, he out on bail,"

"I can't tell you, I don't know Ben, I am in the dark about that," said Bob, enquiring more of his asking, he was now inquisitive as to another puzzle to piece together,

"What makes you ask that question, Ben," said Bob,

Seeking more of a complete answer hoping for something more constructive from Old Ben,

"You copper never took down the wall, did they, they missed all the stolen property it's been chored (steal) from all over, and the chainsaws, grinders and lots of other stuff are still there, so I heard," said Old Ben.

"What wall are we talking about Ben," said Bob, somewhat puzzled at his comment.

"The straw bales governor, like I said the Gun maker had made a false wall in his big barn. He stacks all those straw bales up to the roof, and he has a room behind that bales where he keeps all his nicked gear, did the police not find it," said Old Ben.

"I honestly don't know Ben, but I will find out, I'll check on it when I get back to the station," said Bob,

Old Bens questions had thrown a spanner in the works; Bob made sure that his colleagues. Were aware of everything Old Ben had told him. Also realising why, he kept referring to Ampthill. This farm location had a dry up Water Well on its land. And was somewhat deep and hollowed out at the base, to store stolen property. To Bob's recollection, none of this was ever talked about. Other than a proper arrest and stolen property found at the time, but no mention of a false wall or the Ampthill connection. Bob slipped Old Ben another twenty quid and promised that he would check on what he had just been told. For Bob, it was one of intrigue and a priority to get this sorted. As with Old Ben making mention of it, indicated that he knew that the hidden room had not been discovered among the straw bales, so why not, what had gone wrong with the information he passed over to the other police station that covered the area to where the farm was situated.

Back at the police station next day on early turn (7 am) duty starts Bob decided on a novel approach writing down his information (instead of passing over by telephone) with a request that his intelligence report is given through the appropriate channels for the attention of the CID dept. Of the other police station, more eyes that see his statement the better. As proof of his past actions having been ignored this ought to send alarm bells ringing. As to the previous cock-up or some other reason of untoward nonsense occurring, jealousy is always hard to accept among colleagues, and yet it was an occupational hazard with some personalities across his division, who acted out of plain spite and ignorance through their lack of policing skills.

No sooner had Bob finished his report when came a panic call from the Station Duty office downstairs for colleagues to hit the road as the foreign vehicle was being chased some miles out of their immediate area, but the first reports indicated that shots had been fired from the car at the pursuing police cars. Leaving their meal breaks three double crews scrambled and were soon heading towards the area of the chase. Listening to the radio, it was undoubtedly one of the manic moments with so many patrols trying to speak to one another. Due to the sparse locations of some of these vehicles with poor radio reception is a common factor of frustration for many officers due to the open countryside, and the many hidden valleys and dips in the contours of the landscape. So many black spots made it even more dangerous for officers driving through these narrow back lanes where little warning was afforded to oncoming traffic requiring sensible driving rather than speed as often criminals would leave their vehicles stationary blocking the narrow lanes and escape on foot, more often than not the high banks of the hedgerows prevented doors from opening, being at the mercy of not defending themselves as officers would be trapped in their vehicles and would be easy targets to attack.

Bob realised that the balloon had gone up and all hell was now let loose with shots fired and a vehicle chase ongoing somewhere in the country lanes, this was the most dangerous scenario one could imagine for the general public as these lanes needed to be blocked off immediately, this Bob pursued in haste leaving some residents unhappy about the roadblocks occurring when he had to turn some motorists away and explain the reasons to others was time-consuming, still some of the public found it hard to obey. Eventually, he found some locals prepared to use their vehicles to block the junctions to stop others entering the danger zone of the pursuing police vehicles.

The helicopter appeared overhead, the low decent was deafening from the sounds of the jet engines blasting, and the rotor blades swirling up the dust and lose debris more like a bloody sandstorm he thought as he covered his eyes from the clouds of flying dust. The pilot had come low to work back up the lane to see where the crossovers of the lanes meet and the many hidden locations of sufficient size to hide a vehicle that could be identified for those working the ground in pursuit.

It had been a canny move on his Policing colleagues engaged in the vehicle chase; it was clear from the radio chat that surrounding roads and country lanes had been cordoned off and, in many cases, blocked off by heavy goods vehicles. This placed the onus on the driver of the foreign car, to realise he was on the road to nowhere and ought to stop and surrender. But then whoever else in the vehicle had crossed the line by using firearms and shots fired at the police earlier engaged a more significant police presence trying to bring this vehicle chase to a safe ending. Two police vehicles had been rammed earlier and been pushed aside as the car continued at high speed to escape. The vehicle being of foreign make was on appearances, a heavily constructed vehicle with high ground clearance, and what appeared to be fitted to a long-wheeled base chassis, apparently a sturdy, weighty car now used by the driver as a bulldozer against the vehicles trying to bring the car to a halt.

The driver realised he was running out of options when entering a narrow lane heading towards Forestry Commission land about one mile from the junction, eventually the driver on approach of a five barred gate, left the lane and smashed straight through the wooden structure at such speed the gate completely disintegrated on impact as the vehicle momentarily left the ground on all four wheels before thumping back down to earth, as the driver continued at speed on a forestry track that was now well off any solid road surface, pursuing police vehicles entered the forestry land and abruptly came to a halt as others arrived in a growing number of marked police cars assembled before any instructions were given to continue pursuing the vehicle over dirt tracks.

Local farmers were again alerted and assistance sort regarding large machinery to be brought to the location and deployed in forming a barrier inside forestry land to block any escape route by the foreign vehicle.

Behind the line of soldier-like formation remained the assembled police vehicles along with three-armed response crews and cars. The duty Inspector who was the acting controller on the ground briefed all officers and some farmers who remained behind and had good knowledge of the surroundings. So, it became more of a waiting game for the Helicopter to provide information as to where precisely the vehicle was positioned, while this was happening Forestry staff members arrived with survey maps of the ground area. It was a massive landscape of thick woodland and good ground cover for concealment. Being a local officer from the area Bob arrived on scene and met with the Duty Inspector' who outlined his thoughts and wanted Bob to add any knowledge he could input at that moment, Bob suggested more use of the farmers present as they had years of experience of working the land and would know of every crook and cranny, not even the Forestry staff present could equal their knowledge to that of the farmers. So now a waiting game continued as police vehicles were shunted around the location and parked in some order rather than the melee that first assembled.

It took the Helicopter crew a good thirty minutes to locate the vehicle. By their heat sensors on board there were at least four persons in the car, as before when chasing earlier it was known that there were at least two in the car, one the driver the other the shooter, due to the black tinted windows others could not be seen at the time. Bob gave thought to what had been fed back to the

Duty Inspector and added a further comment with regards to the numerous incidents that had been occurring up and around the gipsy camp.

"There have been two vehicles driving around the area and attacking the gypsy site, this was the case when the dead gipsy youth was dumped at the side of the road and that as you know is a murder, so where is the other vehicle, I passed on the index number of this vehicle and I understand there is a registered address some fifty miles away. We ought to get that address checked out and find the second vehicle, perhaps the local station can tell us more about the address and perhaps the occupants," said Bob, more anxious than ever for this to be taken more seriously regarding cross-border crime.

The Inspector was unaware of the second vehicle and requested by mobile phone to his station to have this address followed up by the local station shown on the vehicle registration. So now all officers were aware that the vehicle had been located and that the four occupants remained in the car and were parked about half a mile from the current Police positions. This became a more significant frustration as by staying in the vehicle. Attack dogs could not be used against them, so how was it going to be possible to entice them to leave the car and remain on foot. Furthermore, were they armed was the real growing worries of the Inspector, although, our armed response teams were present, it was more of a game of patience and not to have officers lives endangered any more than it has to in the current circumstances, at least the vehicle was off road and not a danger to other motorists, so it was one of containment being the first priority, the car certainly wouldn't get past the tractor barrier across the woodland and dirt track entrance, it remained a wall of solid steel and very imposing with so many machines parked up and facing inwards so if darkness should fall without resolve vehicle lights could be used to trail blaze the dirt track.

An hour later the situation was a stalemate as no movement had been detected by the Helicopter and of course, there was going to be a time when they will have to leave for refuelling, and that would be a vulnerable time for officers on the ground. Word came back from the other Police force concerning the second vehicle; it was found parked up at the address. It appeared the occupants of the house were a mixture of Russian and Romanian, gangster types involved in burglaries, protection racketeering and prostitution. Local police had been engaged concerning their loud parties and drunkenness over the summer months, and locals were fed up with their behaviour and the comings and goings that were occurring right through the night.

The Inspector put out a call to the army base for an armoured vehicle to be borrowed to approach the foreigners holding up in the woods. The request had to go through various channels of police and military levels of command and then the wait as to whether permission would be granted, considering there was little danger to the occupants of an armoured vehicle it was agreed along with two servicemen as driver and navigator, so a further wait entailed whilst the arrangements came into play. One officer had taken the small police van into town and came back with cold and hot refreshments for the waiting officers as time was passing rather slowly and boredom was now the most significant worry and the loss of concentration by some officers.

Eventually, the army arrived with the mobile armoured

vehicle, and soon the Inspector and armed response officers were quickly packed into the car as it trundled on down the dirt track towards where the foreigners were hiding. Now it was a tense waiting game, whether they would surrender without a fight or whether they would shoot it out was anyone's guess at this time. After hearing the loud hailer echo the voice of the Inspector, as he addressed the foreigners. Then shots could be heard, crack, crack, crack echoed out and then much shouting and once again the Inspectors voice could still be heard of the loud hailer appealing for them to surrender, then more shots rang out, it sounded like a mini-war was taking place deep in the woods. After some minutes the armoured vehicle reappeared and returned to the assembly point of waiting officers. It was about to become a nightmare scenario as to how to get them to move from their position so long as they remained in the vehicle the dangers were visible, it could not be done safely without death or injury, the risks were too high, and something more would be required at this time.

The helicopter provided video footage relayed back to their headquarters which provided a clear view of where this vehicle was positioned and whether it would be an easy task to remove them or were they too wedged in for officers on the ground to approach them. It necessitated a senior officers conference to be urgently convened and included an invitation to the local military base for their expertise. Other senior officers more local began to arrive as it was clear that this situation would be picked up by the media and then they would all be clamouring for a position to the unfolding rodeo.

More was to come from this situation as it was decided that the address which had earlier been checked out ought to be subject of a 'Search Warrant' as this was going to require a support team from that force area,

to turn the place over. So, it was organised at a high command that when ready to deal with the concealed vehicle the other force would raid the address first to avoid any mobile use or instructions being given as to what may be found at the property, so it was to be one of coordination.

At the same time, Bob was released to return to his Police Station as his presence was required concerning another operation that involved the 'Gun Maker', arriving back at the station Bob was pleased to see Sgt Anderson had returned from sick leave, it was him who had requested Bob's return. Sgt Anderson outlined the results of the other stations 'Search Warrant' that had been executed on the 'Gun Maker'. It had been more than successful once they had found their way into the hidden room, then it meant all the hay bales had to be removed, which in turn revealed an Aladdin's gold mine of stolen property. The false wall had obviously served a criminal purpose for the individual for years, and why there was never any success in this area of criminality, now the local CID had their claws into this fellow, and he was singing like a canary and what do you know Ampthill came up time and again, the exact location of your information, so from small acorns grows one bloody big operation that is going to take some clearing up but already the crime book§ are out and being browsed for clear ups, Bob you have hit one of the biggest crime busts of your service. So, more officers are being brought in as a joint operation with support group units doing the farm at Ampthill. They are currently waiting on their 'Search Warrant' so this has all the forces talking at this point as it's a mismatch of finding officers to make up the teams, Bob sat back and smiled as Sgt Anderson continued speaking, you could hear in his voice the excitement, it was the shot in the arm that they had all been wanting for months, to get stuck into the crime wave that had been boiling for many months and now that big break and faces full of smiles and many will be thinking of the overtime from this. Sgt Anderson took Bob into the kitchen for coffee making, as he was ecstatic and could not stop praising Bob enough for all he had done throughout. It took time for this to hit Bob as to the enormity of what he had achieved but also realising that this would never have happened if it weren't for Old Ben Witney sending him on his way with puzzles to solve.

"Skipper do you know how things are progressing up in the Forestry", said Bob.

"No not really, it's clear they have no protection at Headquarters they are having a conference about what steps to take, I suspect they will have to get help from the military, it's interesting that none had broken cover but stayed with the vehicle", said Sgt Anderson.

"Makes you wonder who we are dealing with, could they be from a military background. They seem organised and not bothered if we see them, certainly not shy, to say the least, they don't seem to care about anything", said Bob still with a suspicious mind about the background of these foreigners.

Sgt Anderson informed Bob that he had left a fascinating document in his docket with a note attached for comments.

"When you were on that month's course, did you ever hear about a large crime caper happening in the Bristol Area. It happened around the same time as the Manor

House fire, and of course with so much going on down here. We have not shown any real interest as it only affects us by the very fact of finding the stolen property. Well, what's in your docket is an outline to what's been stolen. It's taken months to put together; it was a well-run operation. They had no bodies were in custody. So, the appeal has gone out to all forces and to try a resurrect some interest that is positive, they have no leads, the document is a brilliant piece of writing in laying out a very complex situation and no forensics either to go on, they are fucked for answers", said Sgt Anderson.

"Well why not take a look at this lot that is on us now, clearly violent criminals and prepared to use firearms, I mean where had they been all night parked up somewhere, I had seen them chased off the gypsy camp they had been spying on, what a time to be turned up on a vehicle chase, they had not been up to any good I bet you a bottom dollar that is the case and now they are trapped up in the woods, there still are some missing pieces to this puzzle, as Old Ben was certain there was some exquisite quality jewellery stolen and he thinks that's why the foreigners are chasing the young travellers, but none of that has turned up if that is the case", said Bob, pondering on his words he stood shaking his head.

The front office informed Sgt Anderson that the incident was now a siege and it was all about containment and nothing more until they were able to resolve the equipment to use in flushing them out. The vehicle was apparently built like a tank and equipped with a potent engine giving fast acceleration, so it was a tall order to try and unseat them without the right equipment on hand.

Bob was well satisfied with his days' work and wanted to get off home to relax. So, finishing at three o'/clock, he was soon out the back door of the station. Avoiding other ranks who were sorting out the personal numbers and those who were going to be allocated overtime to stay on duty and Bob did not want to be compromised, out of sight, out of mind was his motto of the moment. When leaving the station yard, it was obvious the cat was out of the bag as the press and media were hovering at the front of the Police station looking for their story.

Early turn shift Wednesday saw Bob back on duty and the news of the day was good to hear, the army had challenged the occupants of the vehicle, well it was considered to be more sinister and possibly one of a terrorist act so under the 'Terrorism Act' the authorities decided to act and to stop media speculation as many were amassing, although, prior Bob heard that the Search Warrant executed at the vehicles address proved very fruit and was a fantastic result in finding a number of young prostitutes, drugs and lots of other bits and pieces, so a good result by all. Senior officers were well chuffed with so much cleared up in a matter of hours. This meant that he could catch up on his briefing board and study the Bristol intelligence document thoroughly in more detail.

Later that day it was 'Sandy's phone call to Bob which he dreads the most, her husband was returning home from abroad the following Tuesday. She urged Bob to spend the whole of the coming weekend with her at the house. For what was most likely to be their last time together as she had previously suggested or rather hinted that her husband was coming home for good, possibly taking early retirement, although, Bob was none the wiser as to her husband's occupation.

At eleven o'/clock on Friday morning a couple approached the front desk of the Police Station requesting the presence of PC Bob Benyon, the man gave his name as 'Lenny Burns', when Bob heard the news he nearly fell of the bloody chair he was sitting on, he turned at colleagues and clasped his hands to his face,

"Fucking hell, what next, I cannot believe that he has shown up", said Bob,

As he left the briefing room and bounded down the stairs in such a rush that he nearly came a cropper on the bottom tread. At the front counter, he introduced himself to 'Lenny Burns' who in turn presented him with his original letter.

"Right hold on a minute let me get the property from the store", said Bob,

Within minutes he had returned with a large cardboard box. He asked 'Lenny' to check the contents for him, and then explained the reasons for the contact and to return the property. He continued to explain how this was left in the local pub, although that night he left on a month's course and was away from the Police Station. When he returned the landlady of the pub had told him that the box had been left for him a month earlier by a fellow he had met in the pub and shared stories about the gipsies. This made 'Lenny' more forthcoming and appeared more relaxed at the story told by Bob; it was then that Karen closed in and hung onto Lenny's arm as if to reassure him that everything was okay, whatever that was supposed to mean, but then only they both knew the answer.

"The fact is I must hand it back, I can't use or keep any of it, only we found our way into your man cave at 'Marshalls Green', and it's taken us awhile to identify you the owners of the manor house, so tragic, so sad, but it must have been your friend who left this for me, ('Tommy Sands') only it was suggested that he and I believe a young lady companion had perished in the fire, as yet the cause has not been established, so on finding the man cave we Police alarmed the property due to the continuing gypsy problems we are experiencing, the alarm has now been removed and handed back to the agents of the property. More importantly, no bodies were found among the fire debris, although, we did have death occur that was somebody in the petrol tanker that crashed into the building", said Bob as he searched the face of Lenny for clues.

"Petrol tanker you say crashed into the house, I don't understand as to how that could have happened, we are on a gradient hill and well off the lane", said Lenny with a rather curious but enquiring comment, "That is strange that is".

Bob realised that this was not known by 'Lenny', it came like a bolt out of the blue as he watched his face look confused.

"I assume as to what I have told you. You weren't at the house on the night of the fire, and it must have been yourselves who collected the three dogs as you were both captured on the security camera at the pub, that is how I was able to locate you", said Bob.

So the whereabouts of your friend 'Tommy Sands' is not known and he has not been subject of a missing person report, other than the fact you are both occupants of the house and now destroyed by fire, leaves just the property in your man cave as you need to be sure that it remains secure as the gypsies are everywhere at the moment as we have had some nasty incidents and two murders all this since the house fire, we do have other matters pending with regards to foreigners either Russian speaking or Romanian.

"I need a signature on here please, and that is it, so please pass on my regards should your friend appear and thank him for his thoughts on the box", said Bob.

Lenny signed the receipt, and he and Karen left the Police station with a cardboard box full of electronics, Bob was well satisfied with the result another job well done, and he had met 'Lenny' for the first-time face to face, he felt good and realised how attractive Karen was in the flesh. But Lenny never gave any indication that he knew Tommy's whereabouts or whether he had spoken with him since the fire, typical villain always playing matters close to one's chest.

CHAPTER SEVENTEEN

The Affair was to End This Weekend

So, it came to be that Bob at short notice managed to take two annual leave days for the coming Saturday and Sunday respectfully. 'Sandy' was ecstatic at the news as she decided on making this the most memorable weekend together. Memories that would last their lifetime as for him it was to be the last weekend of the 'Long Penis' that reached deep into the darkness of her pudenda, a forbidden and yet highly sought after a place that left the richness of man's gift to be nurtured into a new life.

So, it came to be that Bob finished his early shift at two o'/clock on a Friday afternoon. Straight home to change and reorganise himself and by late afternoon 'Sandy' had arranged a pick-up point away from his house, within a few minutes' drive she pulled into her open garage as Bob was hiding on the backseat of the vehicle. Entering the house through the side gate the couple were soon in the kitchen locked together in one passionate moment, and that moment became a greater urgency. As he stripped 'Sandy' naked as he laid her back onto the kitchen table, as he knelt on the floor and placed his lips up against her vagina as he gently placed kisses around and along her inner thighs.

At the same time, he also was undressing with awkwardness as he continued to kiss her inner thighs, this also made 'Sandy' smile as she felt the warmth of his breath up against her slightly open vagina. Finally, back on his feet and almost naked with his trousers round his ankles. He took hold of her legs and placed each over his arms, his hands gently cupping her knees as he parted her legs and dragged her body across the surface of the table. As his penis poked, poked and poked at her letterbox, it needed oiling as both could hear the squeakiness of her lips gulping, inhaling and exhaling air as he opened and closed her legs with his actions, looking down her pouting lips were like that of a Carp out of water gasping for air. Finding the right moment and without a hand on his penis he pushed and entered her, his momentum continued back and forth, like a turning piston that revolved as her body polished the surface of the table as he gave meaningful looks into her eyes having created a highly sexual atmosphere between them, an environment that was so mountainous that he had already taken 'Sandy' to her first orgasm, as he saw her face beam and lightened her eyes then close and at the same time showing the tip of her tongue moisten her dry lips. Bob was somewhat surprised by her silence as normally when she reached an orgasm, she was the 'cavewoman' echoing loud deep throaty grunts, sounding like a Donkey sound, a see-saw noise. By this time Bob was still up and hard as he continued to bring her off for the second time, although, this time she was dripping wet as with each movement a squelching noise echoed as flesh met flesh in the heat of their highly charged passion. He lowered her legs to hang over the table as he leaned into her body grasping her nipples and cupping her breasts. He was gentle as he stroked her belly and up under her arms and back round to her breasts and nipples. When finally, he managed to take hold of a nipple between his lips. At the same time, 'Sandy' held the back of his head, her fingers foraged and rubbed his scalp while he sucked her like a babe at teatime wanting milk. It felt good in the way he continued to manipulate her nipple and breast; it made her give out deep sighs as her chest heaved and relaxed under his weight across her body.

Finally, he came in long warm spurts that she acknowledged as she wriggled making the squeaking noises of her backside rubbing on the surface of the table. When Bob stood upright and back from the table 'Sandy' reached down with both hands and placed them on either side of her vagina. As her legs bent at the knees came to rest with her feet on the edge of the table her legs wide apart as she gently massaged her flesh into the crevice of her inner thighs.

(The rhythmic movements of their coitus energies was the beginnings of a lasting sexual journey that would engage the whole of their weekend together, and where orgasms never needed to be compared to the last, as each was a new adventure in its self, as to the many positions they tried in advancing their lovemaking techniques, without burning the candle at both ends where soreness and discomfort to their sexual parts would foreclose on their shared experiences)

Exchanging smiles 'Sandy' reached down and retrieved her briefs from the floor and wiped between her legs, Bob saw the perspiration on her back shimmer with her wiping motions; he grinned to himself about the number of calories they had both used in the last thirty plus minutes. While both still naked 'Sandy' beckoned Bob into the lounge where she had prepared some canapés, with small triangular sandwiches plated under cling film and a coffee dispenser spouting steam with a choice of milk or cream alongside. This amused Bob, as clearly 'Sandy' had gone to a lot of preparation to make this a final moment for them both to cherish. As time slowly ticked away before the final curtain came down on their shared affair and they went in opposite direction of their lives, as Bob felt this was to be their last time together. He knew very little about her, where did 'Sandy' originate from, what her background was and how their affair began as if 'Sandy' had specifically chosen him in the beginning when they first met in the car park, fascinated to know the answer to his questions as he had questioned on other occasions then dismissive of his thoughts, it didn't matter in the least as he was the one who had been fucking her for weeks, so his questions were irrelevant to the moment as he also agreed to be her 'Friend with Benefits' and no questions asked and he the Policeman should accept her confidentiality on the agreement they both shared.

From eating and drinking coffee together, it soon became an endearment on 'Sandy's part to stand in front of Bob, and stare into his face. As with one hand she took hold of his floppy penis and led him from the lounge, up the stairs and into the bathroom, Bob trotted along with her actions as she had taken charge of the moment as she ushered him into the shower with her. While showering Bob paid attention to the area around her clitoris as 'Sandy' stood with her legs apart and her hands rubbing shampoo into her hair. At the same time as Bob stood behind her with a finger on her sexual button as he continued to play with her 'Quincy' 'Sandy' remained well lubricated from their earlier fucking as he entertained her 'Muffin' with his penis. Hitting the jackpot at the right moment and on target as he felt the smoothness of her silky lining squeezing and squeezed as she tightened her muscles and held him. As he took hold of his balls at times that pressed right against her gateway of femininity.

It was no more than around seven o'/clock by the time they both settled down on 'Sandy's bed wrapped in large bath towels, as he cuddled up to her. As there is a horny moment when Bob turns onto his side and exposes her breasts as he leans in and covers a nipple with his lips, teasing as he used his tongue to touch the tip then to hold the nipple between his teeth with gentle pulls and nips, he felt 'Sandy' react as she wriggled, and her legs began to thrash around as the heels of her feet were at times pushed deep into duvet cover, as with one hand on the nape of his neck she pushed him hard against her body as she whimpered and once again Bob saw her complexion redden under her chin and across her chest. As he realised she was on a right royal flush of multiple orgasms, then turned towards him and held him tight. As Bob felt her tremors and shudders shake them both before she finally relaxed laying across his body as her lips were buried deep into his neck. As she had taken the opportunity to kiss and suckle his flesh as he felt the warmth of her lips move up to his own, and then engage in lengthy passionate kisses that gave real meaning and depth to their lovemaking as her fingers rummaged through his hair, then slowly her movements became less as she stopped and remained cuddled up to him as he heard her sighs as she appeared to fall asleep from her exertion as he heard her purring lips breathe out in gentle whispers.

So the hours ticked away into the early hours of Saturday morning both remained naked on the bed, having already felt Bob muff dive as he had gently parted her legs once again as he placed his tongue round her vagina lips, but at the same time she felt the coldness of the lubrication as he was using one of her sex toys to penetrate her which made her shiver at his first attempt, as he used a finger to entice the door to focus on his touch and easy on the hinges so that he could ease into her the lubricated toy which he played with in gentle motions and at times rocking from side to side. 'Sandy' became more awake by his actions to where he withdrew the sex toy and lifted both her legs back up towards her shoulders. This was a right missionary position for her as she felt the pressure on her chest as Bob placed his penis right deep into her, as she let out a sequel. As he went deep into her from his position and it felt good from 'Sandy's point of view. As she had all his Penis length inside of her and possibly accompanied by his balls. As it really felt fantastic it was a right meaty moment as she let Bob work her silly, then those long withdrawing thrusts that came thundering back with such force that he was pushing her up the bed, as she had hold of his arms at the time, his deep penetrative technique had certainly reached her deep shagging well which she found exquisite and way beyond her desires as Bob's hand had slid underneath their bodies, As he took a finger and rimmed her anus with such sensitivity that it made her squirm violently in trying to escape, as she felt her mind exploding, with a penis 'like-rock' deep inside her with a pounding chest and heart beats ringing in her ears, this was pure ecstasy, this was an indulgence she never expected, especially occurring in the early hours of the morning as she joined in the thrashing that intensified as again she felt the orgasmic explosion rip through her body and her screeching voice that echoed and bounced off the four walls of the bedroom it was deafening when she finally came to rest she was all of a fluster,

"Oh! My God, what has just happened, what a fuck you have given me Bob, Oh! My God, you have fucking nailed me with that rendition. Bloody hell my hearts thumping, bells ringing in my ears and a fanny that is on fire and my arse is buzzing," said 'Sandy' somewhat perplexed as to the new heights Bob had taken her, "I am drained of energy Bob, God! you have fucked me hard tonight. You know how to surprise me, where does it keep coming from."

"Practice makes perfect, my older mentors from my teenage years my girl, being a toy boy and being able to self-control and go the greater distance. Otherwise, one spurt and I am like the rest blown a gasket, roll off and roll over and sleep for a couple of hours to recharge my sperm count," said Bob with a big grinning smile that was so infectious it made 'Sandy' laugh along with him.

The early morning events were more than overwhelming for both to have slept late and so the new day began like the night before with interrupted sleep and lots of engaging physical sex that reaches depths and heights in some of the most extraordinary ways possible from taking her in a: -

(1) Doggy position that was animalistic, fucking her on all fours was a godsend, as it was hands free to caress her hanging breasts with one hand and the other to stimulate 'Sandy's clitoris, where allegedly the elusive 'G'-spot sits in the roof part of the vagina wall whilst still being able to have a penetrative penis pushed deep inside of her, this made her sing out like a melodious Nightingale.

(2) The Wheelbarrow partnership by entering 'Sandy' from the rear, raising her hindquarters as 'Sandy'

balanced on her hands, as Bob had mounted her deep between her widespread legs. This she enjoyed and squealed and laughed a lot as he moved her around the floor.

(3) The Spooning effect post-coital cuddling up from behind with both hands-free to roam and touch her body parts intimately, perhaps also this is a fast track to orgasm by massaging her breasts., as it was a comfortable position to be inside the vagina. 'Sandy' loved her close-up cuddles and Bob obliged as he held her tight while he stroked and touched her flesh in kind.

(4) The Sixty-Nine position is a great position for hearing all those sucking noises of the flesh as both sets of lips attack from opposite sides of the spectrum giving a close-up view of each other's undercarriage, with one mouth on the vagina and the other gobbling the penis.

(5) The Missionary position is the most regular of positions that most afford for a good shag. Either lying down or standing with one's arse pressed up a brick wall made a minor difference so long as you got the penis inside, so face-to-face fucking is looking into each other's eyes as the penis reaches up and tickles the inner lips while standing or deeper if laying down on top of the woman. Either way, it's quick and easy without having to strip off naked, just pull the panties to one side and you are in. Her dress remained on but pulled up to the waist, fuck for as long as you can from the male's point of view, she stands with a wet dripping pussy.

It was as it began a 'Friends for Benefits' arrangement agreed between two participating adults. Who was more than sexually compatible, for 'Sandy' she sought the experimental excitement of an affair with a partner able to maintain standards by varying and trying the many styles and positions of making love, it was the quality they both sought and provided each other? While Bob's position was very different to 'Sandy's, being separated and believing that his marriage was finally to end with his wife having left the matrimonial house some weeks before to stay with family. 'Sandy's appearance was more by chance, although, it did cross Bob's mind as to whether he had been chosen, either way, 'Sandy' was married and alone with a husband having long working spells away from home, much seemed to be abroad somewhere in Europe. She was a tall woman with a slim, lithe figure, obviously extremely fit, her bust line was neat with a well-shaped leg, she was the dream woman of any man's desires, but above all, she had a personality. Always smiling with sensible makeup attire around the eyes with soft and inviting lips that needed little colouring, she was in hindsight a natural beauty who displayed the real sides of femininity and not pretentious, speaks with a soft well-spoken voice that had its twang of an accent that drew one to her.

There was a moment in the latter moments of their relationship where Bob gently prized a little more of her side as he complimented on her is not only a desirable and willing partner but one who had no inhibitions with him that made their affair even more unique in what they shared together. Bob described that first moment they met then their first Fuck that electrified him to wonder if it was a one-off. He was very candid as he spoke and maintained his manly dignity but stressed that if there had been another time in their lives, he would have been chasing 'Sandy's arse up and down dale and that they would never want to leave the house. But more seriously he found that she would have been a fantastic choice for a wife. One who engaged in the right way, who was experimental but more to the point of having that kind of endearing personality that was unflappable, one that needed to have siblings suckling her breasts and choice was never too much for her to moan and groan as he also had been with her during her period times of menstruation, she was a well-balanced all round woman that dreams are made of and he could not hide his feelings any further as he explained what he had found in her as someone exceptional and your husband is a bloody fool to be away so often. 'Sandy' having listened and smiled as her hands stroked his face before leaning forward and passionately kissed him, even the saliva joined them both at the lips as she parted from him. Bob explained his reasons for voicing his opinions as this being our last time together. I just could not let you go without you understanding my thoughts and feelings being uppermost for you to know that any time in the future you will know how to reach me should you ever need help and at no time, no matter what, you are never to be alone in my thoughts.

Neither had been dressed from their Friday teatime encounter in the kitchen, so it seemed rather strange to see 'Sandy' naked and sat on a chair with her hands clasped between her legs as she bent over in deep thought on this Saturday early evening. Bob stood back and left her side as he went off to make coffee for them both, 'Sandy' remained in deep thought and obviously chewing over Bob's words, minutes later 'Sandy' entered the kitchen and placed an arm round Bob's waist as he turned to face her, 'Sandy' placed her head on his chest and clung to him without any words being uttered, Bob realised that he had touched a raw nerve as he saw the tears trickling down his naked chest, 'Sandy' was quietly crying to herself as he too could feel her emotions building inside of her as again she turned and kissed him with a greater and more urgent passion, he realised how tough this had been on her and now there was that final moment when with one day left before they finally parted as her destiny remained unknown as it all hinged on her husband's decision and choice as to where or what he intended for the couple's future together and this would happen after his return on Tuesday.

The remainder of the weekend continued in the way of their choosing being sexually charged and fucking each other like no tomorrows, with Bob being on a Rest day on Monday it was decided that he stay over and leave sometime during the morning. So come the Monday morning both had continued to remain naked throughout the weekend and it was that one moment when he was about to follow 'Sandy' up the stairs when he grabbed her waist from behind, 'Sandy' bent forwards with her hands resting on a stair tread with her naked arse exposed to Bob as he leaned in and began to prise his tongue towards her hidden vagina between the crease of her thighs, she in return parted her legs wide as Bob stood up and took hold of his growing member and aimed towards her pillar box in the undergrowth, by which time 'Sandy' had gone to ground with her arms now supporting on the stair tread with her knees perched on a lower tread as Bob had mounted her in this fashion, and both became more of a contortionist in this position and very uncomfortable, even though he was inside of her he decided to withdraw and chase 'Sandy' up the stairs to the bedroom to finish off what he had started on the bed. It was that loving feeling that made this so special and so intimate for the last time of their togetherness, it should and was dramatic in the way it happened, so slow and gentle, he withdrew time and again to her open vagina lips and then eased in and out in such a rhythmic way that 'Sandy' was reaching a frenzy as she was taken to a peek to orgasm and then he relaxed and continued to move gently back and forth to a point where she placed her legs round his waist and her arms round his neck as she pulled him into her as she bucked and rocked her torso on his penetration, he was buried deep and he was pushing hard against her pubic bone as they both came together with that final explosion of a dripping wet and moistened vagina and a penis covered in a white membrane of sticky love that had spurted deep into the silky depths of her womanhood.

'Sandy' agreed for Bob to video his last withdrawal from her in memory of their last fuck together as vagina and penis partod company for the last time of their ending passionate affair. As fitting to their perpetual lovemaking, a lasting private and comforting moment in time that will never be lost between them. Later Bob sent a copy to 'Sandy's mobile which included the time and date it was taken and now set in stone always of the secret they shared.

Later that morning after a late breakfast 'Sandy' and Bob left the house by the back door, as he climbed into the back seat of her car, hidden from prying eyes as she drove to Bob's drop off point for the very last time. The ending was emotional for both of them as Bob left a small gift on the passenger seat as he alighted from the vehicle and walked off without looking back; turning a corner he was out of sight of 'Sandy' as he continued to walk home, those last few yards were monumental in terms of the loneliness he felt as if from behind every curtain eyes were upon him as if the whole street knew of his secret.

Once indoors Bob soon showered and went straight to bed, his mind swirling with many imaginative thoughts about 'Sandy', her husband, his marriage and the time he had left in the Police service, but above all he was physically knackered from such a long weekend of pure unadulterated sexual pleasure the likes he had never experienced, with his balls on fire and a very aching penis that needed to be calm and not aroused on this very hour of his tiredness.

CHAPTER EIGHTEEN

Life is Full of Unexpected Surprises

It was the following Saturday that Bob on High Street patrol at around eleven o'/clock caught sight of 'Sandy' outside the local supermarket with an older man the couple were engaged with two of her friends whom Bob had recognised. Bob realised that 'Sandy' had married a much older man, clean-shaven, balding and grey-haired wearing wire-framed glasses, height around five feet eight inches. Sporting the overlapping of a pot belly held back by the belt of his trousers, in fact not the kind of man he pictured as her partner, they were like chalk and cheese together. So, what was the attraction the connection that kept them together, he did not look the virile type with energy to pleasure and fuck his wife in the manner she was accustomed to him. Here was a man some twenty year's older than her, with no children from their marriage and she very much remained a single woman in her husband's absence. So a professional man who wore sobering clothes and his wife the complete opposite in her dress code of wearing vibrant colours and modern styles of dress with above knee length dresses, often going without underwear were very much describing a woman who enjoyed the sexual freedom that endorsed her openness and her lack of inhibitions this coupled with her passion for life that displayed her raw femininity and exercised her personality that was uplifting to any male ego who saw her as a challenge and who would be very disappointed as to where her loyalties lie with only one man who reciprocated her loving and accepting her nakedness at all times. When the group parted 'Sandy' and her husband entered the supermarket, as he moved on further down his beat, so their paths would not compromise each other. Although he slowly walked with many thoughts churning over in his mind about her, his memories and a video clip of their last fuck together, he nodded and shook his head with a grinning smile in disbelief as to his affair with her; it's what all men dream of and one without complications.

Weeks passed and not one sighting of 'Sandy' during that time, although she was not far from his thoughts, although, his wife had returned home in the meantime and somewhat pregnant. His wife appeared without warning midweek after he last saw 'Sandy' and her husband that previous weekend. Having returned home after finishing an early turn shift, he entered his house by the front door only to find the hallway littered with women's underwear of all colours and shapes from bras, panties and slips. It was that moment of sheer panic that sent a chill down his spine and a stomach-churning sickness. Not knowing what to believe then his thoughts turned to 'Sandy' had she gained access to his house. Was she in the house, when from the kitchen his wife appeared naked in the doorway, she turned sideways to show off her bump, Bob stood perplexed and confused at what he was seeing, his wife seemed to be pregnant, but how?

"Bob, I am pregnant, we ought to have spent more time at the bottom of the garden, don't you think", said his wife with a smiling face that glowed with her delight and motherhood growing inside of her.

Bob was lost for words as he sat on the bottom tread of the stairs with his head in his hands not knowing what to believe. And yes, the seduction of him by his wife before she left to be with her family made sense. But why the secrecy he thought, why, as if this was some game she was playing, none of this made sense he was left alone by her absence and not one word of sorts had he received from her. His wife closed the front door, and stood in front of him and bent over, as her hands rubbed his back. He lifted his head to be staring at her swollen stomach, and her neatly trimmed pubic-line that he hadn't seen in months that was staring back at him as if to say a 'job well-done mate'. Bob explained to his wife that he could not comprehend what he was witnessing and why was there such a secret, why he believed their marriage was over and much more besides in the way their relationship had been heading and expected that a divorce was on the cards. He ached inside from others knowing of his pain and separation that had been tormenting him for many months and it had been sole destroying for him to believe in the cruel way she had left their home to join her family and not one word of comfort had she left him on the day she went.

"It's a boy, Bob, look here is the picture of the scan," said his wife,

As she handed him the picture, by this time Bob was crying tears flowed down his cheeks as he wiped away his sniffles as he took the picture from her. Apparently, it was a time for talking and once he had come to terms with her return and the very fact that she was pregnant made it even more difficult to relate to her at this time. It was a strange scenario on seeing his wife naked at this time, and the way she had seduced and fucked him before she left. It didn't make sense, so their conversations continued long into the evening and the days that followed as Bob had requested a 'DNA' test as it was going to be necessary for him to accept that he was the father of the child she was carrying. His wife had agreed to his demands, by the way, she had acted, and her mistreatment of him, and her departure from his life, without warning over the many months of the past. And now she was trying to salvage their marriage. And to go back to where they once were, as a couple. But both knew that it was going to be a long and winding road they shared to make things right and not necessarily would the birth of a child make it right for their future together. It took weeks for this situation to be accepted and acknowledged by all in sundry, especially finding out that his parents knew of her pregnancy before he did, which helped him understand her sincerity and her responsibility towards his parents, as they hoped and longed for a grandchild of their own. With so much confusion in his personal life, Bob felt it was time to revisit Judy Stokes. At the pub and bring her the news of having met 'Lenny Burns' and his female companion 'Karen', and that the cardboard box containing a variety of electronic equipment had been returned to him and on behalf of his friend 'Tommy Sands'.

He also informed her that his wife had returned after months away and she came home pregnant, Judy stopped in her tracks and with one hand over her mouth blurted out,

"Oh! My God Bob, I am so sorry to hear that", said Judy very apologetic and concerned at the news.

Bob leaned on the bar with a very glowing smile,

"It is mine Judy, it's a son, well a long story but she ravished me before she left home to be with her family, now we are to be a real family, I am shocked as to how it's all come about, I really am, anyway, it's happened and we are soon to be parents, so I have work to do in organising a nursery", said Bob.

Judy just remained open-mouthed and stared at him,

"Well, congratulations but you have taken the wind out of my sails Bob. I am shocked, I don't know what to say, but so thrilled for you both", said Judy,

With a smile and a tap on the arm as she went to pour him a fresh drink.

It was at that moment he realised that he was not alone for they're next to him stood 'Tommy Sands' whom he recognised from his criminal photo,

"Please, let me buy you that drink, I am sorry for all the trouble I have caused", said Tommy in a friendly voice.

Tommy went on to explain that weeks before the fire they had been plagued with so much trouble from the young gipsies, and at the same time, his companion 'Lenny' had been a casualty in the big motorway accident that hospitalised him. We had just met the girls and felt that we were starting a whole new period to our lives, so when Lenny came out of the hospital, his girlfriend took him away to convalesce. So, my girlfriend Toni (was beckoned over to join them at the bar) and I soldiered on but still troubled by the bloody gipsies. So, as it happened, some mutual friends of ours had decided to holiday abroad on that Saturday, and we were persuaded to join them, go with them in their car. So, knowing Lenny and Karen were coming home early Sunday morning, we decided on clearing out late on Saturday evening, having exercised the dogs earlier that afternoon and leaving them with plenty feed and water we felt comfortable in doing what we did at the time. All we needed was our suitcases packed and ready for being picked up. So, I left Lenny a note on the kitchen table as to where we had gone, locking the house up with the security cameras fully working we left the house and off we went. Being abroad we were on the French and Italian borders way out in the countryside, then across to Tuscany. We had no one to bother, so we didn't use our mobiles and no television available, we had many weeks of bliss and a relationship to cement, our friends returned to the UK, and we stayed on to enjoy ourselves. Obviously now sad to learn the house has gone, but whether we rebuild or sell up is debatable, but what is clear we have decided to go back abroad and see out another year before deciding. My equipment is being packed up and stored that's why we are back today, brought in a team of security people to organise our affairs and my old mate Lenny, and his girlfriend will be joining us this time, and the dogs are coming with us.

After the explanation, the couple left the pub and Bob knowingly realised that Tommy's story was plausible to believe. But he felt the story was very convenient in its telling and at that moment, but Bob's gut instincts that effects many good Coppers in knowing more about the truth that often the villains realise themselves that once a villain always a villain and going off abroad is an excellent reason to remain off the radar of the British Police, out of sight, out of mind?

Within the week a hurried Divisional Parade had been arranged for all officers and ranks to attend unless on operational duties at the time of the parade. The Chief Superintendent had decided that it was necessary at this time to thank all staff for their fantastic work which had been achieved in the past weeks. He first addressed the two gipsy murders and a CID Det/Insp, and a Uniformed Inspector attended each of the two funerals and flowers left in attendance in respect of the families.

Secondly, the third deceased body found in the Petrol Tanker remains to be identified, although, he is not thought to be local to us and enquiries continue by the Incident Room. There are individuals officers who have done a fantastic job in displaying all the best virtues of good police work, resulting in another sub-division recovering a large quantity of stolen property that appears to have been stored on farm premises and where the occupier has been arrested for firearms offences, plus the fact there was enough sweating fertilizer to blow up the surrounding area (laughter from the audience) Again this snowballed to another force area and again a large quantity of stolen property was found in the bottom of a dried-up well. So, it's worth remembering when executing search warrants as to the versatility of today's criminals, false walls, holes in plaster etc., so what I intend to propose is to organise a series of one-day training programs concerning buildings and search techniques as we cannot leave everything to our sniffer dogs. Of course, the house fire at 'Marshalls Green' was arson caused by the young gipsies over prior aggressions against the householders, although, again we have since established that the building was empty at the time and the only casualty was that of a dog from the property. The illegal gipsy site is to be moved to a more appropriate location on the sub-division and will be supervised by the local council, so that will leave the lanes free of obstruction and debris.

I also want to touch on a group of crimes that occurred

weeks back and very much became a national news story. The incident room of that force has published a 'Bristol Intelligence Document' that I would like you all to read and digest the contents. That is where the focus will be in the coming weeks. As now, there are no suspects and no forensics to any of the crimes. A very professional set of circumstances, so once again my sincere thanks for your efforts and the teamwork displayed that has made this such a success for the Division – Well done all.

The parade came to an end, and all ranks began to leave, with the soundings of much muttering among many officers. Others had other ideas, some had a quieter moment to reflect on the achievements and PC Bob Benyon was one of those who still believed the answers to many of the problems very much concerns 'Marshalls Green' and the two occupants 'Tommy Sands' and 'Lenny Burns', the overall irony came much later for Bob to learn that Karen Black one of the girlfriends was a former Customs officer who resigned her post sometime after the house fire?

It was some months later that Bob met 'Sandy's two girlfriends out shopping, and it was them who broke the news to Bob that 'Sandy' found out she was pregnant before she moved away, as she and her husband had moved abroad believed to be in France somewhere near the Italian border. Bob finally found out that her husband was a diplomat from the Foreign office who took early retirement and she had come from a very affluent family in the West Country, hence that lovely twang she had with her accent. Bob remained in awe of the news and that finally 'Sandy' had flown the nest with only her memories and a short video clip of their last moments together, the time and the date was important for him to remember, although, he refrained from making personal comments other than to say she was a really nice person, who had a caring and sincere personality, she always chatted when I saw her. Her two friends bid him goodbye as they left carrying their shopping to the car park nearby. Bob moved on and smiled to himself could this be the answer he sought, was he chosen to father a child, could that be why she was so open and uninhibited with him and why their fucking was so intense. Could it have been an agreement as her husband must have realised that he was not the father, unless she had been artificially inseminated by an anonymous source or could be as the result of 'IVF' treatment, Bob's mind went into overdrive at the news, in many ways he was excited for her and in another way terrified that this may come back to haunt him in the future, a son or daughter turning up on the doorstep unannounced would just about do it, he smiled and grinned at the thought, his seed was perhaps the growing seed in her belly, what would she be like with a swollen tummy to see her naked once again in the undress of her pregnancy.

A further thought had crossed his mind, he accepted that 'Sandy's forth coming pregnancy was as the result of their affair without questioning that another man could be responsible and yet with his own wife he had requested a 'DNA' test for the parental facts of whether he was the father, due to the extremes of their turbulent marriage of recent times and like his thoughts none of this made any sense as it was all arse about face as he ought to be questioning a 'DNA' test from 'Sandy' instead of his wife. No one would ever believe this story as 'Fact was stranger than Fiction'; he continued on his way with a face full of smiles and two women pregnant, not bad for a few months' works, neither intentional, neither planned?

Five months later Bob's wife gave birth to a son and so made this a life changer for them both as a family and so ended a very unique chapter in his personal life, although, somewhere in Europe there was another chapter still to close and would remain unknown as to the child's birth and the unanswered question as to whether he really was the father of 'Sandy's child?

POSTCRIPT

Months later PC Bob Benyon received a personal letter addressed (C/O) to the Police Station, intrigued as the postal markings were foreign. His mind began to speculate as to where this had arrived from. Once opened he soon realised that 'Sandy' had addressed to him her original writings. Concerning personal relationships, she had often referred too when speaking of her girlfriends, and their bad relationships. Which were very frequent among some of them and their shared experiences that had been mulled over as rather heart-breaking and distressing in their poor choice of men.

Bob felt the hairs on the back of his neck stand up on reading her letter. As his old memories, although, recent came flooding back to what they had shared together and the bond and fellowship that grew between in such a brief time of trust and confidentiality.

Bob was more mesmerised by her words of confusion, Q. Garden needs seeding, then refers to new life that grows, and Blue has a real meaning in her life, and always indebted to him forevermore? Bob spent ages just chewing over her words in silence, he was alone and needed to be at this time as he began to mentally answer her riddles.

He decided to decipher her words bit by bit **1**. Seeds and new life that grows (her friends mentioned that she was pregnant when she left) **2**. Always and forevermore indebted to him (He was the father of her child written in a subtle way of hinting rather than coming to the point) **3**. Blue held real meaning in her life and the card she had sent was mostly printed in Blue and Blue is a colour for Boys?

Slowly Bob began to grow into the fact that he had fathered 'Sandy's child and her signs indicated a son, but nothing more in the attached correspondence. As he read through her notes and writings and she certainly had put together an interesting argument. About relationships and the sexual practices that were unfulfilling for so many. Very much about the plus and the minuses on what she had researched during their time together, although, she had refrained from mentioning their relationship in all her notes, very much a door left open as to their futures and what that might hold for him in the long run. He sat just tapping the desk and chuckling to himself – Know one just no one would ever believe his story – Fact or Fiction it didn't matter, he lived the moment of something beautiful and something sexually shared and mind blowing to them both and now a closing chapter in their past lives together.

RELATIONSHIPS OF A PERSONAL KIND
MALE & FEMALE
The Sexual Beginnings
Between Couples of Either Sex

Where and how does one begin an intimate emotionally charged sexual relationship between male and female species? Is it by whispers between mates or the banter of adolescence about the feminine shape as to what they each wear under their clothes. Such mystery, such humour, such tales, what is the truth of what goes on in the heads of male youths. In a mixed family of either sex, one sees undergarments on washing lines. But none of this comes to mine, even when perhaps a female relative glamorises their looks in socialising as it never is noticed in the thoughts of male youths, just taken for granted that a sister or a female friend dresses up to go out.

It is only when young males become interested in girls for the first time when puberty strikes at the most inconvenient time having watched from the side-lines for whatever years it has taken for them to be attracted to the female sex. That moment of giddiness, hot flushes, and feeling as if one's eyes are going to pop out. That moment of euphoria a misleading state of irrational happiness and behaviour. When one's 'PENIS EJACULATES' and you end up with dampness in your underwear that holds no explanation as to what's happening, but a sudden warmth and exhilaration strike at the very heart and mind of the individual young male where few tell and share their experience with others.

Some are embarrassed; some are already aware of what they have experienced as they have been informed by somewhere else. Others are confused, some are disgusted, but always it is the personal view of the person as to how they digest and appraise that moment that takes their lives from being a youth into manhood for the very first time of what nature provides for reproduction in the species of the sexes.

The learning curves to this are when young males make haste to clean themselves and change their underwear. Does the realisation set in to know that one's Penis expands and rises by the flow of blood to make it stiff and ready for intercourse? For some, the Penis will relax to soon after ejaculation, for some, it can last longer and perhaps with some embarrassment to others as the Penis remains rigid and presses against one's underwear and can be evident to others.

It is natures time in telling you that one's body is ready in making babies and at that moment one needs to take care as the Penis is not designed for fun as nature intends it for another purpose. The fun part has been created by science in birth control whether for male or female intimate sexual relations has now become big business in the way people have designed for themselves a more recreational way of enjoying their shared physical experiences. In later life, men do experience erectile dysfunction, and this can be a very disruptive force in any relationship,

- This can be caused by one a medical condition,

- Not wanting further children,

- Or a host of other reasons including bereavement for a close person,

• To be in debt and worrying,

• Through work-related practices and pressures (conditions & hours)

• Or for many merely lose interests in the physical side of a relationship,

• Fallen out of love with a partner,

• Perhaps having sexual relations elsewhere (affairs) always tired,

• Maybe either has put on weight and is undesirable to each other's feelings,

• Disgusted by the whole physical side of life beyond the purpose of having children (feeling dirty & unclean),

• Even to the point of being pressurised in one's faith of religion,

• A partner who is perhaps more a nymphomaniac who requires regular servicing to the end of the male becoming exhausted and disinterested.

It is why some mothers do not like seeing their daughters sitting on the laps of boyfriends because of the arousal factor. That often occurs once puberty has found a release, such as the fun times of young lives when being ignorant in the absence of sex education on such personal matters of hygiene, especially those who have not been circumcised as the foreskin needs to be drawn back and the flesh needs to be cleaned. To rid the tissue of the white sticky secreted sperm mucus from one's body and of course drying in underwear leaves a crusty starched material and indicates a clean change of clothing as often this can reach into the fibre of the trousers and males beyond the underwear change often forget this.

The giveaway signs to wives, mothers or other interested parties are either an indication of (a) puberty having occurred or (2) an extramarital affair is the source. As discharged sperm has an aroma all its own and is a dead giveaway if one is not clean in their habits. Even so with a clothing change soon after a sexual encounter, one needs still take precautions as to the continued secretion will emerge from the Penis tip, so tissues are handy to have to wrap around the penis for times of self-comfort.

With girls/women, they are more likely to have tissues available or will use their briefs/knickers to wipe themselves. If a toilet/bathroom is nearby, they are more likely to use the facilities and endeavour to clean themselves. Depending on the location and circumstances there are those females who will douche their sexual vessels internally for vaginal irrigation. As women are more aware and well informed on hygiene matters than their male counterparts, and it follows that as soon as practicable the female will bathe or shower soon after intercourse.

Again, the male is more likely to make do with a quick wipe of the Penis and either to drive home as it remains in situ or to fall asleep should it be at home and not be bothered so much about the stickiness that follows. This also relates to a woman's period as it can often happen that a female's period will start during or be ending in intercourse and that is only noticeable when the physical act has finished, and she cleans herself.

Again, women are more Intune with their bodies than males and for apparent reasons of monthly periods. Such knowledge and teachings will be coming from their mother's or older female members. To explain the actions that would be required by the female and to avoid accidents in one's underwear and outer garments. It can also be embarrassing to the woman but then it is a natural monthly event, and I would have thought that most men would be switched on and to ignore any rude comments and banter about such situations, more so in the disgust of the individual making it. Perhaps women, in general, do not realise that many a male gets uttered good verbal warning from their counterparts over obnoxious comments and maybe far more than women recognise as fellows are not tolerant about such lewd remarks of women and that I can honestly assure you.

- One of the most prominent traits of life is the sniffing of dogs around the crutch area this naturally causes embarrassment and annoyance if the animal persists and you are not able to stop it for whatever reason of the animal not being adequately controlled by the owner.

  Now that Puberty has arrived in the mind and penis of the youth its knowing what to do next and this is where curiosity comes alive as there is an overwhelming lack of understanding when it comes to the arousal of the penis as this is more about swings and roundabouts.

Meaning it can happen at any time as there is much to learn about one's body and the mental control one needs to engage and exercise. So now the individual being of youthful age and without a full sexual experience with a female is unclear on their part as to how one approaches such a pure experience with the opposite sex without proper instructions rather than groping, fumbling or being a bull in a china shop.

The most obvious by standards of curiosity is to masturbate and there again lies many myths and legends about experimenting in this way. Going blind or it will wilt and drop off, or it won't work at the right time, such comments and remarks are commonplace with older males especially in the workplace with much male banter and teasing of the youth.

One of the biggest teasers related to Asian woman where their vaginas are positioned in such a way as to resemble their slit eyes, then of course whether the youngster is well hung like a donkey, all these comments are commonplace among young men and often confirmed ingest by the older man if approached for confirmation. All this is very much a world unknown to women in general terms as such behaviour is very much contained in the male bastion of their privacy.

When puberty occurs while still at school or some sporting activity. Then that requires shower time with other males then it becomes an exercise of self-confidence, examination and comparisons of other men, the school would naturally be of the same age, sports could well have involved outside groups shared with older men. So, puberty among young men is a learning curve as to size, colour and shape, there are occasions when some youths will not engage and that maybe because of body size or embarrassing hair cover, either way, one should not interfere rather ignore and leave others to adjust to their circumstances of puberty.

• There are other matters of concern for males of all ages, the cause of penile ruptures relates to handling one's penis in violent or vigorous masturbation that would indicate that the individual is doing it wrong and this is more than likely to be pointed out should it involve hospital medical treatment.

• As the average male orgasm lasts six seconds and the average female orgasm lasts twenty plus seconds. A female orgasm releases endorphin, which is natural painkillers, and oxytocin provides the feeling of being connected to the partner. As the nerve ending (multiple of thousands) in the clitoris includes the area of pubic growth which is why grinding against your partner provides that good feel factor for many females. A females Breasts also increase in size when aroused and where nipples especially become very sensitive to touch.

• The average size of a man's penis is approximately 6 inches in length a more extended size in inches is of a small percentage of the male population.

• The male can also orgasm without ejaculating, and that does not mean he is faking due to the lack of sperm. As sperm is mostly made of Sugar.

• When it comes to penetration of the vagina then it is mind over matter for the male as to learn the mental control of himself and how he physically behaves towards his engaging sex act with his partner and this comes with practice in perfecting his own physical skills in being a good lover, rather than being negative in the approach to lovemaking. For the lower part of the vagina narrows for a better grip of the penis during intercourse.

• There is much criticism by women generally as to how rushed the actual sexual act can be. Leaving them high and dry emotionally and physically unfulfilled by their partner. More of the male's selfishness with little thought in applying a foreplay role. (as foreplay stimulates an area of the brain called 'Hippocampus') of engaging physically with their partner, this can be by massage, a touch of the fingers or toys and oils it depends as to how open one's relationship is and whether equally shared, as variety is the spice of life and action speaks louder than words and words well to be remembered for the future.

• By the early thirties, a female's clitoris is four times larger than at puberty.

• The average vagina is three to four inches in length and expands in size when sexually aroused this is an intervention by natures very own. Orgasms provide real strong factors for women lowering the risk of heart disease, breast cancer, strokes and mentally aids depression and very much provides a well-feeling element of contentment and may well help to burn off the calories through the physical exertion and the efforts made in taking the lead in pleasing her partner. The most orgasmic sex for women is playing Solo with themselves, second is Oral, and the third is Penis penetration.

• Kissing also provides millions of exchanging bacteria, so again mouth hygiene is another crucial factor in a sexual engagement. Male sweat becomes saturated with perspiring chemicals that link to female arousals.

• Women are as susceptible as the male to wet dreams when blood flows to the vagina area as it does to the penis. Men often wake to be 'Piss proud' where the penis is erect and rigid. Few possibly due to early mornings ignore the sexual apparitions of the moment due to work, whereas it would be an appropriate time to fuck the partner as both would be more relaxed and Intune with their bodies to reach orgasm together.

• As climaxing increases with age for the women then perhaps one can understand why older women feel more rejected by the lack of sexual fulfilment by their partner as age. Mental and physical conditions are a direct effect on the male's prowess. Meaning erectile dysfunction is often requiring medical assistance and a good reason why females in their prime can feel isolated from being sexually active and right to seek an intense extramarital affair, merely to satisfy their physical needs, rather than trying to break up a marriage or relationship that provides them with family contentment and long-term security. As lousy sex in a relationship is a real ball buster as women are as capable as the male to think about sex at any time of the day.

• Sex surveys do occur throughout the world by scientists and it results in a variety of findings and especially for women to recognise they are not having as much sex as they would have liked, as the male is more stereotyped than is fact in thinking of sex in any one day as women are just as equal in feeling the same.

• For the woman a more intense climax is deep penetration for her by raising the hips and to squeeze the pelvic muscles before orgasm, this can be supported by placing pillows underneath the buttocks for the partner to penetrate deep into her vagina. By stimulating either the penis or sex toy can significantly increase vagina stimulation.

So how does it all begin for the young male once having reached puberty, it all starts with the eyes which tend to be the physical reasons as the main attraction towards the opposite sex? Females are more attracted to emotions and personalities, love and future security in a relationship are important choices in the values of choosing a male partner. Rampart feelings are the fun aspect of a sexual relationship, and the feel-good factor is very much to hand in the mind is experiencing the desire to experiment in the physical act of intercourse and foreplay, but foreplay is not much understood among the young as to the importance of understanding a female's emotional needs. For the most part, the beginnings of a youthful experience are boosting one's self-esteem. To feel the naked flesh of a woman and whether one can hold on and not ejaculate before penetration of the vagina, again how worldly and experienced is the female likely to be, perhaps she is more akin to a sexual relationship in the first instance of being with a youth who has just reached puberty. So how does the relationship from eyes meeting to Intercourse occur as males tend to endorse the visual clues and cues as to whether a female is prepared and ready for a sexual encounter with a youthful partner?

As females are as curious and lustful in wanting to experience new sexual encounters and of course, comparisons do occur between close female friends over partners and their choice of male lovers. To engage in sexual matters of fulfilment can be caused by boredom for the female, perhaps revenge or through drunkenness and bravado including a wife's tale of burning off the calories (fact or fiction – does it work) overall and out of self-sexual gratification and not necessarily one of love and commitment. Again, this depends very much on the female's personality and what she is seeking and intending by engaging in numerous sexual affairs in the short term as its clear that some women cannot be satisfied by one or several partners in the short term. An old saying is a wise saying that 'Quality over Quantity' should prevail over common sense above self-gratification for the very sake of it and does nothing to equate one's self-esteem in the long term of holding down a healthy relationship with one of the opposite sex by choosing an inexperienced partner.

The physical act is just a small part of a relationship, as at times the action can be overstated. But more importantly nature provides other senses of the mind and body and often ignored for a variety of reasons, hearing and talking able to converse and how many couples take time out to engage with each other, to speak face-to-face with their other half. It remains so easy in social gatherings to converse but also shared with others. Personalities do shine at times and are noticeable with one's partner, and yet when isolated as a couple it seems that each has run out of things to say, but why, what is the reason, apart from talking about other people there is little or no focus on the relationship. Knowing how to keep a relationship alive not for an hour or a day but long term. What is interesting in either partner, what engages the most with one's other half, Is this a long-term commitment or an experiment of a third kind. In chopping and changing partners (like changing underwear) for the most sexual fulfilment that one can gain from another and will such actions be life-changing for the future of one's life. Being a restless wandering soul does nothing long term for a relationship to hold its course for a long-term commitment that includes children and family life after that, only she the female can answer the question, but sadly neither communicate between themselves and boredom sets in and that is a recipe for disaster in the relationship.

Medically it is understandable that the female 'Menopause' can also be disruptive in a relationship, but again it all comes down to the emotional needs of a woman. As she experiences Hot flushes throughout her body and this being disruptive in a relationship. There is an overwhelming lack of understanding when it comes to the female sexuality to her general likes and dislikes and maybes from orgasm to her being dysfunctional in the main.

There is inadequate knowledge of the female anatomy among both sexes, lots of myths and legend that gets passed down over generations, but little advice is given in the teachings of either sex and the makeup and differences of her anatomy. It is sadly more or less left to the groping and fumbling of the male individual to go it alone and find their way of experimenting with a female. From the first date, there are boundaries that one doesn't cross and that is more of the common-sense values of not wanting to offend, so closeness and holding hands is the beginning to kissing whether short pecks or kisses of more profound meaning, without suffocating the female. But again, this is where the youthfulness stands more of being a young adult by not being over exuberant and eager to move on to that of a more sexual nature, by touching and stroking the female's breast over her clothing. To being more personal and intimate as the kissing continues as hands wander under the dress, gently pushing back the boundaries and whether there will be resistance on her part, and yet little conversation occurs between them as to the point of the Bra underwear being undone and removed, possibly with short whispers from him, perhaps the female has shown little resistance as to the hands of the male touching her naked breasts, then the grasp of the nipple between fingers and he listening for sounds of her contentment.

In doing so, it all becomes a learning curve in relationships for the first time of touching and cradling a naked breast. The softness of her flesh and whether she responded with the male's touch, it is also a crucial factor to note that the female nipple is an “Erogenous zone” for pleasure although, biologically, the nipples of both species remain similar. It all is part of the male's makeup in the natural sense of curiosity. As the female would also recognise the males breathing pattern that edges on excitement. Indicating to her that the arousal factor is the sexual kind and building up to be rampant. As the male's hand will wander onto her tummy and downwards, inch by inch a hand will tempt providence as he side moves into the female’s briefs, will she resist, little by little the hand will continue stoking and touching her pubic area? For the female may show willing in helping her partner by parting her legs a little giving a hand an opportunity to move down further to the vagina area and the clitoris. But the clitoris is not likely to be known as to its position by the moving hand

and the ignorance of the partner. She perhaps will arch backwards to allow the hand more space to move as already at the top of the vagina. Will a finger penetrate her, will he be caring and gentle or insert in a rush, will she be hurt by his touch or will she pull the hand away and back up to her breast, where the hand starts from the very beginning?

Will she have conversed with her partner as to her likes or dislikes, will she guide him to her, will she provide more encouragement in slowing downing the sexual act to last longer than a five-minute wonder, she wants foreplay, to experience more of his touch upon her flesh. But then where is this liaison happening outside in the open, standing up in an alleyway, on a sofa or in a bedroom, but perhaps more likely for it to be in a motor vehicle parked somewhere somewhat secluded where both parties can guarantee privacy. It is the motor vehicle that carries the most weight of occurring more of the sexual practices in relationships between the unmarried or the extramarital affairs by far than any other place of convenience for intercourse to follow.

For many young males being unaware that the woman's clitoris is designed for pleasure and that is it in a nutshell. But and the but is one where the youthful partner is not going to ask. But would instead feel his way to stupidity in the eyes of the female realising that her partner is not well experienced in finding the clitoris. That is where a penis, finger or sex toy can stimulate the shaft and internal clitoris which would significantly increase. Her sexual feelings by the nerve endings of the vagina and for her internal functions to lubricate the channel to assist and aid penetration as a dry vagina would provide extreme discomfort to the female in the absence of fluid. Some women squirt, how this develops within her anatomy is hard to describe. But can add significant stimulus in heightened sexual play, some males might well find this abhorrent it's all about taste and attitudes in developing a relationship with one who is described in medical terms as a squitter, there is nothing sinister about the occurrence and not defined in its analysis as excreting urine during intercourse.

A woman deserves hot sex it's not something she does to please her partner by her sense of duty to gain some satisfaction from her sexual experience. Again, if her sex drive is impaired it could be by medication that causes the problem, so best to seek medical advice rather than just mopping about the absence. Perhaps to keep a diary or some commentary on one's feelings and desires as to when her mood is right for fucking.

If married it could be a host of problems that stand in the way of self-satisfaction especially with a growing family and children needing attention. Keep track of the biological clock concerning menstruation as this also affects as to feeling ones sexiest when ovulating around two weeks before one's period. Some women feel at their most sensual just before or during their periods when you know it is the safest of all days to engage in intercourse without birth control.

It is all about body types and nakedness as some females refuse to be seen naked by her partner or having sex with the light on or in daylight without being undercover for the privacy of the sexual act. This often comes down to the changing body type of the female. It is about loving one's self in building up one's confidence and self-esteem. To enjoy a full sexual relationship that bears all the fruits of great satisfaction, but then how much impute and encouragement comes from the partner or has the change been accepted without acknowledgement of the moment as conversation and opinions no matter occur between couples.

Women should be more adventurous in themselves without even being embarrassed by their feelings even when alone. Explore the intimate side of one's personality as to what turns you on whether by erotic literature, by sex toys or also consider the various positions one can try with a partner, take control of one's situation and tell your partner what you like and dislike. Whether you want to experiment with your partner, or fantasies by making love in the garden at night or in open spaces.

Stop feeling as if sex must be over and done in a hurry. Like when your partner finds you at the kitchen sink, and suddenly you are engaged in a quickie from behind as an act of sexual pleasure, it may be that the suddenness of the moment and actions of your partner heightens your sexual feelings at that time where comfort is much appreciated above all else. To remember what dramatically aspires your needs from being intimate and how your sexual preferences can be held as a priority in your life or lives in sharing a loving relationship that engages in the variety of lovemaking and how one can engage without any inhibitions being blighted by ill judgements on the part of the female.

As overall it does not mean that one must be married, engaged or in a deep relationship to having great sex. Great sexual experience with another does happen often, and it can happen by experimenting with one's self. Or may well be and what most would regard as the norm of a male appearance which is unattached in prior contact in knowing you. Or perhaps a long admiration that has been exercised from a distance by a male figure and gone unnoticed by the female as there were no signs to read, however, nature can play blinders on one's emotions, and it happens regularly with either sex to experience higher satisfaction with an acquaintance or a stranger. Where the after-effects of the female merely have blown away the cobwebs that have remained dormant for such a length of time within her. Thoughts and experiences in longing for satisfaction in her free moments of wanting to be fucked with a clear conscience of not being troubled in the way she has felt and acted previously.

Females do and act with regular frequency in being flirtatious with males in general. Again, it's all about being perceptive on the male's part, whether it's by the meeting of eyes and smiling and does the eyes and smile mean anything of a sexual nature or one of just being courteous in the acknowledgement of one's presence. Some signs indicate something more personal without touching a female especially when the woman is known to the male, and she sees the man in a different light than any time before. It could be the quirkiness of the personality or showing a robust, manly approach to surrounding matters by exercising one's practical skills that had gone unnoticed previously.

For the male to experience the closeness of the female standing directly in the mind's eye and follows provocative comments, banter exchanges, enquiring her needs for help. But by holding just inches from one's body is an indication that the female needs attention. She is wanting to be appreciated for the right reasons and not ingest of being laughed at. For the male who feels her energy and vibes is a question as to whether he reaches out and kisses her on the nose in playful terms, draws her close and gives a cuddle or places arm around her waist and walks her off to part their closeness. Such are the thoughts of the female form on her part. This is likely to be a regular occurrence as to what she is missing in her married life. Or with a partner if one has good reason to be around her whether, by work-related issues, sports events or some other social matter that allows this to happen, what becomes problematic is such incidents occur to be in public and not in private.

Would this occur in private, would this be the signal to go further with the closeness? The contact by kissing and cuddling her and whether she is likely to pull away or allow the males presence to continue in feeling and touching her body. Where the cuddle has now become more intimate in feelings between them both and would it mean that the female would allow herself to be moved and possibly undressed for a full-on sexual experience due to her lacking in affection and sexual pleasures in her own life, as a married woman or with a partner where she feels neglected and seeks that closeness and that touching to be real in her release in the way she feels at that moment in time.

Not every relationship is sexually compatible at the time of choosing one's partner as other motives and reason take priority in the hope that matters will change when spending more time together. If the female is more sexually experienced than the male it can be a source of irritation to her in making comparisons to other lovers, but at the time of choice it was one of long term security and having an affordable life where wealth is not an issue to their lifestyles with children playing an essential part in their relationship, to the point where the children are of an age that leaves the female feeling bereaved due to the absence of her siblings who are out socialising with their friends or away from home for reasons of education, and she remains in an empty house.

There are couples who have intercourse per day of their relationship, it is there connection and loyalty to each other that keeps alive their partnership where conversation and feisty, passionate times are shared, where sex is a massive player in their lives and where both can explore and experiment without displaying an awkwardness that inhibits either from expressing their likes and dislikes.

There are other relationships that beggars belief in the attitudes that couples can display to each other, having their privacy and space is a big plus for any couple, the handicap to sexual intimacy can have an adverse effect by being always together that detracts from the urge of wanting regular sexual relations all the time, although, there is no chink in the relationship to cause alarm as sex has decreased by their consent as sex is now about quality than quantity as was prior to coupling as being in a permanent marriage or relationship, although, this too can have its handicaps as their arrangement can be too regimental with particular times for particular chores, meaning time for bed, time for showering but more time together is about parenting coming first in the household with a growing family.

Tiredness plays a more prominent role in being destructive to any regular or spontaneous sexual activity between couples and does strain relationships especially if the female bears the brunt of family life and the male is working long hours to support family life. Again, family life can be more difficult if living far from other family members (parents/grandparents) who would have been ideal to help take the strain by babysitting occasionally for privacy to enhance the couple's sexual feelings elsewhere or with an empty house and no children. Again, some couples do set time aside for intimacy, but often the planning will go out of the window. If siblings encounter vibes of their own and can be a bloody nuisance and hindrance at the most awkward of times to parents. When parents act differently to the standard pluses of the day, and this takes the biscuit. With the phones not turned off and ringing every few minutes, call it intuition, call it what you like it's still a frustration that causes sexual tension in the relationship with promises to improve in the future of making more time available for sexual activity. But it's not about long term it's about now, this hour, this day you cannot be a victim to be a robot with one's personal feelings as planning never happens, and age creeps and creeps upon us each year so who wants to live with memories as to how it once was.

Not all women have masses of sexual partners although. In a modern society sexual freedom is more prevalent than ever before in the history of birth control, as with such freedom sex was more playful and experimenting without having full intercourse, and of course, it removed the worry of pregnancy and the freedom also made it as equal to that of the male figure. Respect very much played a crucial role in relationships and became more enjoyable to know that the freedom genuinely liberated the female, and that sexual activity and intercourse was very much available most of the time as it was now one of choice for couples to choose the moment without falling pregnant.

There are taboos in relationships in the way males physically treat their partners. As love bites (hickies) are not as harmless fun as people think. However, being ignorant of the apparent dangers is a poor excuse for not understanding that by sucking one's flesh in this manner. As one can often see on the necks of individuals the bruising, that occurs, but more to the point of sucking too hard on someone's neck can cause a stroke by leading to an artery blockage.

Either sex does exaggerate about their orgasms and do fake the occasions as and when it suits them best, excuses can be alcohol-related, stressed or reasons for exhaustion. For the men it is a weak reason for not being sexually creative with one's partner at the times they share but not to the point of being a contortionist or a ballerina working out on her bars and tiptoes, be expressive make noises other than listening to the sucking noises of the vagina inhaling and exhaling the air that the penis drives home on the back and forth of thrusting.

Men are not the only ones to get turned on in their sleep; women too experience “nocturnal orgasms” sexual pleasure can stimulate at the centre of the brain as you dream of having a subconscious desire of fucking a female of the erotic kind.

The average size of a penis is 5+ inches. So, it’s not about quantity as many males would argue it knows how to approach the clitoris and vagina in understanding how the stimulus works for the female in how she receives real sexual pleasure as the nerve endings are around the first inch of the vagina. This is followed up by the healthy signs of the male partner being overweight where the overhanging stomach can quickly cover the base and diverts blood away from the penis; smoking is another example of neglect that has some effect on the arteries in reducing the size of the erections.

More about the self-neglect by the males who fail to perform and always in a hurry to finish that sexual act, and where the partner remains feeling neglected and frustrated by the lack of sexual attention that is denying her from experiencing any real pleasure from her sexual activity at the time.

Other myths - Popping the virginal cherry is not what is claimed at all, a woman's "Hymen" long regarded as a fleshy seal broken for the first time by vaginal intercourse, although, the seal is formed in female embryos it dissolves before birth.

Also, further from the truth is the more sex a woman has the looser the vagina becomes and of course no one vagina is like another as size plays an integral part in the relationship to a woman's body.

Natural childbirth can cause a loss of muscle tone, and this is where pelvic-muscle exercise can help the female to tone her muscles and has no bearing on sex with a male even if the man was well-endowed size is immaterial.

Having sex more than twice a week helps to boost the immune system the more sex you have, the more of the antibody "Immunoglobulin" being the first line of defence against colds and flu.

Premature ejaculation associated with immature youngsters who have only just reached puberty and lack the control of their ejaculation as practice makes perfect, for men over thirty years it could be erectile dysfunction, tiredness & fatigue, anxiety or depression and other reasons that can interrupt intercourse at the wrong time by taking breaks during sex or one's train of thought is elsewhere and lacks concentration on the partners needs or the female climbing on top causes some difficulty for the male in ejaculating to early by the very touch or movement that interferes with that moment of truth and where only it can happen to anyone at any one time of trying to make an effort to please one's partner.

Never say never is an understatement that exaggerates the unwelcome truth, and the misconception that one cannot get pregnant standing up or having sex in water, the reality is that nature has never devised a barrier to pregnancy sex is sex and is possible to get pregnant each time you have sex.

Penetrative sex is unlikely to result in orgasm for the female. A substantial proportion of women do not achieve and requires clitoral stimulation which ought to show the immense importance of foreplay in the mentioned area, even toys to help the woman climax. Again, not all women orgasm as there is a condition known as "Anorgasmia" but does not mean the female cannot enjoy sex it is more of the lack of knowledge and the experience of foreplay by the male, its more about how to get the result of where the female has much pleasure as possible during the sexual act of penetrative intercourse. It is a testament to the skills and understanding of the female's emotional needs by her lover that would shine through in providing and servicing her needs.

People do not understand that to get pregnant eggs must compete against thousands of other eggs in the vagina to become fertilised it is not about the fittest of the fit as there are millions of sperm swimmers competing in the ovaries. There are many reasons as to why women search for the affection they are not receiving from their husband or partner, no matter how beautiful the person may be in other ways of the relationship and the family man he may be. The argument is, the lacking in the bedroom of self-confidence as the male shows no real affection towards the female. Even when the female requests more togetherness from the partner. To touch her, to cuddle her, he only reaches her in bed when he feels duty calls in fucking her and she must initiate sex in the first instance at his request and is all over so very quickly that she is left confused and feeling rejected as only to be used as a sexual vessel to satisfy his immediate needs in a sterile environment that is explicit in a coldness that no women can accept in the long term without considering an extramarital affair to satisfy her needs and requirements as a woman and to show that she is still capable of sharing sexual pleasure with one who appreciates her company and energy.

The most prominent issues couples have is when the male partner rejects the physical side of the relationship; the partner explains that he does not think about sex and that his partner is confusing sex with love. So, what is love other than a word that can be described in thousands of different words and expressions? It is a simple means of a verbal statement, so how can it be confused with any sexual intimacy. As sex is sex and apparently the male partner is missing the genuine issues of the emotional values, concerns and fulfilment of his partner. As sex is an integral part of a loving partnership and should not be divorced from the physical actions of a grumpy old male who shows no sexual chemistry towards the female, it could be in real terms of the man having a genuine low sex drive that requires medical assistance of some kind, being honest and frank about one's situation rather than ignore the real underlying issues of neglecting sex and the partners affections and sadly all too frequent of the older male and the stubbornness of seeking professional help.

- Unless individuals or couples make an effort to spice up their sex lives in a more knowledgeable way before embarking on some scatty performance then their experiences are likely to be less fulfilling and may well become problematic between the couple and one that could well destroy their relationship, so be wise before the event and take heed of the warning, think through one's actions.

- Not everyone or even couples feel confident in talking to each other about new practices or trying new things in spicing up their love lives.

- It could be that one partner is afraid of what their other half may think of them, it could be a big turn off in suggesting something new into their sexual preferences that may not have been discussed or agreed between them, this could have a daunting and unsettling effect on a partner.

- Most are curious about trying new ways but again it must be by the consensus of both parties and not browbeat the other half in trying something new against their will, and of course the change in attitudes and the question of consent to regular intercourse may be agreed and going outside the boundaries may well place you liable to criminal prosecution. So, one needs to show more of an intelligent attitude to overcome and avoid these problems before they start.

- There are so many ways of being passionate so to be crude or to introduce dangerous practices or instruments is undoubtedly going to make your partner wonder where the hell you have been living, sensible methods, agreeable practices, but then it is extraordinary that stripping off and having penetration sex (Fucking in real terms) that a partner is uncomfortable or embarrassed to discuss introducing new ideas in experimenting in their sex lives, whilst touching every nook and cranny of the most intimate of their partners body, when you are already knocking at the door by dipping your wick in the most private of privates and the giving and sharing of intimacies one can experience in open nakedness. It doesn't make sense not to speak with an original tongue that is not judgemental on your partner or to pressurise or compromise the person.

<u>FEMALE</u> - Trying to engage in sex by convincing your partner to make love is never the right answer and almost never works in the satisfaction one would expect at the time and more likely again to be problematic by creating mood swings between you both. When a person is sexually aroused bodies release a chemical

"Adrenaline" into the bloodstream. This chemical gives you the energy to make love, so it's more about approaching the partner in the right way to arouse the person and 'YES' it could work even when one is tired.

Period Sex is not off limits – Has been a trending factor for years. There are those who find the thought repulsive, and those who prefer to enjoy that time of a month. Where a woman is menstruating for the increased arousal and lubrication feelings. Since the woman's body is preparing for reproduction and of course it is believed that woman feel more sexual during this period.

PERSONALITIES

Sadly, people do change in several ways by physical appearance and being overweight and by attitude which can be devastating should that happen and there remains a stubbornness of refusing to get help obviously places a massive strain on any relationship. Anxiety & Depression are perhaps the main causes of change in a person, but also a medical diagnosis can also have an immediate effect on a relationship – 'Asperger's Syndrome'. Again, an unwanted pregnancy or being in debt, it very much depends to the level one has reached in a relationship. Is one generally open and a communicator or one who is generally a day to day worrier and ready to argue over the smallest of incidents. Sleep deprivation plays a vital role in causing a great deal of distress, especially among women, then of course there could be hormonal changes occurring in the female body. So, a change in attitude and without communication between couples can have an everlasting effect on a loving sexual partnership, where one partner may or will start an extramarital affair, this could in the singular of a one-night stand or having sex at every opportunity and in the lewdest ways possible without any personal thoughts of having unprotected sex or using drugs to enhance one's experience. The male species often turn to Brothels or Escort agencies, as it offers a quick release but leaves no commitment on either person engaged in a sexual act. Other than a momentary cost or using Adult pornographic sites who charge astronomical fees or even going to the extreme of Alcohol use and Gambling. Whatever, can end in regular addiction and a downward spiral in one's personal circumstances that requires professional help and counselling. So, a simple bad mood can cause an irritation that festers attitudes in relationships, but always whatever the personal problem may or can seriously damage a loving sexual relationship. That once was perhaps perfect or well satisfying to one where a partner will just go through the motions of pleasing or perhaps showing a distinct affliction for acts of perversion and being mean and controlling with the partner as much is often caused by the male. The biggest enemy in any relationship is not communicating, although, there are those couples who have an agreement to be involved on the Swingers scene with set boundaries and at most works for many but can also be open to partners making comparisons for liaisons outside the classroom and an awkwardness in believing that this will not be harmful. But sadly, time is always a bad keeper of catching people out. It is so easy and tempting to be a chancer with a quickie with the boss or a work colleague or even over the fence with a neighbour. It all eventually comes home to roost and destroys one's faith in humanity. How one begins a relationship and how adult and grownup are each in the relationship. Are both equal communicators as perhaps this is where couples should concentrate more on the personalities of each and take counsel from those around you and gauge the depth of conversation and listen more to family and friends before jumping into a situation with both feet.

Perhaps more for the younger male is to engage with older females who are more adventurous due to age and prior relationships or the unfortunate circumstances of a broken marriage as often there are couples who separate for a period and then return to the fold of their marriage and one can be caught up in such domestics. By having a sexual physical relationship is more advantageous, as often the older women are not wanting a permanent relationship more of expressing their sexual prowess with the younger male. So, experiment if the younger male does not become jealous and too demanding and excepts that both are free agents and an enjoyable time to be had. Whether caused by Alcohol or from a teaching perspective of learning the emotional values of the female species and how to make real love and not sex for the sake of sex that only provides quickies, and lacks the real quality of knowing the real depths of a woman's biology and understands the needs of foreplay before plunging and diving straight into whatever Vagina is on offer at the time of looking. Quantity does nothing for one's soul and moral compass in respecting the female body which can have dire consequences in later years of a relationship. Fuck with the right person and not be wronged in one's pursuit for being stupid in one's younger years in seeking an adventure of a sexual kind. Loving making in the real sense is an art and once learnt in the proper way of a relationship will never be forgotten. So long as there is a loving trust between two people who are communicators in sharing each of their own trials and tribulations of daily life.

Also by A.E. Snelling-Munro

After a life of crime in the East End of London, Tommy Sands and Lenny Burns leave prison to enjoy the proceeds. Having purchased an isolated house on a large estate, they leave their past behind. After five years, with their money running out fast, a change of direction was vital. Lenny had taken to drink and they were each getting on the other`s nerves. Tommy decided that one last big job was essential to fund their gracious lifestyle. He adds a few more ingredients to his plan - women. Surprisingly, sometimes this kind of recipe can work. Can it?

Bobbyjac – A.E. Snelling-Munro

ISBN 9781549517648

Published by: Michael Terence Publishing, 2017

A.E. Snelling-Munro

An indentured apprentice to the motor industry who, on completion, entered the Police service as a full-term career.

Since retirement, he is now an established inventor with many concepts to his name.

Interests include serious DIY, family history and writing - including verse and lampoons and the idiocies of British politics.

Available worldwide from

Amazon

---

www.mtp.agency

Printed in Great Britain
by Amazon

69784825R00189